MARC SCHOOLEY

KÖNIG'S
FIRE

MARCHER
LORD
PRESS

KÖNIG'S FIRE by Marc Schooley
Published by Marcher Lord Press
8345 Pepperridge Drive
Colorado Springs, CO 80920
www.marcherlordpress.com

Cover Designer: Kirk DouPonce, Dog-Eared Design, www.dogeareddesign.com
Creative Team: Jeff Gerke, Dawn Shelton, Christianne Squires

Library of Congress Cataloging-in-Publication Data
An application to register this book for cataloging has been filed with the Library of Congress.
International Standard Book Number: 978-0-9825987-5-7

Printed in the United States of America

To: Norman Schnatterer

From: The Schneebrunser…mach schnell & Hook 'em!

Acknowledgments

Thank y'all for believing in this:

Jeff Gerke, constant encourager and editor/publisher extraordinaire, who embraced this story early on and made it happen. This is *our* book. Thanks, Jeff.

Dr. Emil Silvestru, for fact checks and tips regarding Ploiesti, Romania.

David & CL Dyck: Dave, for technical assistance with refractories, ovens, welding, and solvents, which led to one striking image of the ruinous effects of sin. Cat, my critique and writing partner, whose help with this work was instrumental in its success. The honorary Texan applications y'all submitted are currently under review. Hope springs eternal, eh?

First readers: Mother, Dorann, Lauren, and MS Quixote.

Soli Deo Gloria

1

They called me Nebuchadnezzar, and the name suited me fine.

A good name has a way of weaving itself through and around a man until it's part of him. It merges with his soul, for better or for worse, and it augments it somehow. It amplifies it, or maybe what I'm trying to say is it helps reveal it. All I know is that there's a lot in a name. That instant right when someone calls your name? That's what I'm talking about.

These were my first words to my accusers and to my judges after they asked me if I had anything to say in my defense. I sat on one side of a polished oak table in wrist and leg irons, whiskers grizzly, hair matted and gray down the sides of my head, the ebbing remains of a crew-cut on top. The crew-cut had receded from my German forehead, which accentuated my ancient Aryan features, especially the nose. *Ancient* in terms of the purity of my Germanic blood—and the plain fact that I'm now a very old man.

Across the table sat three of my accusers. The ten others lined the cobbled rock walls of my interrogation room, half in and half out of a feeble light emanating from the ceiling. Beside one of them, I saw the remains of splattered blood on the wall, barely perceptible after all these years. I noticed it because I was looking for it. Sometimes we vex ourselves with our memories like insects that can't resist the pink swells of a Venus flytrap.

The interrogation room ran about forty feet square and was dungeonesque in its austerity. Rock all around, dark, damp, cool. I remembered this room. We used it for storage, mainly for fuel: 55-gallon drums full of fuel for the furnace.

My primary interrogator, apparently receiving orders from someone lining the wall by the way he continually looked over his shoulder, was a beady-eyed man with thick glasses and a widow's peak. He was so slightly built I felt I could break him in half by snapping my fingers. Flanking him were two women who appeared to be of Eastern European descent. They never spoke, but I could see their souls nonetheless. Heartless. During the interrogation, anyway. Could have been different on the outside of the Nachthaus.

Everything seemed heartless inside the rock walls of the Nachthaus. When they caught me after 70 years in America and secreted me back to Romania, I was too old to care much. But coming back to the Nachthaus was another story. This place is as heartless as its walls. I shivered an old man's shiver for what might await me. They had no idea how evil this place is.

"Mr. König," my interrogator said, "we're not interested in philosophy. We're interested in your crimes. Names, dates, historical data. If you cooperate, things will be much easier for you." He adjusted his glasses with hands so small they could be a third grader's.

Easier. I knew what he meant. The death chamber was right down the passageway.

"Call me Sascha," I said. "I haven't been called that in a long time."

"Mr. König—"

"Your organization has been hunting me for 70 years. You got lucky. I should already be dead. But I'm going to make this worth your efforts. I will spill the whole load, ja?" Only two days back with these people and already I was sinking back into German-English. I guess that skill had helped me blend in with Americans for so long. "But you've got to let me tell it. And if you do, I'll tell the whole thing. Otherwise, just get it over with. Do we have an agreement?"

One of the heartless women reached over and massaged my interrogator's hand. After looking over his shoulder, he nodded at me. "Continue."

I leaned as far across the table as I could, staring at the diminutive man and his female escorts with my Aryan blue eyes, trying to let them see my features. My eyes are a faded, old man's eyes. But they've seen a lot. More than they should have. And I wanted them to maybe see a bit of what these eyes held right around the sockets where the crow's feet have dug entrenched battle lines.

"They called me Nebuchadnezzar, you see, because I could get that oven hotter than anyone at the Nachthaus. Seven times hotter, if you believed the accounts of my prowess with fire."

• • •

The place was named the Nachthaus because no matter what time of day it was, it always seemed dark inside and out. The Nachthaus had an official German name, what might be loosely translated in English as the *reclamation center*. It was not your standard Nazi concentration camp; it was too cramped to function as a full-fledged death camp. Instead, its limited facilities were directed at extracting information from enemy agents and torturing select dissidents from the eastern front. That may be the reason it's not as well known as some of the others, but for those who knew about it, it was feared above all others.

The Reich established the Nachthaus not far to the northwest of Ploiesti, Romania. Ploiesti was an important industrial and energy hub in Romania, capable of supporting Operation Barbarossa, the German codename for its offensive against Russia.

The Nachthaus was a short drive from Ploiesti. One moment we were driving past factories and oil refineries, and the next we were plunged into a primeval Romanian forest in the foothills of an eastern arm of the Carpathians. It was as if we were catapulted out of civilization, even by 1940s' standards. This forest seemed to have a soul, and one time I thought I saw its face. I could feel it, even when we were driving through.

The forest's soul matched its darkness. Something, I think, had fled to the wood to escape the onslaught of western civilization with its materialism, science, progress, and rationalism. It hid there in the hazy fog of perpetual night among the primordial trees, the rotting undergrowth, creeping vines, and elemental terrain, untarnished by humanity for centuries, unacquainted with ax or saw.

I felt it my first trip to the Nachthaus. I watched the forest pass by out the back windows of the Mercedes I rode in, and

I felt it looking back at me. When you brought me back here yesterday, I looked for it. After all these years, it was still there, and grinning back at me. I heard Robert Frost speak gently in my mind: The woods are lovely, dark and deep.

At the deepest part of the wood, the Nachthaus appears like a stunted castle, right at the foothills of the mountains. From what I gathered of the history of the place, it began as a mining camp. There are probably still some spent shafts behind these walls. In a way, it became our *Volksgemeinschaft*. The Nazis added a Bavarian touch to the camp and for some reason cut stone right out of the side of the mountain to build these interior walls.

The thickness of the canopy and the constant fog create dusk during the day and the darkest of nights at night: black, foggy, starless night. The perfect place for something to hide.

2

I arrived at the Nachthaus in December of '41 not long after Romania joined the Axis powers. When I stepped out of the Mercedes and straightened my Nazi gray uniform, my anxiety was confirmed.

My black jackboots crackled in the gravel as I pivoted around, absorbing first impressions of my new post. With my first sight of the Nachthaus I attempted to locate the all-encompassing preternatural dread I sensed riding through the wood. It was pretty easy. I kept a Luger and an officer dagger on my belt, but they seemed woefully human in sight of the forest.

The one-lane dirt path winding through the forest fed into a hundred-foot diameter circular gravel lot that fronted the compound. Our driver snaked around lofty conifers that drooped their lower limbs over the roof of the Mercedes. All of a sudden, the compound materialized, but there was no real clearing.

The trees were cleared within ten feet of the entrance to the Nachthaus, which allowed a decent view of the compound's face. It was a bulgy face of dull stones, some of them massive, protruding from the foot of the mountain. It reminded me of the Hunchback of Notre Dame's face.

Its complexion was marred by moss and lichen, and the entranceway at the bottom and center of the face was a gaping black maw. The forested mountainside rose into a murky haze above the Nachthaus, giving it the impression of a forest god descending in judgment upon its realm.

The Hitler Youth had instilled in me that members of the Aryan race, and specifically those members of the Aryan race who were Nazis, were intrepid conquerors, members of a super race that had banished fear from their hearts. I learned firsthand it wasn't true, crackling in the gravel outside the Nachthaus.

The noonday dusk unnerved me, and I gathered one last first impression: the oppressive humidity, the limited visibility from the dense forest and the low-level mist, the smell of compost in the dampness, and the utter quiet.

Except the quiet was not utterly quiet. It was odd that there were no birds chirping, no howling of forest denizens, no wind coursing through the trees. But there was, and always would be, this faint groaning, as if all the trees of the forest were bending at once, their trunks laboring not to snap in two. This constant low moan would haunt me as time passed but, as disturbing as it was, it was never as bad as the scratching.

I followed my escort toward the cavernous entrance of the Nachthaus. We passed two personnel carriers, knobby-wheeled trucks with the military-green canopy over the bed. I adjusted my gray Nazi cap, fingering the pewter emblem of an eagle that rested above the cap's black visor. I straightened my formal uniform by tugging at my jacket right above the beltline in a downward motion. The starched jacket was reassuring through my black gloves. I shouldered my backpack of chemist equipment, picked up my travel case of extra uniforms, which held a stash of classic literary works forbidden by the Nazis, and soldiered on.

When we reached the aperture leading inside, I tilted my head skyward to note the transition of the sky to the stone ceiling of the Nachthaus overhead. It invoked a sensation of going from dark to darker to darkest, from hopelessness to despair.

Outside, the forest moaned.

At the end of the twenty-foot, unlit cave, which may have very well been an adit, a sentry flanked either side of a great iron plate blocking the passageway. The uneven curvature of the cave rippled along the iron door, but the floor was fairly level and I detected a groove cut into the rock of the cave floor into which the door was set.

My escort pounded the door three times and barked out a password. The door began to inch open, scraping against the floor as it slid into the cave wall on the far side from where we stood.

It stopped after three feet, and we entered single file through the portal. The iron plate seemed to be about three inches thick. Two guards on the inside rested against a makeshift gate opener to my left. It was a large wooden wheel, much like a ship's wheel on a pirate schooner, connected by ropes to a pulley system that facilitated the opening and shutting of the iron plate door. As we shuffled past, the guards began to turn the wheel, and the iron door scraped shut. A thick *clank* reverberated through the cave as it latched into place.

We were greeted by the tallest man I had seen up to that point in my life. He introduced himself as Sergeant Major Adalbert Falke. He pronounced the surname with two syllables. He must have been six-eleven, and over seven feet tall with his hat.

He saluted with a hand that resembled a tennis racket and his voice was so low, but soft, that it sounded like he had a pillowcase lodged in his throat. He may have been even taller, since he seemed to be stooping, with a noticeable curvature in his spine that forced his head out in front of his body like a diplodocus. His nose was shaped like a butterknife, with deep-set, widely spaced eye sockets to the sides. Oddly enough, I felt I had known him my entire life, yet was unable to describe him clearly.

"Colonel Hayner wishes to see you without delay," Falke said. Hayner's SS title, Standartenführer, exited crisply out of Falke's mouth, which was surprising given the size of his lips. He rotated laboriously and sauntered ahead through the cave like a giant sloth, his hands moving forward and back in cadence with his footfalls like enormous pendulums. Stringy brown hair flowed from under his cap, down a little past his shoulders.

My escort dropped off to the side, and I followed Falke alone, slowing my usual gait to match Falke's awkward, loping stride.

The walls were roughly hewn, if not natural, and supported every ten feet or so by enormous columns. Water dripped from the ceiling at intermittent points along our nominally descending trek, pooling in depressions in the floor. The cave was gloomy, sparsely lit by single 40-watt light bulbs at least 25 feet apart, suspended by a single electrical cord stapled to the ceiling. It was generally cavernous.

Two hundred feet in, the shaft was blocked by rubble. Falke steered himself through an adjoining passageway on the left, about 30 feet before the rubble. The floor was covered by wooden planks constructed like a makeshift pier, or raised boardwalk. It sounded hollow underneath, and Falke's footfalls echoed through the cave. The passageway smelled like a mixture of sewage and a chemical disinfectant, which I recognized as a chlorine derivative.

The passageway was bordered on both sides by deep alcoves, rooms almost, quarantined by chain-link fences and, in some cases, wrought-iron gates. Were they storage areas? Why the fence and iron?

I halted in front of one of the wrought-iron gates. "What's stored here?"

"Don't mind the trappings." Falke continued to lumber forward, the echoes from his footfalls matching the rhythmic cadence of his arms.

I set my travel case and backpack down and stepped off the wooden walkway, splattering a small pool of water onto my pants leg. I shook my leg in a vain attempt to dry myself. Cupping my hands around my eyes to prevent what little light there was in the passage from ruining my view, I pressed my face against the iron gate.

I strained to see through the bars, but to no avail. It was too dark in the recesses of the chamber, though my mind began to play tricks on me. It conjured a nebulous apparition floating in the darkness, more or less expanding and contracting in concert with Falke's diminishing footfalls. Then, as my eyes adjusted, the apparition dissipated and I thought I could make out movement, but I was mistaken. There was nothing in the alcove.

My biology professor at Leipzig University had claimed that the tendency for people to imagine forms where none exist is an evolutionary heritage passed on to us from our ancestors. It always struck me as a "just-so" evolutionary story.

When I pulled my hands from the gate, a fleck of rusted iron swept into my eye. It was excruciating. I fell to my knees, drenching them in the water. I rubbed my hands against my eye, trying to work the fleck out. It burned. Finally, it dislodged against my nose, and I flicked it off. My eye was watery and unfocused. I rubbed it against my sleeve.

When my eye came back into focus, there was a face pressed against the gate inches from my own. An arm darted from between the iron bars and grabbed my jacket.

I fell onto my rear in the water and pushed with my feet, propelling myself backward onto the walkway.

The face was horrified. The eyes were vacant, and its throat was convulsing, as if it were trying to scream—but no sound came out. It was covered with grime. Abrasions were forming on its cheeks from it rubbing against the iron bars. The man's hair was scraggly and protruding from his head in all directions.

At the corner of the man's right eye, something ever so slight began to leak out. I thought it was a tear at first, but then I realized it couldn't be. It was glowing and pulsating. In a moment of dreamlike insight, I understood it as a manifestation of abject despair. It sucked back into his eye and the filthy man disappeared back into the shadows.

In his place stepped a gypsy girl, as if floating out of the darkness into the muted light of the passageway, which cast faint shadows from the bars against her form.

She appeared as a girl, but she could have been a full-grown gypsy princess. She exuded an aura of maturity, as if she were an ancient soul, yet she stood only three feet tall. Her bangs reached down her forehead to her eyebrows and transitioned without seam to manicured shoulder length brown hair, combed so perfectly that no one hair overlapped another.

She wore a checkered blue knee-length dress with a faded white sash tied in a bow around her waist. There was not a spot of dirt anywhere on her. Her skin was a light olive complexion, and she was as flawless as a china doll. But it was the eyes . . .

The eyes were astonishing. They had to be the size of half-dollars. It wasn't possible, but they were, and her three-foot frame accentuated them. I have never seen anything more strikingly beautiful in my entire life, and yet nothing more tremendously unsettling. It was an encounter with the numinous.

Each eye was a radiant blue that filled almost the entire eye socket, except for the outermost extremities in the corners and the slits right above and below her eyelashes. There was not enough light in the passageway to make her eyes shine that radiant blue. But they *shone*.

In the miniscule space around her eyes, starlight broke through in a pulsating resplendence. It was as if she had a strobe light in her brain and someone had cut slits around her eyes with the finest scalpel to let the light out. I'm convinced I'll see those eyes on my deathbed, and I'm certain God will not be pleased with what later transpired.

Because of those eyes, I'm certain there's a God. Something that exceedingly beautiful must have a creator, and only a God could create something that exceedingly beautiful. They say that God is the highest beauty: the *beatific vision*. If that's true, He's infinitely indescribable.

As I sat on the walkway, I felt the water soaking into my trousers, but it was a distant sensation. The eyes were everywhere, and all things to me.

I vaguely felt myself rising as Falke's giant hands lifted me and my things off the walkway, and the gypsy girl floated back into the darkness. Before she disappeared, I heard these words: *Deus et natua non faciunt frusta. Ex malo bonum.*

3

"What *was* that, Falke?"

"Don't mind the trappings." Falke carried me a ways and set me down at a convergence of two corridors. We had left the passageway with the alcoves behind us. There was a solitary light bulb overhead in the junction, with four dark passages leading out of the intersection. "Standartenführer Hayner does not wish to be kept waiting."

"Ja. Mach schnell," I said.

Falke took the passage to the left and resolutely disappeared into the shadows. I chanced a look back, then followed Falke, who was now a hulking silhouette in the dim light from the next lightbulb up the corridor. Under the light he paused in front of an oaken door. When I arrived, Falke brought a clenched fist down on the door like a mace.

"Enter," said a voice. It sounded like a macaw.

Falke reached out and opened the door. It groaned as it opened slowly on its hinges, but I couldn't tell if it was the door or the forest outside groaning. As deep into the mine as I was, it had to be the door. I stepped into the room, and Falke shut the door behind me.

It was obvious these Nazis were not interior decorators. The wood paneling was mixed and matched and tacked up poorly. A few of the panels' corners had detached. They hung out from the wall and nearly all were warped and buckled, so the seams between them were exposed. The floor was musty, with a water spot here and there, much like the floor I had seen on the way in.

A single bulb lit the entire room, which was about 20 feet square. Standartenführer Hayner sat behind an executive desk situated at the back center of the room. A map of Europe hung across the back wall, with magnetized pieces of armies and matériel placed in strategic positions. From the positions of the magnets, it appeared Hayner was about six months behind on his current events.

"Step forward!" Hayner screeched like a macaw again.

I stepped forward, adjusting my pack. Hayner stood, both fists on his desk, knuckles forward. I was soaked through from my waist down.

Hayner's eyes were so black I couldn't detect pupils. He was utterly hairless—not even eyebrows, arm, or chest hair— with isosceles triangle ears that pointed backward at 45 degree angles. Two wrinkly blue veins snaked up his forehead to the middle of his skull on top. His lips were so thin and pale they resembled an overstretched elastic band.

His hands were gnarled as if he had acute arthritis, but the manner in which he easily clenched them made me think he was in no pain. He wore a standard-issue tank top with camouflaged shorts, which revealed a powerful build. His muscular frame writhed with what seemed to be displeasure, probably at my appearance, but with the way he screeched before I entered, I guessed it was standard form from him.

I had thought Falke was the star attraction at the Nachthaus, but I was wrong. Hayner was *sui generis*.

"I demand that my officers be in top form, inside and out." Hayner eyed my wet pants.

"I—"

"Speak when spoken to!" Hayner's black eyes bulged out of his head while he screeched at me. I decided against informing him that he *had* spoken to me. "Your dossier says you are a chemical expert?" Hayner's eyes receded back into their sockets.

"Yes, Standartenführer," I said. "Leipzig. Major in chemical engineering, minor in Liberal Arts."

Hayner lifted his hands from the desk and cracked his knuckles. "The Reich must be getting soft. Liberal Arts. I don't trust a man who loves the arts. Literature makes a man weak."

As Hayner prattled on with his wrongheaded polemic, I squelched a retort from Shakespeare that was insisting to be heard. Then I forgot all about Shakespeare for the time being.

A black slug-like creature oozed from the corner of Hayner's mouth. I thought I had imagined it at first, but it did not disappear when I looked more closely. It began to wiggle out and then twisted its head around as if it were surveying its surroundings. It locked on to my face and began to glare. It didn't have eyes, but it was glaring nonetheless. I could feel it.

I also realized it wasn't a creature after all. Its body wasn't real. It was more like some form of energy. Somehow I connected the slug in Hayner's mouth with the man in the alcove and the thing that had emerged from his eye.

My insides felt as though they had liquefied and seeped into my boots. The Nachthaus began to press down on me. The full weight of the mine was forcing its way into my mind. I was trapped under tons of rock and earth with things I had never seen, all revealed to me in my first 30 minutes.

I forced the thought from my head: What else was down here, even at deeper levels of the mine, and what was it doing here?

My mind conducted a fighting withdrawal to two lines of defense. The first was not too promising: however bad it was inside the mine, it was worse outside. The second line was better: whatever evil might be in here, it had not snuffed out the gypsy girl's eyes. Seeing those eyes was worth whatever price I might pay for being here to see them. It would be a small price, because wherever those eyes could exist, there was hope, even in a place like the Nachthaus was turning out to be.

"Your chemical expertise is what's needed here, Leutnant," Hayner said, using the proper Austrian form of *Lieutenant,* "so leave the arts outside."

Though his phraseology was correct, the rank he called me by was not. Hayner had called me a first lieutenant, though this was an obvious intimidation technique, as I was a second lieutenant, an Oberleutnant. I elected to not correct him.

"Falke will now show you to your quarters," he said, "and then to the fires. I want those fires hot, Leutnant. I want them hotter than any fires in Europe. The Reich will burn its hottest here."

Hayner moved from behind the desk and approached me. As he did, the slug squirmed back into his mouth. "Also,

Leutnant, I want you to develop a solvent. We need to delve deeper into this mine and, as you might have noticed on the way in, we've had some trouble with cave-ins digging with conventional means. This mine is unstable. Look at my walls."

Hayner was now standing directly in front of me. I guessed he was about five-foot-eight, a full five or six inches shorter than I. His skin looked like it had been pulled tightly over his face and attached along the sides of his bald head.

"If it were that easy, everybody would already be doing it, sir. There are some solution mining techniques available, but that works with solubles like sulfur. You've got solid rock here."

"Then I suggest you get busy, Leutnant," Hayner said. "Falke!"

Falke opened the door.

"Show the Leutnant his quarters, the laboratory, and the oven."

Falke led me outside and shut the door behind us.

Behind the door was a loud crash as if Hayner had overturned his desk in a tantrum. It was followed by screeching that continued as we walked down the corridor. By the time we reached the intersection where we had turned to Hayner's office, the screeching was barely audible over the groaning. This time I was certain it came from outside the mine.

4

Falke executed a wide left turn at the intersection like a truck towing a long trailer. I followed and felt the beginnings of a subtle decline. After fifty feet the decline increased until I could feel the mine pulling me down inside the mountain.

Despite what Hayner said about the arts, I was pleased with my classical education and no more so than at the moment Hayner disparaged it. A classical education included Latin, and mine was fresh enough to roughly translate the gypsy girl's cryptic words. *Deus et natua non faciunt frusta. Ex malo bonum:* God and nature do not work together in vain. Out of evil, good.

My head was reeling a bit from the steady decline into darkness, but a thought from Epicurus came to mind in concert with the gypsy girl's Latin:

If God is willing to prevent evil, but is not able to, then He is not omnipotent.

If He is able, but not willing, then He is malevolent.
If He is both able and willing, then whence cometh evil?
If He is neither able nor willing, then why call Him God?

The Nachthaus was quickly affirming the existence of evil, not that I needed confirmation after having lived in Nazi Germany. Evil seemed to exist in bountiful supply down here in this Romanian mine, and I hadn't even seen the torture rooms or the oven yet.

The single bulb on the ceiling ahead must have burned out, because Falke disappeared into the darkness of the mine as we descended. I could still hear his rhythmic footfalls as I entered into the darkness behind him. The angle of descent increased, and the air around me deadened as if the mine ventilation system had shut down. The still air was warmer, and I felt myself struggling to breathe. A smell of hardboiled eggs lingered. The walls of the mine groaned. I walked with my free arm outstretched in front of me, carrying my travel case in the other.

After what seemed five minutes, the floor leveled out under my feet and I found myself in utter darkness. I paused, for I could no longer hear Falke. I groped about, not able to see my hands. I discovered the side wall of the mine and felt along it until I grasped a support beam, which instantly offered me a splinter in my left hand.

I embraced the beam there in the darkness, longing for my Bavarian home where my bride-to-be, Katia, waited on me—I hoped. *"The jaws of darkness do devour it up: So quick bright things come to confusion."* Shakespeare was never at a loss.

Bright things had come to confusion, and here I was in the abdomen of the earth, in the dark, wishing I were alone. But even then, I sensed I was not. I somehow knew—I felt it in my bones—that something was afoot in the Nachthaus. And I wished the rock of the mountain would cover me. I wished as the wicked in the Bible wished for the rocks to hide them from impending judgment. Yet I knew it was a futile wish, even in the dark.

I've heard it said that courage requires fear, and I believe that's true. People react differently to fear and pressure, and I made a choice in the dark that day, clutching that support brace deep in the dark Nachthaus, with my imagination conjuring indescribable evils around me, that no matter what would come for me—and I knew *something* was coming—I'd face it with courage.

I decided on courage because fear is not eternal. They, or it or them, could kill me once and fear would be gone. But courage is forever.

A thought intruded on my mind through the darkness: *What if death is not the end? Perhaps fear could extend beyond the grave . . . what if I were to fly into the undiscovered country to evils unknown? Or what if I were to descend into the depths of evils unknown?*

I scraped my head against the beam and my hat fell to the floor, the black visor clacking against the stone. The moaning of the forest and the mine wormed into my chest, and I felt the outer darkness of the mine. "Courage," I said. My voice barely registered.

"One moment, sir." Falke's voice crept softly through the mine. A light sputtered on, off, and then finally on up ahead.

Falke finished screwing the light bulb in, and I looked over at him, adjusting my eyes to the light. He stood under the light next to a parched wooden door, much like the one leading to Hayner's office. Behind him was a pile of rubble blocking the mine shaft. We had reached the end of the corridor. I reached down for my hat.

"These bulbs burn out regularly, when it's their time, of course," Falke said. "I always keep a spare or two on me." Falke opened the door. "This way, sir." He held out one of his tennis racket hands toward the opening. "First hall to the left, your quarters. The hallway at the end leads to your lab. The oven is on the right. Have a pleasant evening, sir."

I entered, and Falke shut the door behind me.

The corridor was well lit in comparison to the rest of the mine. The bulbs overhead were spaced out about every five feet. The gentle hum of a generator came through the walls to my right, almost counterbalancing the constant groaning I had heard since arriving. A faint odor of charred carbon filled the hallway. It reminded me of when I would clean my fireplace in my home in Bavaria.

I stepped forward to the first hallway on the left. It extended back about fifty feet and had three doors spaced evenly along the right side of the passageway. The hallway ended in another pile of rubble. I set my travel case and backpack down at the entrance to the hallway.

I was more interested in the lab, so I passed the hall leading to my room and moved forward. Ahead was a one hundred-foot passage that was better maintained than what I had seen so far of the rest of the mine. In addition to the better lighting, the walls had been polished down the left-hand side. That, or they had a polished granite façade inserted for aesthetic purposes. I touched the first pane of granite. It was smooth to the touch and cool.

The corridor itself was warm, even a bit stifling. The floor was well-kept. I figured someone was sweeping and mopping on a regular basis. About thirty feet in, the oven appeared on the right-hand side. Two observational slits with thick glass ran ten feet away from a central door in either direction. The glass slits were about six inches in height and about a man's height off the floor. I could already tell they'd resemble flaming eyes when the fires were lit.

The door to the oven was an iron plate like the one at the entrance to the Nachthaus, except this one opened vertically. Two sets of ship's wheel pulley mechanisms were mounted on either side of the door. The oven had been hewn directly into the rock of the mine. I peered through the glass, estimating that the oven was forty feet long by twenty feet deep. The interior was devoid of structure, except for another iron door at the back right corner. The floor was stained black in random splotches.

I turned from the glass portal and noticed the strangest figure on the polished granite directly opposite the oven door. It was a face. Not a face that might be imagined in an ink blot or a cloud, but a real face—a no-doubter. I crossed over to the wall and placed my fingertips to the granite in an attempt to see if the granite had been chiseled or worked in any manner to produce the likeness. It hadn't, that I could tell.

The face was a demon emerging from the granite façade in three dimensions. The eyes glowed, the horns on its head protruded out from the rock, the snout extended into the hallway, and the teeth drooled.

I traced my hands along the granite, feeling the snout right above the thing's nostrils. Its eyes began to root into my mind. I felt the thing rummaging through my thoughts.

"I wouldn't touch that," a voice said.

I wheeled to the voice, which had come from the end of the corridor, presumably from the hallway leading to the lab. My hand remained attached to the granite. The man to which the voice belonged beat it double-time down to where I stood, extracting a folded-over magazine from his back pocket as he ran. Thanks to my love of the arts, I immediately recognized Broadway star Mary Hawkins on the cover. She seemed to keep a wary eye on the granite face from behind the fold. When he reached me, he held the magazine out and used it to remove my hand from the wall as if it were attached to a live wire.

"Leave that one alone." He stuck the magazine back into his pocket and saluted me. "Private Gotthold Moench, sir. You may call me 'Gott.'"

"Is that a standard-issue magazine out here, Obergrenadier?" I asked.

Gott replied without studying me. "I studied theater and dance back home before learning to goose-step, Oberleutnant."

Obergrenadier Gott Moench wore glasses, and he reminded me of a Nazi version of Harold Lloyd: fluid and athletic. He moved like a dancer. The way he moved, he could have been a God in India if he had six arms. Now that I thought about it, I hadn't heard his footsteps as he'd run to knock my hand from the granite. I think genius appears in many forms. Physical genius is one, and Obergrenadier Moench had it.

Gott wore the standard-issue tank top and camo shorts with black boots, much like Hayner. His glasses made his eyes appear bigger than they were and his cheeks bulged out at the sides of his face, rounding it. I imagined if he wasn't so physically gifted, he'd have spent much of his childhood nursing wounds from bullies picking on his baby-faced looks. His hair was cropped along the sides and back, but longer on top and allowed to curl down across his forehead. He seemed to be early- to mid-twenties, like me.

"Nice to meet you, Gott. I think we can dispense with all the formalities down here in this hole." I stuck my hand out to shake.

Gott seemed to make sure I had not offered him the hand that recently was affixed to the granite, and then he shook. His hand was soft, but the grip was firm. "You're different from our last Oberleutnant."

"In what way?"

"I never shook hands with an officer before."

"I doubt you're any more of a man for having done so," I said. "What's with the face here?"

"Permission to speak freely, sir?"

I nodded. "Natürlich."

"I doubt I'm any *less* of a man for it, either." Gott strained his eyes at me through the thick glasses. It was clear to me he was studying me, quickly and intently, though it looked like he was doing it through a fish tank. I wondered if we ever see anyone more closely than that, no matter if we wear glasses or not.

"Perhaps not, Obergrenadier," I said. "What kind of Nazi are you, with black hair and eyes?" I studied Gott's reaction. Two could dance this dance.

"Nazis are not as they look but as they do, sir." His eyes did not flinch behind the glasses. He turned and pointed at the granite face. "We leave this one alone, sir. It'll cloud your mind if you look at it too much. We never touch it, and we don't even linger around it alone. It's the oven's herald—the thing lights up when the fires are lit. Don't ask me how it got there. We don't know, and we don't ask it."

My science and arts backgrounds pitched battle lines in my mind, and dug in. The first salvo from science claimed there had to be a natural explanation for it. Arts returned fire: haven't you seen enough already in this one hour to suggest that not all things are explained sufficiently by natural causes, especially here? I settled on the notion that perhaps the face was a confluence of natural causes working through the granite, and maybe another cause I was not privy to.

"Hmm. A game you play on all the new arrivals." I pointed toward the oven. "What's behind the door at the back of the oven?"

Gott turned and walked to the glass viewing slit on the right side of the oven door. "There's a small room behind it with the oven controls, the generator, and some utilities. When we fire this thing up, someone has to run the controls from behind that door. It's fireproof, obviously."

"How does the generator run constantly without fumigating the room?"

"You'll see when you go back there. There's an exhaust port that connects to lines that run through the mines to the outside." Gott gestured to determine whether I wanted him to take me through the oven to the room.

I declined. "I didn't see any lines on the way in. Are those lines drilled through solid rock?"

"Not sure," Gott said. "The exhaust lines go out the back of the room. Probably mostly set through small drilled holes, but there's plenty of other passages behind the cave-ins. The pipes may run through those somewhat."

"Wonderful," I said. "At any moment a cave-in could fumigate us with carbon monoxide."

Gott shrugged. "Rolf's in the lab. Do you want to meet him?"

"Bitte."

I followed Gott down the hall past the oven. The way he moved, if he made it out of this mine and war alive, he was going to be famous. We reached the end of the hall, which terminated in more polished granite. The only egress was the hallway to the left. This one had two doors instead of three. Both were wooden and both were set on the right-hand side.

We walked down the hall, stopping at the door to the first room, which, my good inquisitors, happens to be the one we're sitting in now. Except back then it was full of 55-gallon drums and chemicals. Gott opened it to allow me a quick look inside. He shut the door, and we walked to the end of the hall.

Gott opened the second door and ushered me in.

Ah, a room whose purpose I could understand. I immediately felt comfortable for the first time since arriving at the Nachthaus. Inside was an under-lit laboratory, fully stocked with beakers, Bunsen burners, microscopes, electrodes, test tubes, workbenches, and, best of all, shelves and shelves of chemicals—liquids, solids, and gases in pressurized canisters. There were several glass cases, the kind with the rubber gloves built in to them so one could handle dangerous chemicals safely inside the case. And there were tables, several of them. They reminded me of operating tables.

The room was as austere as the storage room for the drums of fuel and about the same size. I loved this laboratory instantly. Except for one thing: there was what appeared to be a human body lying on one of the tables toward the back of the lab. It seemed to be covered in leaves, as if retrieved from a shallow grave. The chest cavity might have been open, except it was ringed with spikes.

Gott saw me staring at the body. "I'll explain that later, Oberleutnant. You're not the only scientist here." He pointed at the other side of the room. "Let me introduce you."

A man in a white lab coat was washing scalpels in a sink. He shut the water off and turned around. He was wearing protective goggles. He smiled, revealing the largest set of choppers I had ever seen, and walked toward us. He clacked his teeth together as he walked. They were mostly brown— not rotten but stained tan as if he had smoked for 60 years. When he quit smiling, his lips didn't quite cover his teeth.

"Oberleutnant König," Gott said, "this is Rolf Waechter."

"No salute, Waechter?" I asked.

"I'm a civilian," Rolf said. "Not required." He looked like a heron in the white lab coat.

"Are you a scientist?"

Rolf nodded. The goggles accentuated his head movement.

"No need to salute, then," I said. "What's the thing on the table?"

"Pflanzen-Krieger. A plant warrior. You'll see a lot of those around here. Are you squeamish, Oberleutnant?"

"Not that I know of."

"Good," Rolf said. "Come with me."

We walked to the table where the corpse lay. Gott stayed behind.

At first the body appeared to me like a lump of rotting vegetation lying on the table. It smelled like a compost pile. It was moist and dingy, like it had come from a swamp. It might have been eight or nine feet tall.

Rolf brushed vegetation off the thing's chest—several insects scurried for cover—and pulled apart the corpse's chest cavity. Or perhaps its stem. The chest cavity was a monstrous Venus flytrap. The interior was pink, full of oozing sap, and seemed to lead to a rudimentary gullet. The flytrap was rimmed with spikes. Rolf placed a wooden beam inside the flytrap to keep it wedged open. The plank sank a few inches into the pink walls of the trap. It reminded me of the railroad ties that supported the mine shafts.

The corpse's head was the main concern for squeamishness. It was a bulbous fruit roughly contoured in the form of an elongated human skull without jawbones, tapering down to the rough husk of a melon where the chin would be. An intense red was obscured by a beard of thick, live vegetation engulfing its entire head, with willow tree leaves beginning at its brow and flowing back over the skull. There was a circular hole at the base of the melon that appeared to be a mouth. It was at least four inches in diameter and as dark as a deep well, surrounded by whiskers of grass. I thought I could make out human eyes under the vegetation.

What have you gotten yourself into now, Sascha König?

I leaned forward over the corpse, peering into its black maw of a mouth. It reminded me of the entrance to the Nachthaus. It was fascinating, more so than even the flytrap that Rolf was fiddling with. It seemed as though something was moving in the mouth. I leaned closer. It was a large worm or a snake, perhaps.

A vine shot out the thing's maw, at least four feet long. It coiled around my neck and constricted. I tried to yell for Rolf, but my wind was cut off. Its eyes opened under the vegetation. The plant-man lurched up into a sitting position and howled wildly: *Wooooooooooooooooooo! Woooooobooooooooooooo! Woooooooooooooooo!*

5

Rolf ripped the wooden beam from the flytrap. The ridged opening snapped at his hands, but missed. He took the beam and beat the plant-man's head until it was a pulpy mess. The vine relaxed and the plant-man fell back motionless.

"Sorry about that," Rolf said, tossing the beam aside. "They do that sometimes when they warm up."

"*Sometimes?*" Inside of me, the détente between science and art had ended. "How many of them are there?"

He shrugged. "Many."

I rubbed my throat. "Do you work on these things by yourself?"

"I asked you if you were squeamish," he said. "I sedate them when I study them like this, but sometimes it wears off if they warm up. Something in the plant tissue blunts the effect of the drug, I guess."

Rolf, the six-foot-tall heron, stood facing me with giant teeth and goggles. What a day.

"Do you have more of these in the lab?" I asked.

He motioned toward a door at the back of the lab. It looked like it could be a cooler. "About half a platoon," he said. "A whole forest of them out front, you know."

"Gott, show me to my room," I said, my mind feeling sluggish. "And when do we eat?"

"Do you like salad?" Gott said.

I searched for a hint of the humor on his face and came up empty, but it had to be there somewhere. "Not tonight, I think."

Thirty minutes later I was in my room, reclining on the bed with a bowl of hot potato stew and some sandwiches. The room was a cave with no opening, and I half expected to be required to fight a bear to claim residence. The bed was a stained mattress with a tattered blanket and a pillow lumpier than the stew I was eating. The only furniture was a table by the door and a nightstand with a wind-up alarm clock.

It was two-thirty in the afternoon: two-and-a-half hours since I'd arrived, and I was already exhausted. I would begin my first official day of duty at six in the morning. A nap enticed me.

I opened my travel case and rooted around for my lone picture of Katia. One picture was enough, as long as it was her. She was the beauty and purity we conquered for, the Nazis told us: the face of the Fatherland. Her eyes were Aryan blue to me despite the black and white photo, her hair flowing blond. In the photo we stood together by the train before I departed for the Wehrmacht.

The Nazis had spoon-fed us their doctrine, their *weltanschauung*, but the two of us had spit it out like sour pabulum.

I was conscripted into the army as an officer on account of my university achievements, and I vowed to Katia that I would return to marry her. The army was a stint for me, a tour of duty. I expected to perform my service, remain alive, and return to the academic life . . . and to her. Thus far I had served on the eastern front, but when I'd received a transfer, the last thing I had anticipated was an officer command under the direct supervision of an SS Standartenführer like Hayner in an isolated death and torture camp like the Nachthaus.

I wasn't sure how to handle this new assignment. Fighting on the front was bad, but at least there we were against armed men who wanted to kill us, and an officer had some power to prevent atrocities against civilians. Here were an oven and ghastly torture rooms. In my mind, the latter were worse. I didn't know what to do. Could I last a day here, much less my entire tour of duty? If I deserted, I'd end up dead or in the Nachthaus torture room myself. If I didn't, I'd be party to the crimes here. It was a German's dilemma.

I set my Luger and officer dagger on the table by the door and lay down on the bed, trying to remember how out of sorts I had felt when I was first issued the gun and blade. I remembered only vaguely, as if though a dream.

I shut out the light and the room turned pitch black. You could count on an underground room for real darkness. Outside my thick wooden door, the mine groaned. I was certain the forest outside was moaning, as well. It had been a long trip to Romania, and a strange two hours. I slept deeply—for a while anyway. Sleep was a prized commodity at the Nachthaus, as it turned out.

• • •

A monstrous duck was honking rhythmically. It was an unnatural honk, not sporadic like a duck in the wild, but a mechanical, on-a-second-off-a-second honk. It was raspy and grating, like an overamplified kazoo.

The duck was outside the door of my room trying to wake me from my slumber. It kicked in the door with an enormous webbed foot and waddled into the room. But it wasn't a duck, it was a wading bird . . . a stork, or even a heron. Its webbed foot had four-inch claws, which scraped across the stone floor as it entered. The wooden door to my room crashed against the wall, gashes carved deep into the wood from the bird's talons.

I rubbed my eyes because the bird didn't have a bill. It had large brown teeth and wore goggles. Gott charged in behind the duck, which now resembled Rolf very much. Gott slunk around Rolf in his graceful, athletic manner and yelled at me to wake.

I leapt out of bed, fully dressed except for my jacket and my boots. Outside the door, a red light was flashing on and off in concert with the honking, which now proved to be a blaring alarm. The clock on the nightstand read midnight. Or noon the following day, perhaps. What I wouldn't give for a window.

"Hurry!" Gott's eyes pulsated behind his glasses. "Bring a weapon if you have one."

My first thought was of the face across from the oven. A weapon, though? Didn't make sense, unless the face animated off of the wall from time to time.

I grabbed my Luger off the table and ran out the doorway behind Gott and Rolf. By the time I'd made it out the door and turned toward the main corridor, Gott had reached the end of the hall. In the flashing red light I saw him make a right into the corridor. He was heading out, away from the face. What was it, then? Allied attack?

I slid in my socks at the end of the hall, gained my balance, and sped toward the mine shaft. Gott and Rolf had made it through the door and into the shaft. I ran faster, not wanting to be left in the dark. When I passed through the doorway into the shaft, Gott and Rolf were moving quickly up the incline.

The main lights had cut off throughout the shaft, leaving only the flashing reds of the alarm. The shaft was bathed in a blood-red color one moment and went dark the next. I was glad not to be passing by the face in the granite under these conditions.

The alarm's volume increased as we approached the front of the mine. When I reached the intersection where Falke and I had turned to visit Hayner's office, the alarm and red lights were in perfect synchronization. My eardrums rattled.

I followed Gott forward onto the pier-like flooring that led past the gated alcoves. Without the overhead lighting, it was impossible to see clearly. I wondered if the gypsy princess was still behind bars. I shook off the disconcerting notion that humanity could be so cruel as to lock up a creature like her. It was as if astronauts had returned from another galaxy with the most exotic alien fauna ever encountered and locked it up. It was unconscionable.

I passed the alcoves at a full sprint in a futile attempt to catch Gott. I was gaining on Rolf, though, who seemed to be losing steam. The alarms blared, and up ahead I heard muted gunshots and screaming.

Screaming? What horrors awaited me now?

To my right, I passed the alcoves and I saw those eyes. I didn't need the red flashing light to see them. In fact, they were more visible in the dark. They floated in the darkness of the alcove, shining like binary-star supernovae. They ejected a burst of stellar luminescence that lighted the shaft instantaneously. I saw the gypsy princess in her dress.

"*Ex malo bonum*," she said. And then she was gone.

I made the right at the end of the corridor and sprinted toward the front of the mine. More gunshots rang out. I heard Hayner's screeching above the tumult.

When I got to the front door, what I saw made no sense. Five men were straining against the ship's wheel door closing mechanism. Their brows were rife with sweat and their arms bulged with effort. The rope-and-pulley system creaked and whined under tremendous stress. The iron door was ajar, and I stopped, flatfooted, ten feet from it when I saw why.

Six giant hands held the door from the outside and were attempting to force it open. It was a tug of war between whatever was out there and the five soldiers turning the door closing mechanism. It was give and take—and the issue was very much in doubt, but it seemed the invaders were gaining ground.

The large hands were pallid, as with poor circulation. The fingers were bony with oversized knuckles, with claws extending from the fingertips. The hands were devoid of hair, and their veins stood out as they struggled against the soldiers' efforts.

There were inhuman invaders at the Nachthaus door. Was I in Romania or the netherworld?

The groaning from the forest was audible above the alarm, which was almost deafening. The forest was incensed and trying to enter. Over the low moan, a hideous shrieking emanated from outside the door. From the sound of it, there were scores of . . . whatever they were . . . outside.

I could no longer feel my legs. So much for choosing courage.

Hayner was all action, but he did not seem astonished. To watch him move, a person would think this kind of thing happened all the time. He alternated between the inhuman hands and the five soldiers, whipping the soldiers with a riding crop to urge them on and attempting to beat the hands off the door with a billy club. The club was having little effect, although I know I heard fingers breaking.

Every now and then I could see something try to dart inside. A squad of armed soldiers to my left was firing rifle shots into the gap between the open door and the side of the mine.

An anthropoid head that seemed all teeth breached the gap. Its nostrils flared beneath russet fur, matted like a field of dead grass. The thing must have smelled man flesh, for it cocked its head and roared and its eyes scanned the interior of the mine hungrily. The mouth extended around the sides of its head, and the jaws appeared to unhinge like a viper's. The teeth were grotesque spikes set at odd angles along both halves of the jaw, partially covered by a spongy black hide and caked with decomposing tissue. Strands of gnarled remains lodged between its teeth hung down across its lower jaw.

The head bared its teeth—and was shot. It retreated. There was a horrible moaning right outside the door: a guttural, gurgling, deep moan.

Hayner pounded the hands on the door with his club, but missed once. The club smacked against the iron, recoiling and flinging itself away from him back toward the squad of soldiers. It bounced against the wall and spun a few times before coming to rest on the stone floor.

One of the hands reached inside and grabbed Hayner's arm. He screeched louder than ever and the two blue veins on his head bubbled up. The arm that grabbed him was formidable, but Hayner stood his ground against it, not budging an inch. His own muscular form strained against the intruder.

One of the soldiers charged forward in an attempt to free Hayner. At that same moment, I raised my Luger and put two slugs into the creature, one in the forearm and one in the elbow. The thing let go and vanished behind the iron plating. Hayner vaulted back to safety.

The charging soldier ventured too close to the opening. Another arm grabbed him from outside. Hayner had the advantage of being against the back of the door, which provided leverage. The soldier was directly in front of the gap. He twisted and broke free of the hand's grasp. But when he did, another one grabbed him, then another and another.

The soldier fell to the floor and began to slide backward through the door. He was screaming for help, clawing at the floor of the mine, but the hands kept pulling. The red alarm lights shone intermittently on his face, highlighting his terror.

He was halfway through the gap and it appeared some Pflanzen-Kriegerin—the plant-men—were pulling him with their vine tongues. The soldier was now all the way outside to his shoulders and begging for the soldiers to shoot. They began to fire through the opening of the door, but it was too late. His screams filled with pain, not just fear, and I had a bad feeling that something horrible was happening to the part of his body out of sight.

I saw something emerging from the sides of his eyes and from his mouth. Black snakes of his soul.

He slid out more. Only his hands were left inside. They grasped the edge of the iron door. They held for a few moments, and the soldiers rained bullets into the opening. Whatever was pulling him was able to do so from behind the safety of the door. Abruptly, the screaming ended. The soldier's hands relinquished their hold and disappeared into the darkness.

The six hands forcing the great iron door open were winning the tug-of-war against the soldiers trying to close it. The pulleys creaked louder under the strain, and it was obvious that the door was about to give way completely. It shuddered open another inch, then two. Then it lurched an entire foot.

I was thrown back to my right. I stumbled and fell. A short blast of fire hit the iron door. Falke had thrown me out of harm's way as he'd passed. From the floor I saw him lumbering forward with an outstretched flamethrower. The tanks strapped to his back looked as big as full-sized compressed air tanks.

Falke again blasted the opening with fire. It streamed through the gap, and the creatures outside wailed. The hands roasted and released the door at once, slipping into the dark. The soldiers at the wheel began to turn. The door inched shut while the forest outside moaned.

Falke kept a stream of fire trained on the opening and pressed the flamethrower nozzle all the way through the door, no doubt spraying anything within a thirty foot distance from the door. The door finally closed. Two soldiers rushed to set the locks.

Outside, the scratching began. The sound seemed to come from every inch of the iron door, as if those things were mindlessly searching for a way in. I remembered the size of those claws and imagined them digging at the iron facing.

It would continue every night for my entire stay at the Nachthaus. Every night: constant and continual scratching until morning.

"You complete buffoon!" Hayner whipped one of the soldiers with his crop. The crop was fitted with a silver swastika on the handle upon which a flaming skull with ruby eyes was set.

The soldier kept his arms around his face and head in defense, cringing at the blows.

"The door stays shut at all hours, and especially at night. Do you hear me!" Hayner's crop came down hard on the soldier separately for each of the last four words spoken.

"Gott," I said, "you must tell me what this place is." I leaned back against the side of the mine, attempting to process monsters, mines, forests, and my descent into strangeness. My Luger had seen some action on the eastern front, but here it was my first day at my new post and it had already been fired in combat . . . against inhuman beings with giant hands. "Gott, help."

Gott steadied me against the wall. "Give it a moment or two and it'll seem normal again. This place is *unheimlich*—weird—that way. Before you know it, the oddest things will somehow not bother you much. Trust me, you'll see worse than that, and if you're not careful it *won't* affect you." Gott pointed at the other soldiers. "Do you see anyone worried? Do you see anyone mourning their fallen comrade who just died a horrid death? This place causes that, Oberleutnant."

Hayner's black eyes found me, and two slugs like the one I had seen at the corner of his mouth were hanging out his nostrils. They quickly popped back in. "König, come here please." Hayner had regained his composure and appeared to be schmoozing me to the best of his ability. He actually smiled a wry smile at me, his tight skin straining. "Did you get a good look at that?" he asked, pointing back at the iron door. The scratching seemed intensified now that the mine's alarm system had shut off.

My legs were steadier than I thought they'd be when I pushed off the wall, so I walked over to Hayner. This was a madhouse. A wisecrack might help suspend my disbelief. "I put two bullets in your dance partner's arm." I searched him for a reaction, but got none. "I'd suggest you get a prettier date next time out." A bit sycophantic and self-serving, but I was pleased with my response.

Hayner squinted at me, apparently unsure. Score one for the liberal arts. He smiled again and put his hand on the back of my neck, guiding me into the mine. I could feel the coiled power pent up in his muscles as his arm rested across my back. "Sascha," he said, "you begin in the morning. We need that solvent." He halted our walk and pointed back at the door. "Work on the oven's fire too, but get that solvent ready. It may be our only chance."

I looked at the door and then back at Hayner. I combined the door, his statement, and the rubble I had seen all over the mine. "We can't get out, can we?"

"Don't ask too many questions, Sascha."

"But I had no trouble coming in yesterday."

He almost smiled. "Getting in is easy."

I remembered the way the forest had stared at me on the way in. "You can radio out," I said. "You did to get me here, evidently."

"We seem to have no trouble with those kinds of messages," he said. "But other kinds of messages—such as my many requests for reinforcements—never get through." Hayner squared up in front of me and put his hands on my shoulders. The slug was back, hanging out of the corner of his mouth. "You may be our last chance, Sascha. Work on the solvent."

"I'd probably need at least six months, Standartenführer. And then what's your plan? Chemically burn a way through the mountain?"

"That's about the size of it, Sascha," Hayner said. "There are other shafts and exits, and we need to get through to them. And don't worry about the six months. We have much more time than that if we need it, as long as they don't shut down our incoming supplies. We've held out longer than that already, and we still have a lot of work to accomplish before we leave."

I was still holding my Luger. I holstered it. "Accomplish?"

"Don't ask too many questions," Hayner said. "Go get some sleep."

On my way back to my room, I paused at the alcoves. The gypsy girl's eyes had been calling me, and I wanted to see them again.

Thus far I had hid from the Nazis my disbelief of this place. No one in the Nachthaus seemed to acknowledge the existence of the strange creatures assaulting the mine, nor the life and death struggle we seemed to be engaged in. No one cared for their dead, no one challenged Hayner's seeming insanity, no one expressed a sense of dread of the spiritual oppression coming from the Nachthaus itself. No one seemed worried that they were trapped.

I couldn't reconcile this inconsistency with our situation and the behavior exhibited in the mine, so I hid my disbelief from the Nazis for fear that they would turn on me if they knew. The terrifying thing, though, was that I could feel my own shock and panic fading away. My own rational disbelief of what I was seeing was fading—quickly too, as easily as rationalizing my reasons for not visiting my grandmother when I had the opportunity.

This terrified me more than the creatures, more than the death of the soldier I had witnessed: that I might wake up one morning dead to the evil in the Nachthaus, with a seared conscience no longer sensitive to the horrors around me—a sort of spiritual dementia.

All these things haunted me, and the gypsy girl seemed the only one in the Nachthaus that might possess a rational explanation. Those eyes promised she did, and I sought them.

I grasped the bars of her cage, rattling them. Nothing came from the darkness of the alcove. "Please," I said. "I need help." I waited for a response that did not come. Then I muttered dispiritedly, broken by the recent events that flooded my mind. "Please."

Glorious light saturated the alcove, encompassing my entire field of vision. In the center, two blue orbs hovered. A voice came from the light. "You are free, Sascha König. Why would you seek help from the captive?"

I considered this. "You are not my captive," I said. "I think *I* may be a captive of this place as well. I'm afraid." The sublime light I stood in was so alien to the Nachthaus. I feared it would cease.

"You will do what you will do, Sascha," the voice said. "I must not speak with you further. Awake, thou that sleepest."

The light extinguished and I stood blinded for a moment, now hearing footsteps approaching from the main shaft. The clarity afforded by the light vanished, and I lamented. The Nachthaus sprung upon me again, working its disorientation into my mind. I stumbled off toward my room.

I slept fitfully that night. The continual moaning of the mine and forest reached all the way down the mine to my room like a plumber's snake unclogging a drainpipe. My thoughts switched from Katia, my betrothed, to killer humanoids, to chemicals, to the gypsy girl with the eyes.

And, of course, the face. No wonder Gott had warned me about it. I could feel its presence in my room. It was calling me. It had permeated the solid rock between the polished granite and my room, or perhaps it had drifted down the open hallway and entered under the space between the wooden door of my room and the floor. I wasn't sure, I only knew it had come calling on me in the dark of the night.

I turned the light on, preferring the light and my picture of Katia to the unwelcome presence of the face. When I finally drifted off, I dreamt of Nebuchadnezzar and the fiery furnace. The king ordered the furnace to be lit seven times hotter than normal, and the three Hebrew boys were bound and tossed into the fires. And then one shining like the son of man was among them in the flames.

6

Gott, Rolf, and I stood between the granite face and the glass-slit eyes of the oven at 6:00 a.m. sharp. Gott and Rolf looked well-rested, and it caused me to wonder how often the events of the previous night transpired.

I scrawled notes on a pad, ripped the page off, and handed it to Gott. "See that I get these without delay. Your chemical inventory is somewhat lacking."

Gott ambled to the door to the mine as gracefully as Fred Astaire, pausing to depress a buzzer. He sat at a desk and waited.

I turned to Rolf, who was standing in front of the face. The face's 3D effect made it seem as if it were about to bite Rolf's head off. "Do you always wear those goggles, Rolf?"

"I mounted two monocles in them," Rolf said. "I can't see very well at all without them." His tongue darted in and out of his mouth between the big brown teeth as he spoke.

"Okay, Rolf. Give me the tour."

Rolf brushed past me and began to turn one of the ship's wheel door openers. The iron door began to rise, making no noise as it did. "Sir, would you turn the other wheel, please?"

I went to the other wheel and turned. The silence with which the great door rose surprised me. At the end of the hall, a soldier entered. Gott handed him my note and issued instructions to have Hayner authorize the requisition immediately. I could hear Gott over the rising door, which also surprised me.

When the door was fully open, Rolf latched his wheel, and I did the same. We entered the oven, Rolf leading the way.

The oven floor was sooty, as I had seen. The soot chafed against the bottom of my shoes and a light particulate hung in the air. There was the distinct fireplace smell from the soot. It was dark in the oven, the only light entering from the open door, and to a lesser degree through the slits. If it closed, it would be near dark.

The iron door was suspended only by the latches on the wheels, which was discomforting. It must have weighed a full ton, and the thought of it breaking the latches and crashing down, trapping us in the oven was sickening.

Rolf guided me to one side of the oven and displayed a set of louvers that covered the entire wall. "These shutters open remotely from controls in the back room." He pointed across the oven to the other side. "There's an identical set over there. When open, the jets are exposed. The jets flood the entire oven with fire instantaneously."

"This doesn't remotely approximate German efficiency," I said. "Who engineered this atrocity?"

"It was here when I got here," Rolf said.

"Nonsense, Rolf. Why would miners build a furnace such as this? It is not designed for smelting or refining. It doesn't make sense." I walked to the side of the oven and traced the walls with my hand. "How long does the oven take to cool?"

"An hour, usually. There's a built-in cooling system." Rolf pointed at a hole in the ceiling less than a foot across. "Runs to the back and connects in with the generator exhaust. Sucks the heat out."

"Definitely not German," I said. "The cooling system is not efficient. Rapid cooling of a blast furnace like this would compromise the shell integrity. Ruin the refractory material."

"Maybe it's repaired from time to time," Rolf said. "I'm a scientist, not an engineer."

I doubted the oven would burn as hot as Hayner desired, but the professional challenge excited me. The thought of what my expertise might be used for did not. I sidestepped that line of inquiry.

"Rolf," I said, "doesn't it strike you as odd that there's an 800 square-foot oven in the center of a mine?"

He didn't flinch. "It's the glory of science to progress."

"'Tis the infamy of man to misuse it." I gauged his response. This time he showed signs of breaking, his lips peeling back over his brown teeth. I pressed. "What exactly do you burn down here?"

Rolf swiped at the soot with his shoe. "You saw those things last night, didn't you? Remember the plant creature in the lab that grabbed your neck."

"Is that it?" I feared something much more insidious.

"Except for Hayner's projects, sure."

Rolf headed for the control room door at the back of the oven. He opened the door and waved me in.

The room was around twelve feet deep and six feet wide. A control panel was mounted on the left wall, running half its length. It featured the controls for the oven, the generator, the lights of the mine, and a communications grid. A map of the mine illustrated the location of each light and communications station.

The generator was much louder in this room than it had been outside. Rolf had to raise his voice a bit to be heard. I walked past the control panel to the end of the wall, where the room made a left turn and extended about twenty feet before terminating. A rusty generator ran smoothly, anchored atop iron I-beams. The generator exhaust pipes disappeared into the wall along with the oven cooling pipe as Gott had indicated, but the odor of fumes lingered in the air.

Gotthold Moench was entering the control room as I came back around the corner. "Your supplies will be here soon, Oberleutnant."

I nodded and went over to the control panel. "Since I need to fix this fire, you might as well show me how this thing works."

Gott and Rolf each waited for the other to man controls. Gott lost. He flipped a six-inch toggle switch at the top left-hand corner of the panel. "Shut the door, Rolf."

Rolf pushed the control room door shut and secured it by a latch and a sliding iron bar. Gott rotated a red knob clockwise. A whirring noise arose somewhere outside, which Gott attributed to fuel pumps. A meter in front of Gott registered the fuel, and in fifteen seconds, it was ready. Gott depressed a switch and a lamp labeled "pilot light" illuminated green. There was a distinct *whoosh* outside.

Gott opened a door on the control panel. It swung open, revealing a master switch. "When you're ready, press this switch."

I stepped up to the switch, the smell of the fuel faintly reaching into the control room. I was already lightheaded from the generator fumes, and the smell of the oven fuel increased the sensation. I rested my fingers on the switch and distinctly felt the granite face outside burrowing into my mind. I pressed the switch before it could get in.

The ensuing roar was louder than a blitzkrieg. The mine seemed to rattle around me and for a moment I thought the control room door might not hold. The roar was louder than cannons, freight trains, bomb blasts.

I staggered back against the wall of the control room. The blast furnace was all-consuming. The roar disoriented me and all I could see around me was flame, ever-encroaching flame. Gott's and Rolf's voices faded away, and the lights of the control panel doused. I fell against the wall, and the flames set in.

I writhed in a pit of flame, yet the flame burned darkly. I was in an outer darkness, but it was replete with fire. First I sensed a presence, and then multiple presences. Something, or somethings, moaned incessantly in this pit. The groaning crept closer and grew louder.

The flames licked at me and I tried to move, but was caught against the wall of the pit. In the flames, the granite face leered at me, again burrowing into my mind. Just before it could succeed, the face exploded in flame. My arms, legs, and torso were afire.

I screamed and my screams alerted whatever was in the pit. The moaning grew louder, and a horde of humanoids resembling the ones attacking the front door of the mine appeared. They approached me methodically with gaping, toothless mouths, empty eye sockets, and outstretched hands with fiery talons.

The nearest set of talons closed on my right leg. The next on my arms. A third around my neck. They shook me violently, the talons digging into my flesh.

The humanoids separated my body and spirit. I floated away from the carnage, free from the fiery pit. There was a brief frigid sensation as I passed through the iron control room door into the oven.

The oven was a sea of fire.

The shutters had opened revealing the jets, from which it seemed the power of the sun had been released. There was not an inch of space in the oven free from the flames. Adrift in this ocean of flame, I heard the cries of the oven's victims. Their cries reverberated off the walls of the oven, echoing through the fire, forming faces and likenesses of their bodies.

It was a chorus of agony. The souls of men and women from every tribe and nation throughout human history swirled in the fire, lending their voices to a discordant refrain that lamented the evils of the world. It was not the flames they bemoaned— it was evil itself: human evil, natural evil, demonic evil. And there was no shortage of iniquity for the dirge performed by this nameless choir.

The pictorial wickedness bled through the flames in all its infamy, yet was not consumed. From the most banal acts to the senseless to the thoroughly heinous—evil was on display in its naked villainy. The world was a butcher shop and, to my horror, I felt a part of me reaching for it. *Embracing* it.

The roar of the oven ceased, the flames subsided, and instantly I was wrenched back into the control room and reunited with my body. Instead of flaming talons, it was Gott and Rolf shaking me from my stupor.

• • •

I extended a hand to assure Gott and Rolf that I was fine. I contrived a story on the spot that claimed I was given over to mild convulsions periodically, but I suspected those veterans of the Nachthaus knew better.

When the oven had cooled enough, they guided me out of the control room, one man holding me under each arm. Halfway through the oven, they dropped me. I fell to my knees. Gott and Rolf rushed to the iron door, which had mistakenly been left open. They seemed worried. I pushed myself up and followed them. They stood in the doorway arguing, each blaming the other for leaving the door open.

I reached the doorway, standing directly under the suspended iron door. Gott was to my right. Rolf moved into the corridor to accommodate me. "Why does it matter?" I asked.

"It floods the entire hallway with fire," Rolf said. "If anyone had been standing here they would have been incinerated." The two looked both ways down the hallway.

"Gott," I said, "check the halls to the lab and our rooms. Check outside as well to be sure."

Gott took off toward the lab. In a few graceful strides he reached the corner. "Clear!" He started back toward our rooms.

"I'd think you'd have a failsafe," I said.

Rolf started to speak, his teeth separating, then didn't. Gott passed between us on his way down the corridor.

"I'm pretty sure we killed someone," I said, looking at the face.

Rolf's eyes widened behind the goggles.

Gott yelled "Clear!" again as he passed the hallway to our rooms. Seconds later he was through the door to the mine. Finding nothing, he started back.

"I don't understand," Rolf said. "Why do you think someone was—"

"Take a look behind you." I pointed at the granite.

Rolf turned to look at the wall. Gott came up and we approached the face together. It was gone. Burned away by the flames escaping through the open door. Even though we didn't dare touch it, there was obviously no residue on the granite, just a blotch where the face had been.

"Fascinating," Rolf said. "Maybe we were lucky to have left the door open."

I exchanged a glance with both Gott and Rolf. "Perhaps."

That night the writing began.

7

I awoke to Hayner's screeching. It was like owning a demented rooster that had swallowed a megaphone. I hurried my clothes on and got out of my room, moving down the hall briskly. It was five in the morning.

Hayner stood at the end of the hall, pointing his riding crop at the door leading to the mine. Hayner, the subterranean horseman.

He whipped me with the crop as I rounded the corner at the end of the hallway. The crop slapped the nape of my neck and stung like being popped with a wet towel.

I spun on Hayner reflexively, attempting to take the crop from him. I probably would have done it anyway had I thought it through first. Some things have to be done, and this was one of those times. It proved costly, however.

I was a half-foot taller than Hayner and outweighed him by 20 pounds. It didn't seem to matter. He grabbed me by the throat and lifted me a foot off the ground, gently bringing my face down toward his. It was phenomenal. The muscles in his arm flowed like the swell of a gentle sea, and I was helpless against the depth of its power.

His taut face contracted, and the two blue veins on his head stood at attention. The slugs came out of the corners of his eyes and dripped like black molasses down his cheek. I hoped he wouldn't smear any of it on me. Our faces were inches apart.

With his other hand he thrashed the crop across my ribs with a compact strike. Air stampeded out of my lungs. His hand tightened on my throat. The crop descended again on my thigh. It felt as though he were injecting fire directly into my veins. His thin lips smirked.

The crop came down on my calf, and my legs buckled backward with the pain, but my body did not swing in the least under Hayner's grasp. I tried to rub my legs to ease the pain but the crop swung down on my wrist.

I wanted to weep. I wanted to squeal. Yet I bit down, clenching my teeth with all the force I could muster. Hayner sensed the insurgence in my eyes and brought the crop down again and again.

As I felt my mind swimming in the shadows of a lack of oxygen, I trained my eyes on Hayner in defiance. I blacked out, but not from the pain. I made sure Hayner knew it.

When I came to, I was propped up against the granite façade in a sitting position. It felt as though one side of my body had been soaked in meat tenderizer. Hayner and a squad of soldiers were milling around the door to the mine. Gott and Rolf were at the end of the corridor past the oven. They seemed to be conferring in private.

I rose to my feet, favoring one side. Hayner noticed, and waved me over as if we were old friends. I strolled to the door and realized the source of the commotion.

On the door were written these words: *Mene, Mene, Tekel.* The words were written in the purest white, which seemed to penetrate the general murkiness of the mine. The effect reminded me of the gypsy princess's eyes.

"The patrol discovered this on routine rounds this morning." Hayner gave no indication of any lingering animus over our previous incident. The crop hung from his belt, the ruby eyes of the skull gleaming at me. "Do you know what it means?"

"Ja. I know what it means." I folded my arms in front of my chest, careful not to wince. Defiance is a lush garden when watered properly.

Hayner placed a hand on the hilt of the crop. "Do you care to explain it to me? No one else seems familiar with it."

"It means *God has numbered the days of your reign and brought it to an end. You have been weighed upon the scales and found wanting.* The book of Daniel, I believe."

Hayner peered deep into my eyes. "No one else knows what it means, Leutnant König. How would you explain that? Perhaps it means you did it?"

"Someone's lying, perhaps? It is a well-known Bible passage, Herr Hayner." I tried to dilute the sarcasm lacing my words. "Or perhaps the same way you would explain a siege of our front gate by giant hands or any of the other *unheimlich* things going on here?"

"Ja. Good point," Hayner said. "I happen to know you didn't leave your room last night anyway." Hayner's thin lips did their best to form a smile. It looked like someone had drawn a mouth on a beach ball with a marker. "One cannot be a Nazi and a Christian, Sascha. Do you believe that?"

"What could be clearer, Standartenführer?"

The soldiers had busied themselves trying to remove the cryptic message from the door. They appeared to be rubbing it with turpentine and rags.

"What's clearer is what we do with them and their ilk, Sascha. You'll see a crystal clear demonstration tonight." The slugs popped out of his eyes. "Now, determine what's on that door and mix up a solution to remove it cleanly."

I dispatched Gott with specific instructions for two chemicals from the lab, which he was to mix in a three-to-one ratio before bringing it to me at the door. I asked him for clean cloths, as well. He sauntered down the hall toward the lab.

I called Rolf over to the door. *Mene, Mene, Tekel* remained, despite the soldiers' efforts to remove it. "What do you make of it, Rolf?" I asked.

"Many strange things happen here, sir." He ran a finger over the lettering.

"That doesn't tell me much," I said. "What do you think it means?"

Rolf adjusted his goggles and leaned closer to the lettering. "I'm a scientist, sir. I could tell you more if I were allowed to analyze samples of the—"

"Rolf. Look here."

Rolf turned and looked.

"What's going on here? You've been here how long? Two years? What's going on?"

"I've been here two years, sir. Since they opened the mine. This craziness started recently. Maybe almost a year ago now. I don't know what it means. I only know it is. I'm a scientist. I'm still holding out for a natural explanation, actually."

I put a hand on Rolf's shoulder. "I don't think that's going to be possible, my friend. Come with me." I led Rolf down the hall slowly.

On the right, the oven grew nearer and nearer as we approached. The iron door was still open. I noticed again how similar it looked to the front of the Nachthaus itself. The door was a gaping maw and, after my experience in the oven yesterday, the oven looked sinisterly hungry. The glass slits that formed its eyes followed us as we walked toward it.

When we reached the door of the oven, I guided Rolf to the granite façade where the face had been. I pointed at the granite. "What do you make of this?" I asked.

Rolf adjusted his goggles again. "It can't be," he said. "It can't be."

The face had returned. I recalled that there had not been residue on the granite after the oven did its work on the face. There had been only a disorganized blotch. Now the face had returned and the blotch was gone. There was still no residue on the granite. The face was *in* the granite somehow, a part of it. Perhaps it was a part of the mountain. What I was sure of was that no one could have put it there—no one human, anyway.

Gone was the demon face. In its place was indubitably the face of an old man. Its nationality was difficult to determine, but that it was human and male was unmistakable. Its jowls hung below its lower cheeks and it had a deeply furled, tripartite brow over deep-set, brooding eyes. A bulbous nose took full advantage of the 3D effect caused by the granite, protruding to where it eclipsed a portion of the face's cracked lips. Of all things, the man had white hair. I don't know how the granite did it, but the hair was white: long and stringy. The granite's composition endowed the face with a rough and grainy complexion.

"The blotch is gone, Rolf," I said. "That's the strangest thing. The blotch is gone. The face is clear as day."

"There's got to be an explanation, sir. This can't be."

Gott turned the corner and, when he saw the face, dropped the beaker of chemicals he was carrying. His fluidity of motion allowed him to catch it before it hit the floor, but it was close. "What—"

"Come closer, Gott," I said. "I want to try something."

Gott set the beaker on the floor and stepped up to the face. The three of us were a foot from the granite, Gott on my right, Rolf on my left.

I placed my fingers inches from the wall. "I want to touch the granite to see if there's any trace residue on the rock. Maybe that will tell us if someone etched it into the rock."

"I don't know, Oberleutnant König," Gott said. "We don't touch this thing. Remember?"

"I'll proceed in the name of science. Right, Rolf?"

Rolf smiled with his oversized brown teeth.

"Then use this." Gott handed me one of the cloths he had brought from the lab.

"If something happens, knock my hands off the wall like you did before," I said.

Gott and Rolf nodded.

I wiped the granite with the cloth, right under the nose of the face. Nothing happened. The cloth was spotless.

"Okay, here goes." I placed my naked fingers on the face.

Instantly I was standing deep in the forest outside the Nachthaus. Except it wasn't the Nachthaus anymore; it was a lush and fruitful mountain that stretched to the heavens. As it rose, the upper reaches of the mountain disappeared into the most beautiful spectrum of light I have ever seen. It was even more stunning than the gypsy girl's eyes.

I couldn't describe these colors. I wasn't sure they even were colors. They might have been the radiance of being coming from something above the mountains—something that dwelled in the height of the mountain or, most likely, in the ineffable region above it. I would have stared at it forever if I were able. It was that beautiful.

The wood around me made me wonder why I had considered my Bavarian home beautiful. Here was an untamed garden of indescribable delight. It was pure wilderness, except that its wildness was not what we would think of as wild. It wasn't threatening or dangerous. It was nature as the *natural*. Nature as it was intended to be. It was the perfect amphitheater for an audience to view the mountain and the glory above it.

But then there was a crunch in the wood to my left. I looked over and saw a woman far more beautiful than my own Katia. In her hand was a fruit resembling an apple, and the pulp of the fruit was still on her lips.

Suddenly, the mountain lurched and the earth quaked around me. The unutterable glory above receded into the mountaintop and was replaced by the lingering dread of perpetual dusk. The forest groaned under the quaking of the earth and aged a thousand years in seconds. Blight covered the trees, the smell of putrid death hung in the air, and the most unnatural noises filled the air. I say unnatural because against that first sight of the wood they were unnatural—noises of pain, struggle, and death. The sound of claw, fang, disease, and pain.

I witnessed the ugliness of human history on a grand scale. There was at first a murder, and the ground ran red with blood. Then the floodgates of sin opened and an unending tapestry of violence spread out in front of me. Strands of lust, pride, envy, hate, gluttony, greed, and limitless malevolence wove themselves through history.

The armies marched, the swords dripped with blood, the bombs burst, the forests burned. The grafters came, the politicians lied to the people, and the people lied to each other. Men became lovers of themselves when they could have become lovers of the paradisiacal wood and the departed glory.

I desired to weep. The evil was so entrenched, such a fabric of humanity and the world—and it seemed it never had to be this way.

The wood was angry about me. Natural evil struck back against man, lashing out with earth, wind, fire, and flood. And with fang and claw. In the wood, it appeared some quintessential element was groaning, seeking recompense or revenge for its unchosen fate.

I felt the presence in the wood closing in on me. I rushed through the underbrush of the forest, certain the presence was on my heels. I felt it gaining on me as branches scarred my neck and thorns thrashed my arms and legs. I ran and ran, deeper into the wood and the perpetual dusk. The brush became thicker and slowed my pace, and I could feel the breath of the forest on the back of my neck.

I met the side of the mountain headlong in my flight. Flush up against the rock of the mountain, I could go no farther. My hands groped above me for a handhold to scale the great rock in front of me, but my search was futile. The breath was upon the nape of my neck now, warm and moist. I turned to stare the world in its face.

The scene was hideous in its realism. The souls in the oven sang out their chorus in a dissonant and revolting two-part harmony: one part agony and one part devotion to the very evil they decried.

I awoke to Gott and Rolf slapping my cheeks. I looked up at their faces from the floor. They were obviously concerned. They pulled me to my feet.

The face was in front of me on the granite façade. It stared back at me.

"How long was I on the wall?" I asked.

"Maybe five seconds," Gott said. "You went into a trance and then started one of your convulsions. We knocked you off the wall almost as soon as you touched the face. We let you down to the floor to revive you." Gott's voice wavered a bit. It was the only time I ever remember it doing so.

"I'd swear I was gone for hours," I said.

The visions brought by the oven and the face were as much evil as I had seen, even as a Nazi. But they were a close second to what was to come that very evening.

8

My chemical order arrived that afternoon along with a substantial food and water shipment from Ploiesti as a testimony to German efficiency. For whatever reason—evil is as unpredictable as it is consistent and continual—there was no trouble with an incoming shipment through the forest. In fact, Hayner had managed to sneak in two heavy machine guns and a squad of soldiers in the process. He had Falke and the soldiers mount the guns facing the mine entrance.

The chemicals were delivered in crates loaded in a personnel carrier with side and rear mounted guns. Hayner commandeered two of the guns and five of the soldiers, and sent the truck back to Ploiesti much lighter than it had arrived. I guessed he hoped that an officer on the other end might question the missing guns and soldiers and send a detachment of troops to the Nachthaus. They never came.

I'm not sure the truck ever made it back to Ploiesti, but it probably did.

The officers on the other end didn't care. The Nachthaus was influential enough in those days to commandeer what it wanted, and they most likely didn't want to fight it, especially with their attention turned to the east. It seemed as though it would have been easy to send a message with the driver, but no messages were allowed out of the forest except those that were acceptable to it, even with the radio.

I spent the remainder of the day in the lab organizing. The oven upgrade would be child's play, but the rock boring solution would require some genuine chemical engineering expertise and some good providence. Hayner sent a reminder memo with the chemicals to expedite the solution.

Around six, Gott, Rolf, and I ate a warm supper cooked on the burners in the lab. We ate hastily, as Hayner had sent notice to have the general quarters in top shape for the evening's affair. After eating, Gott and Rolf swept and mopped the floors, and I finished cleaning the lettering off the door leading to the mine. We looked around, satisfied with our work. We dressed in our formals and awaited our guests. I didn't think to ask Gott what the occasion was, not that he would have known. I'm glad I didn't know beforehand.

At eight o'clock sharp, the three of us stood facing the oven's iron door with our backs to the granite face. When the mine door opened, we straightened and saluted.

Hayner strolled into the corridor in full regalia, followed by a contingent of soldiers. I could barely make him out from the corner of my eye. Protocol kept my head forward until Hayner acknowledged us. Hundreds of feet below the earth, and in a secluded forest miles from any war, we were following military protocol under a deranged colonel. This was insanity.

Hayner was goose-stepping and flinging his right arm forward at a 90-degree angle as if he were a band leader holding a baton. When he reached us he halted and spun with precision to his left to face us, not more than a foot from my face. The train of soldiers halted with him. He clicked his heels. Hayner screeched without diverting his glance from my eyes. His breath was stale. "Obergrenadier Gotthold Moench. Scientist Rolf Waechter. Open the door."

Gott and Rolf didn't seem to realize what Hayner meant at first, but it was painfully obvious to me. I swiveled my head to the right briefly, and then brought it back to Hayner. Gott motioned to Rolf and they walked to the oven door, each taking a wheel. They began to turn the wheels. The door rose.

Hayner whispered to me. "You will not break the code of conduct, Leutnant. Head forward at all times."

I didn't feel like a follow-up demonstration of Hayner's prowess with a crop, so I kept my head forward. But it was too late for my insides to stay in line. What I had seen behind Hayner had left me horrified.

The door was halfway up and as silent as it had been the first time I saw it rise. Gott and Rolf kept turning, like skeletal servants on a death ship sailing across a foggy sea. Two lines of soldiers stood in rank file behind Hayner, eight in front and eight behind two captives. Falke brought up the rear, lurking behind the procession in front of the mine door.

The captives were the scraggly man and the gypsy girl from the alcove.

There were rumors of atrocities circulating through the German army's ranks, but mostly they were thought of as rumors only. I had heard vague whispers about death camps, and even stranger tales about the Nachthaus upon receiving my orders to come here, but no one gave them much credence. They were like ghost stories at bedtime.

Certainly Hayner was bluffing. He wanted intel and was using the threat of the oven to scare the prisoners into talking.

The door reached its zenith and disappeared into the rock ceiling. Gott and Rolf performed an about-face and stood at attention.

"Control room!" Hayner screeched like an owl in the night diving at prey.

Gott and Rolf marched into the oven. A few seconds later I heard the control room door open, shut, and latch. This should not be happening.

"Forward march!"

The lines of soldiers marched forward past Hayner's back until the captives stood directly behind him and in front of the door to the furnace. The scraggly man was whimpering.

"Halt!" Hayner's thin lips receded as far back from his mouth as possible, exposing a full set of rickety teeth. He looked like a wickedly bald Cheshire cat with pulsating blue veins.

The gypsy girl had a hood over her head. The old man did not. I guessed Hayner had it placed there to quell the light from the gypsy girl's eyes. They showed dimly beneath the fabric.

I felt my throat welling up and I fought tears. I think one may have escaped down the side of my face. I'm not sure because I was too busy fighting to keep my composure with Hayner staring at me. I was sore afraid: both from fear that Hayner would throw me in the oven if he saw my emotions, and from fear of my own cowardice.

Hayner must have sensed my pain because the slugs were studying my face from the corners of his eyes. They jumped from his eyes and landed on his cheeks, burrowing into his taut skin. Hayner's face became an undulating mass of blackness from the slugs, like a disturbed pool of used motor oil. The black oil began to drip from the corners of his open mouth. Apparently he couldn't feel them. Apparently no one else could see them. It was a theater reserved for me alone.

I stared at the gypsy girl. The hood over her head was a blasphemy. *Ex malo bonum. Ex malo bonum. Ex malo bonum.* I thought the words as hard as I could, attempting to teleport them through space to the gypsy girl, but in the end, I was too cowardly to even whisper them to her, much less try to put an end to the atrocity she was about to endure.

"In!" When Hayner screeched, the motor oil circulating under his skin left. He rotated toward the open door and watched the soldiers lead the two captives into the oven. The soldiers deposited the captives at the center of the oven and returned to the door, where they manned the wheels. They turned the wheels and the door slowly descended.

Before the door closed, I grasped an image behind Hayner's head that seemed foreign in this mine, yet as resolute as the granite it was carved into. With the oven door open, the glass viewing slits created the horizontal arms of a cross along the vertical opening of the door. The door and the glass slits were dimly illuminated, and the cross they formed shone against the darkness of the oven. In the bowels of this evil earth, I saw a cross, if even through dim glass. The contrast with Hayner's writhing head was striking, but it saddened me the gypsy girl couldn't see it through the hood.

The scraggly man's whimpering increased to wailing. He dropped to his knees and pleaded with Hayner, hands outstretched and cupped together in a praying gesture.

The door was down about a quarter of the way. The cross was fading and I knew soon the glaring orange eyes of the oven would displace it. The man rose and charged the door like a berserker. When he reached the aperture, Hayner grasped him by the neck and cast him across the oven where he landed on the floor and skidded into the wall. The man's wailing became screams. He pulled his hair out in clumps.

The door was down halfway when the gypsy girl pulled the hood from her head and cast it to the floor. The oven burst into light. Light flooded through the closing doorway and created an instant silhouette of Hayner. The glass slit eyes of the oven shone, and for a last precious moment the cross illuminated in glorious light.

It was like the creation of a star. I gazed at it in wonder, not caring if I might be blinded. It would be worth a life of blindness to have once seen such a light.

The soldiers at the wheels ceased turning, and the door hung right above the line of sight to the gypsy girl. The two soldiers peered into the opening, evidently curious at the phenomenon. The rest of the soldiers were straining to see from their positions, and a few of them broke ranks to get a better glimpse. Falke even trudged up from the rear to poke his long neck through the oven door.

I caught one last glimpse of the gypsy girl's eyes. Her blue orbs sought me and locked in on me. They pled with me not one bit, not even for a moment. I was thoroughly ashamed of myself, but though I wanted to look away I couldn't do it. It was too beautiful.

Hayner, facing me, must have seen the face in the granite behind me bathed in the light from the gypsy's eyes. I detected ambiguity on his features for a moment, and the slugs dove for the cover of his eyes. He twitched a couple of times, and then turned into the light, screeching.

The crop was out and it descended upon every soldier in reach, with the exception of Falke, who lumbered back to his post. "Get those wheels turning! Get back in line! Mach schnell! Duty!" In Hayner's grasp, the crop whirred through the air like a propeller. Soldiers sped for their positions. The wheels spun furiously, and the door began to plummet.

The iron door hit the floor with a thud. The light was doused, except as it exited the glass slit eyes of the oven.

My heart sank with the door, and the moments of wonderment in the light were replaced by an awful realization. What was I going to do? Or was I going to do nothing? There could be only moments before Hayner screeched out the commands. How could I stand here as an accomplice to this crime?

I started to speak through the lump in my throat, but whatever I might have said was drowned out by Hayner's orders screeched to a soldier by the intercom link to the oven control room.

"Ready!" Hayner's muscles rippled under his uniform.

The soldiers had all returned to their stations and there was a moment of silence. Soldiers stood in ready posture in two lines down the corridor. Hayner stood in front of the door. The two soldiers at the wheels stood at attention. Falke craned his neck from the rear by the mine door. I stood at the back of it all, in front of the face.

In the silence, the light beamed through the slits and the scene burned a singular impression in my mind. We stood in the light of judgment.

The whirring noise of the fuel pumps broke the silence. I thought of my vision in the fire when Gott and Rolf had first demonstrated the oven for me. The thought of the gypsy girl joining that choir of lost souls tormented me.

I thought of the tapestry of evil I had witnessed in my forest vision and the atrocity of man. Now I was soon to be a part of it. But it crossed my mind that I always had been. I was a butcher in the abattoir asylum, the slaughterhouse of the mad. This violent and rebel world quarantined in a remote corner of God's creation. *Is this a dagger which I see before me, the handle toward my hand? Come, let me clutch thee.*

There was still time to prevent it. The light from inside the oven began to strobe, and then waver. There was still time.

Whoosh! The pilot light lit. All that remained was Hayner's command and the oven would fire. Perhaps Gott would refuse to fire the oven.

The light seemed to regain its luminosity, and it surged through the slits. This was my last chance.

I could hear the scraggly man wailing again, as if he sensed the moment. Another few seconds and he would not have to pull the rest of his hair out. The oven would do it for him. Last chance.

Nothing.

Hayner screeched. "Fire!"

The oven's shutters flew open and the oven roared.

The light extinguished. In its place, the orange glow of fire shone through the slits. The oven glared at me like a demon in the dark with glowing orange eyes. It was no longer just an oven. It was alive. It was human iniquity, and it was grinning at me in the depths of the earth like a vicious older brother.

The madding firelight reflected off Hayner's face. This was evil. And Hayner was cackling.

9

The soldiers filed out of the hallway into the mine, goose-stepping behind Hayner. Falke left last, closing the door behind himself after craning his neck around to take one last look. His eyes met mine, then he lumbered out.

I approached the glass slits and tried to look through, holding out a vain hope that the gypsy girl was still there. The slits allowed light through, but the thickness of the glass made it nearly opaque. I was not able to discern anything beyond a few amorphous and nebulous shapes. With regard to those, I wasn't sure if they were there or if my eyes were playing tricks on me in hope that the gypsy girl had somehow survived. I cupped my hands around my eyes and stared as hard as I could, but it didn't help.

I moved to the door, distinctly feeling the face peering at me from behind. I placed my palm against the door, jerking it away quickly. The door was steaming hot, and I felt the beginnings of blisters forming on my palm. From inside came a whirring sound, and I concluded that the cooling and ventilator fans had kicked in.

I sat down against the side of the oven with my back against the wall right under one of the wheels, and waited for Gott and Rolf. The face was indeed staring at me.

"How often have you seen this?" I asked.

The face stared back at me with its tripartite brow in deep thought. I picked at my burnt palm. The blisters weren't bad. Naturally, I was avoiding the obvious.

I had done nothing, I had stood by like I was the one affixed to the wall, while Hayner had roasted the most beautiful thing on earth. Roasted alive. What stuck out in my mind was how the light had shut off. One moment it was there, the next it was snuffed out, replaced by the hellish orange flames of the oven.

But what could I have done? The best I could have hoped for was a beating at the hands of Hayner and the soldiers. The worst would have been to be cast into the torture rooms, and then into the oven. What good would that have done? I still would not have saved the girl.

I sat and wondered if that's how cowards always respond. The face was no help. He sat there on the wall and stared.

Then it occurred to me that I wasn't at all concerned with the fate of the scraggly man that had perished along with the gypsy girl. A dark irony pressed in on me: the man was the one calling for compassion, and had received none. The gypsy girl had seemed resolute and steadfast to the end. The man had cowered and wailed, yet my thoughts had not settled on him once.

Which simply meant that I had not cared that much at all about either one. I must have figured deep down that they had done something to deserve their punishment. I don't know . . .

treachery against the Reich, perhaps. Or maybe they had conspired in a murder plot in Ploiesti. Who knew?

All I knew is that I hadn't cared at all. I wasn't a coward, then. I was worse.

I had cared about the gypsy girl only because of those eyes. Those radiant eyes that filled dark places with light. I had never seen anything like them. The eyes had made her a novelty. No, not a novelty. An attraction. A spectacle. I had wanted her alive for the vision of the eyes, and for that alone. She was my entertainment. It struck me now that I hadn't been affected by the fact that she was locked in a dark alcove.

I trembled, recalling the roar of the oven and the dousing of the light. Kurtz's last words from Conrad's *Heart of Darkness* came to me: *The horror! The horror!* And here I found myself in a dark wood beneath tons of rock, in the heart of darkness itself. With dark, evil hearts all around me.

But the darkest heart was my own.

After the oven cooled, I heard the unlatching and the opening of the control room door from inside the oven. I stood, wiped my eyes, and began to turn the wheel to open the iron door. When it was knee high, Gott scrambled under it effortlessly and went to the second wheel.

When the door was up, we joined Rolf inside the oven. The gypsy girl was in fact still there. She was lying on her back in the center of the room. The scraggly man was still against the wall in the back of the oven.

I knew now why the oven floor was soot-stained, as I had noticed on my first walk-through. Gott and Rolf would be sweeping and mopping soon, but the soot wasn't ever likely to be totally gone. Our sin left a permanent mark, as I suppose all sin does. The particulate hung in the air as it had before, and I took a handkerchief out of my pants and held it over my face. The smell was still reminiscent of a fireplace, but currently stronger.

I knew also why they had called me in as a specialist. The fire wasn't quite hot enough to do the job right. The bodies were burned, but not fully cremated. I'd fix that first thing. I figured it was a combination of the lack of a white hot fire and the placement of the jets in such a large room. The gypsy girl's eye sockets stared up at me. The eyes were gone. I desperately hoped the fire had been hot enough to kill her quickly.

I bit down on the handkerchief to keep it in my mouth and reached for the girl. I've never been quite sure why I did it. Part of me thinks I wanted to hug her, to somehow let her know how sorry I felt over my cowardice. But I suppose I was cowardly to the end, because even now, in the aftermath, I was still attempting to console myself.

The texture of her charred body was repulsive. I jerked my hands away and they returned to me covered with soot. My palms were black with char. I snatched the handkerchief from my mouth and rubbed it vigorously between my palms.

It had an adverse effect. Instead of cleansing my hands, the handkerchief was smearing the soot, working it into the lines and crevasses of my palms. The soot had worked its way into the creases between my knuckles, into the cuticles of my nails, into the lines of my wrists, into the open blisters from my burns from the door.

I scrubbed harder and faster like a man wishing for a genie to come from a barren lamp. The friction from the scrubbing heated my palms. I imagined the heat fusing the sooty stains into my hands.

"You clean this mess up," I said. "I'll be in the lab."

I darted out the door and made straight for the lab. I could smell my hands now, and when I entered the lab, almost at a run, the smell of the soot overrode the chemicals. I panicked, imaging that this smell would never leave me. It was the smell of sin, and I was stained with it. My hands were as dark as the Nachthaus.

I grabbed a beaker of astringent from a shelf and poured it into one hand over a basin half full of water. I rubbed again using the cleanser, slowly gaining speed as my panic intensified. The astringent was having no effect. It seemed to be making it worse, opening the pores of my skin and giving the soot a deeper foothold.

I held my hands in front of my face. They were foaming black mittens. I plunged them into the basin, realizing full well through the water that they were still stained. Worse was the realization that I was more ashamed that my sin would be obvious than I was of the sin itself.

I ran for my room to search for my gloves. They were black, like my hands. But they were supposed to be.

The next morning I was back in the lab, mixing chemicals with my gloves on. Rolf showed up around 6:00 a.m. and began tinkering with a Pflanzen-Krieger corpse. Gott showed up around 6:30 with breakfast. We cleaned off a workbench and ate together. They never mentioned my gloves.

"Rolf, can you spare me a plant-man or two?" I asked. "I'll have the new fuel mixture for the oven done today and I want to test it."

Rolf paused from nibbling a piece of toast long enough to respond. "Can't we wait for the next execution?" He must have seen my glare, because he immediately offered one of his plant warriors from the laboratory cooler.

"Excellent," I said. "Have it ready to go and lying on the floor in the oven where the gypsy girl was last night. Come to think of it, Rolf, put two more in the oven. One in a corner and one at the back of the oven where the old man was. We'll make sure we've got the entire oven covered. And throw some extra items in—shoes, bones, clothes—whatever you can find."

Rolf nodded without nibbling the toast.

"If Hayner wants a fire," I said, "we'll give him a fire. It's the least we can do for those poor souls caught in it. Make it as quick and painless as possible."

Gott poured a cup of coffee. Black, no sugar. "Hayner wants that oven hotter so he can avoid having evidence lingering around." He poured another cup and handed it to me.

"Nothing I can do about that, Gotthold. We've got to help those folks out, and the hotter the better." The coffee was good. Thick and pungent, but not as pungent as the soot smell coming from my hands. Even with the gloves on I could smell it. I wondered if Gott and Rolf could.

Gott handed a cup to Rolf. Cream and sugar. "Don't worry about the plant-men, Rolf," Gott said. "When I was up front this morning, word went around that Hayner's opening the door tonight. He's going to test our new defenses with the machine guns. It'll be a slaughter. Plenty of new plant matter, I think. We'll need to report up front around 2300 hours."

Or, I thought, plenty of new Nazi corpses.

"Hayner's nuts," I said. "Better get some rest this afternoon. Any other news?"

"They're expecting a transport of new prisoners today. Maybe as many as fifty or a hundred. It's about to get busy around here."

"We'd better hurry then. Be ready for the test at 0200."

I spent the rest of the day preparing the oven, more concerned than a chef at a five-star restaurant. It had to be right.

10

Gott showed me the fuel lines for the oven, which were back behind the generator in the control room. I was stunned that the generator was so close to the fuel, but that's the way it was, so I proceeded with caution, hoping I wouldn't be the next victim of the Nachthaus. The generator wasn't overly warm, and there was a makeshift heat shield between the generator and fuel lines, but all the same it was a bad idea, consistent with the shoddy engineering of the oven and the location of the control room.

Gott and Rolf dollied in some fresh 55-gallon drums of fuel gas, which we would later plug in to the lines. After evacuating the lines, I welded a new line, grafting it into the main line leading to the oven. This new feeder line split into two a foot below the main line. I ran one line to a compressed air tank, which I would fill with oxygen or some unstable ozone if I could swing that instead.

For the other line, I planned to heat up a special mixture into a gaseous state and feed it with the ozone into the main tube to mix with the fuel. That would give the fuel a real kick when it lit up. Dicyanoacetylene was the hottest burning chemical known to man, coming in at right over 9,000 degrees. With my special mix the oven never got quite that hot, but it was hot enough.

After the welding was complete, I cut the torch, took off my mask, and handed it to Rolf. In the process, he dropped a hammer we had used to tap in a beveled connection, and it landed hard on my foot.

The Nachthaus leapt on me without warning. I hurled the hammer at the wall and turned on Rolf. He cowered from me, eyes growing large behind his goggles, his tongue darting in and out beneath his oversized brown teeth.

The Nachthaus disoriented me. It called to me in my rage. The flames of the oven danced around my eyes. I wanted to pull Rolf into them.

In a moment, Gott was between us, and the spell passed.

"What was that, Gott?" I asked. "I lost myself."

"Another day in the Nachthaus, sir."

I was a newcomer still but I already knew what Gott meant: another day in the Nachthaus. Except I sensed all the days were the same, blended into one uninterrupted span of existence beneath the faux light from 40-watt light bulbs, which itself was only a weak representation of the muted light filtering through the forest outside.

I managed to release some of my anger against Rolf, and I trudged past him to the back of the control room to retrieve the hammer. The Nachthaus must have infused my rage with a special power, because I had thrown the hammer so hard it had dislodged a rock from the wall.

It occurred to me as I picked up the hammer what such power could do in the hands of a man like Hayner. It frightened me more than the inhuman things scratching at the gate trying to claw their way in. Worse was the thought that it could happen to me. And worse still was the thought that the Nachthaus was not transforming me, as I had thought. No slow descent to horror. No, I had entered as a fully commissioned vessel.

By 0200, the test was ready. I coached Gott on the method of heating and inserting the mixture into the line with the fuel and left Rolf at the controls. I went out front and shut the iron door. With the plant corpses in place, Rolf fired the oven and it roared. I hadn't thought it possible, but the oven was even louder than it had been.

My concern had been that the oven jets weren't properly aligned. But I found that, with the increased heat, it didn't matter. The oven was now truly a beast of hell. All three corpses were incinerated into ashes. Nothing remained: not shoes, not clothes, not bone.

Nebuchadnezzar had come to the Nachthaus.

I spent the remainder of the afternoon and evening before the midnight massacre mixing more chemicals. Since the test had been such a success, I turned my attention to Hayner's other project: rock solvent. Gott brought some rock samples into the lab for testing.

"I took these from a rubble stack at the end of the main shaft, as requested." He set the samples down on one of the workbenches.

"Thanks, Gott. You and Rolf take the rest of the afternoon off and rest up for tonight." I jiggled a couple of the rock samples in my hand. They felt compact and dense. This was going to be a challenge.

Gott paused at the lab door before leaving. "Are you pleased with the oven test today?"

"I prefer to call it Dante's inferno." I kept jiggling the rocks and focusing on a set of chemical equations written on a pad on the workbench.

"Dante's inferno," Gott said.

"Ja," I said, not looking up. I studied my equations.

That night the alarm sounded a little before the time we were supposed to meet at the front door to the mine. I rushed from the lab, bringing with me a knapsack full of carefully sealed beakers, and met Gott and Rolf coming out of their rooms. They were both armed, so I asked them to wait while I retrieved my Luger.

Minutes later we were entering the alcoves where the gypsy girl had been caged. Hayner and Falke were there with a contingent of soldiers. They were pointing at the wall of the mine to the left of the alcove gate, about chest high. We walked up to join them right as the alarm ceased.

On the mine wall were written these words in the same piercing white lettering as the first message had been: *Thou art the man!*

Hayner saw me coming up. He was in full battle gear for the upcoming open door ceremony. "Leutnant schoolboy," he said. "Get over here and tell me what this means."

I stepped in front of him and looked at the wall. The letters were hastily drawn, but in fairly good script. Their contrast with the dark mine was striking.

Hayner slapped me on the back of the head. "Do you know what it means?"

I turned slowly, trying to decide if I wanted to reveal to Hayner that I knew. If I told him what it meant, it would be two out of two, and he might blame it on me. I might end up in the alcove, in the inferno, or worse, in the torture room.

But if I didn't tell him what it meant, he might also charge me with the crime. The first writing would seem infinitely more complex to Hayner since it was in a foreign language, even though it might be more well known—or certainly less cryptic—than what was on the wall now. If I tried to act as though it were a mystery, he'd think I was lying. Tough choice . . . and I was on the clock.

"Yes, sir," I know what it means." Option one seemed the lesser of two evils. I smirked at the thought of a lesser evil in the Nachthaus.

"Something funny, schoolboy?" Hayner grabbed the back of my neck and squeezed. It was not a signature Hayner squeeze, but he could get it there in a hurry if he wanted to.

"Look at Falke," I said. It was the best I could think of. Hayner was a disorienting presence.

Everyone around us in the mine turned to Falke. He stood there with his mouth open and head lurched forward on his long neck, craning down from above us.

First Hayner snickered, then the soldiers did too, then Gott and Rolf, then I did, after Hayner released his grip. Finally, Falke joined in. I was the one laughing hardest, because I had outfoxed Hayner.

"Tell me what it means, schoolboy," Hayner said. Recess was over.

I adjusted the knapsack hanging on my shoulder. "It's another story in the Old Testament, like the other inscription," I said. "Nathan the prophet told King David a tale about a rich man who had taken the prized possession of one of his poorest neighbors. It was a lamb and dearly beloved by the rich man's poor neighbor. It was the one thing the poor man had of value and he loved it with all his heart, soul, mind, and strength. It was like a daughter to him."

I paused for a moment to let the story sink in, kicking at some pebbles on the floor with my foot. One skidded along the floor and underneath the wooden pier that ran down the middle of the shaft.

"The rich man took that lamb, killed it, and fed it to a guest. When Nathan finished this story, King David rose up, incensed and indignant, and swore oaths against the rich man in the story." I paused again.

The Bible must have a strange power over the hearts of men. Here below in the heart of darkness, it appeared to be penetrating into these men. Even Hayner was rapt with attention.

"At the height of King David's oaths and indignation, the prophet Nathan said to him *'Thou art the man!'* For King David had stolen Bathsheba, the beloved wife of a man named Uriah the Hittite."

That was the one time I ever remember the Nachthaus quiet.

Hayner broke the silence. "Who is it talking about, school-boy, since you seem to decipher these riddles easily enough? Who is the man? Who is the lamb?"

I was composing an answer when the groaning and scratching started, and a cry arose from the front of the mine.

Hayner ordered the soldiers to the door, and we all rushed to the front, except for Falke, who plodded along behind.

The scratching on the great iron door sounded like a freight train coming to a screeching halt. It was as if men were outside with crowbars scraping with all their might down the face of the iron door. After that night, I fashioned earplugs out of wax and carried them with me wherever I went.

Hayner commanded the soldiers into position with glee. It was obvious that he thought he had the upper hand with the addition of the machine guns. The guns were mounted into the floor of the mine with steel rivets about thirty or forty feet from the door. A soldier manned each gun, with another on the floor to feed the ammo belts into the guns. It was an iron-clad deathtrap ambush for anything entering the mine.

Behind each of the gunners Hayner had instructed the soldiers to mount two spotlights. Twenty feet in front and to the right of the line of fire, a squad of soldiers manned the door opening wheels, which had been encased in an iron-plated protective covering. The rest of us—Hayner, Gott and Rolf, myself, and the rest of the soldiers—were positioned behind the gun nests.

Hayner commanded the door to be opened.

The scratching outside suddenly ceased. Only the moaning of the forest was audible. Slowly, the iron gate began to shift in its track, grating against the stone. It cleared the side of the mine and opened a few inches, then a foot, then wide enough for a man to walk through—or be dragged through.

"Halt!" Hayner said.

It was quiet outside except for the moaning. We focused on the gap created by the partially open door, craning to see what was outside. Beyond the door, the entry tunnel of the Nachthaus on the outer side of the door was like a rifle barrel, cold and dark, a smoking instrument of death. A light haze wafted in, bringing with it a faint smell of compost and a distinct sense of cornered animals. It was the usual pitch black night of the forest beyond the shaft outside, as if I could be shot out of the Nachthaus into utter darkness.

"They usually charge right in." Hayner's voice was the lowest I had heard it.

I stepped over to him. "You're being had, sir. They're baiting you."

"How could you possibly know that? You think you know everything, schoolboy?"

"You order that door open further and you'll know it too. It's too big of an advantage for us with the door almost closed like it is. I think they know that."

"Silence. They're animals. Proceed!"

The soldiers up front resumed their labor over the wheel that moved the gearing system. The door began to gain speed in its track.

"Sir," I said, "all they would need to do is get something in the groove the door rides in. If that happens, we'll never get a door that heavy shut again." I removed the pack from my back and set it carefully on the floor.

"Halt!"

The door was halfway open now. The forest should have been in view, but it was concealed in the dark. What Hayner forgot that night was that there was only a ten-foot clearing in front of the Nachthaus. It wasn't as if something had to cross a 100-yard gap through machine gun fire to enter the shaft. Plus, we were in a cave. He seemed to have forgotten that there could be things hiding right around the corner and that it was only 20 feet from the door to the outside of the mine shaft. Thankfully, he had ordered the bullet-proof encasement constructed around the door operators.

Hayner was making a tactical mistake, but I couldn't tear myself away from the scene I felt coming. I figured I could retreat back to the lab with Gott and Rolf if things got too bad.

We watched for movement, but it was nearly impossible to get a good fix on anything. The moaning continued, and it sounded as though things were crackling around in the gravel outside.

Hayner motioned for the spotlights to be activated. A burst of light saturated the shaft, illuminating the mine all the way through the door to the forest outside.

There must have been hundreds of them.

Their open flytraps reflected red in the light, as did their eyes. Most of them resembled the Pflanzen-Kriegerin warriors Rolf had shown me in the lab. A few of them were treelike, but the majority of the plant-men were conglomerations of assorted vegetation splotched with leaves, mud, roots, and branches growing out of their bodies.

They were neither completely brainless nor fully cognizant of their surroundings. They seemed to be halfway between plant and animal in their behavior. The light stirred them and the charge began. They closed their traps with a collective whacking sound like an ancient army slapping their swords against their shields in unison. They emitted a howling *Wooooooooooooo Wooooooooooooooo Wooooooooooooooooo* as they charged. It wasn't train-like; it was the way a violent wind sounds rushing through large trees, deafening in the closed confines of the mine.

Their appendages appeared to be fleshy trunks, with jagged hawthorn leaves covering their hands and feet up to the elbows and knees.

The horde was at the door within seconds. The rush occurred with such speed, we didn't recover from our shock fast enough. They had the jump on us.

The first of them to breach the door had a mutated, oversized head. Its mouth was a foot across and its vine shot in and out to a distance of six feet. It was pressed from behind by a swarm that flooded the entire shaft. An endless sea of heads and bodies trailed it.

I noticed with a shock a tattered pair of pants under the vegetation on its—his?—legs. Why would plant creatures wear clothing?

What *were* these things?

The plant-man with the oversized head trained his attack on the encasement protecting the door operators. He broke for it immediately. That was not a good sign, as it showed at least some modicum of intelligence. I prefer my Pflanzen-Kriegerin slow and stupid.

I reached down and unbuckled my pack.

At the same moment, Hayner broke from his shock at the mass of nature descending upon us. "Fire!"

The machine guns erupted and the initial carnage was devastating. Plant-man parts dispersed in all directions, littering the floor in a heap of pulp and splattering the walls of the mine and the back of the great iron door with sap.

The bullets shredded the stalks of their appendages and obliterated their heads, which were evidently full of sap. A shattered head seemed to kill them, exposing an interior like that of a rotted melon. A shot to any other part of their body did not seem fatal, but repeated damage to their arms and legs was debilitating.

Several plant-men followed the first one over to the encasement. They were cut down instantly. One was sliced in half by the swath of gunfire, but was still living, using its vine to lash out, grab hold of something, and pull its severed body forward.

I searched the attacking horde for the creatures I had seen attacking previously, the ones with the giant hands. I saw none and wondered where they were and what other nasty things the forest might be able to launch at us. I also wondered what had prompted the change in tactic.

I thought back to my lush Bavaria, its greenness, and its gardenlike peacefulness. What a contrast. What was this place? Was I delusional? My aches from Hayner's beating argued that this was all real enough, but an attack from overgrown and ambulatory plants? Great Birnam Wood to the Nachthaus shall come, indeed.

The machine guns roared. In the confined opening of the mine they were every bit as deadly as Hayner had imagined. The problem was that he had imagined the slaughter taking place outside the entrance to the Nachthaus. Instead, it was occurring within our gate and the bodies were stacking up at an alarming rate. Already the wall of corpses had grown to half a man's height and was effectively dampening the effectiveness of the guns.

The sheer mass of bodies entering the Nachthaus pushed the wall from behind. It inched forward slowly, and it was obvious that we would eventually be overrun, forced to retreat into a mine with no outlet.

The guns roared on. The creatures fell in stacks.

With the dead on the floor, I saw clearly now that most of them had at least one article of nearly disintegrated clothing. Some wore Nazi jackets beneath the growth on their bodies, some pants, others belts. One even had a Nazi cap like my own, but with twigs and grass growing through holes in the cap.

I couldn't process the disjunctive information fast enough. It seemed they actually were plant *men*, as if the forest had reclaimed war dead to send against us. I imagined nature consuming these war victims, their appendages converting to stalks, their skulls becoming sap-filled fruit, the vegetation of some swamp intertwining with and transforming their flesh.

Then the guns fell silent. The first belts of ammo were expended. The soldiers feeding the guns raced to rearm with new ammo belts, but there was not enough time. The enemy scaled the wall of death, spilled around it, and charged straight for us.

Finally, Hayner screeched orders for the door to close. The wheel began to turn, but I didn't see any way for it to succeed against the sheer volume of the tide of invaders pressing their way in. The gap managed to close a foot against the current, but then, as before, the giant hands grasped it from the outside. We'd perish if we couldn't secure the entrance, and I didn't see a way to fight off the horde and handle the hands at the same time. He should have listened to me.

The creatures banged on the encasement protecting the door operators. It sounded as if they were sounding a huge gong. If the encasement fell, we were doomed.

Meanwhile, the invaders assaulted the machine gunners as they were reloading the guns. The front line of plant-men switched tactics, opting for strikes from their arms and legs instead of their vines. The jagged hawthorn leaves on their appendages rustled like they were caught in the cool wind preceding a thunderstorm. The leaves receded, exposing bristling, two-inch thorns the width of pencils narrowed to tips. It was as if they were literally armed with miniature stilettos.

There was a cry from the men loading the guns as they were slashed and gouged by the thorns.

One of the gunners pulled his pistol and fired wildly into the horde. He managed to explode three heads before his ammo ran dry. Vines coiled around him. He battered an open flytrap with the butt of his pistol. Then the trap closed around him.

I heard a hissing sound and the upper part of the man's body must have dissolved within those jaws, because the rest of him was pulled inside and gone in seconds.

His partner retreated from the machine gun nest and regrouped with us behind the guns. The plant-men halted momentarily to dispose of the other gunners, and those precious seconds allowed us to organize a skirmish line across the mine shaft, about ten feet behind the guns. I stood to Hayner's right, with five more soldiers to my right. There were another five to Hayner's left. Another ten soldiers formed a line behind us with Gott and Rolf. Behind them was a third line.

Mounting the machine guns to the floor had been another mistake. We now faced the horde with only rifles and small arms.

Up front, the plant-men were still attacking the encasement. I was not sure how long it could hold. They had quit beating on it randomly and now appeared to be searching for a weakness in its construction.

Falke, armed with a fully charged flamethrower, stepped into the second skirmish line next to Gott and Rolf. The sight of Falke encouraged the soldiers, but I feared he might set the entire entrance on fire. I motioned at him to hold off for now. He nodded.

The door closed another foot and now was five feet or so open. It might as well have been a chasm, because more of the large hands latched onto the door from the outside and the door mechanism began to strain. Outside, behind the plant-men and the humanoids, which I was now thinking of as great apes, I swore I saw a menagerie of animals. It made me think of Noah's ark.

Then, inexplicably, everything stopped.

From outside, a bellow arose and filled the mine with the sound of a foghorn. The mine rattled with the blast. The plant-men halted in their tracks, and so did we. It blew twice, for about five seconds each time, with a pause of about ten seconds between each blast. The sound was all-encompassing. During the pause between blasts, I realized how much the Pflanzen-Kriegerin stank. It was a rotting, mucky-swamp smell.

We heard something walking outside. It must have been enormous. The earth pounded with its footsteps and the entire mine shook with each step. Dust fell from the ceiling as the earth shuddered. And then it stopped.

Something shot through the door above the plant-men's heads. A huge vine. It was moss-covered and sinewy, and it looked greasy. Moist, matted clumps of rotted vegetation dripped from the vine and splattered on the floor. It wrapped itself around one of the spotlights, tightened, and ripped it out of the mine.

It smashed through several plant-men on its way out, caught briefly on the iron gate, and disappeared with a clanking rattle. In half the light as before, the plant-men resumed their attack and advanced toward us.

This was a last stand. If we gave up our line, the mine was breached and we were lost. We fired off a first round from our line like English redcoats on an open battlefield. Ten plant-men dropped in front of us, their heads spewing pulp. One husky skull split in two, the halves splatting on the floor. The body fell straight forward upon its open trap.

The vine zipped back in through the shaft and wrapped around the second spotlight. The light shattered and a puff of electric smoke wafted into the air. It was dark again. Hayner screeched for the alarm to sound, and the mine filled with the alternating red lights.

The Pflanzen-Kriegerin had advanced several feet in the darkness before the light came on. We fired another round and retreated several paces backward.

I holstered my pistol and dropped to a knee, rummaging through my pack. I brought out several vials as another round from our skirmish line rang out. We were almost overrun. Ahead, the plant-men could have the encasement down in minutes. They had succeeded in wedging their limbs between two iron plates and were wiggling one of them back and forth.

We had been forced about sixty feet from the door now, and in the intermittent flashing red light, I could see the giant hands straining on the gate. It was a difficult target to hit, having to throw between the ceiling and the plant-men, but I had no other options. A volley erupted from our line, and ten more attackers dropped.

With that suddenly clear view, I lobbed a vial forward. It burst three feet to the right of the hands, splashing chemicals on the gate. A very good throw in those conditions, but not good enough. The chemicals hissed and smoked, but merely burned a plant-man that had been milling around the center of the door.

The enormous vine whipped in through the opening and reached all the way to our skirmish line. I almost didn't see it in time. When the red light flashed on, it was halfway to us and headed right at me.

I ducked, and it wrapped around a soldier to my right instead. The soldier screamed, and then the vine tightened, forcing the air out of his lungs. It dragged the soldier outside through the horde.

I threw another vial, but it struck a plant-man on its way through the door. It shattered against his skull, causing the foliage on his head to smoke.

Our line fired off another round, and I threw another vial. This one hit the mark, a foot above the uppermost hand on the door. The acid drenched that hand and the hand below it, a puff of white smoke rising from the burning flesh. The hands spasmed and receded behind the door.

I threw three more vials. One smashed against the head of a plant-man in the doorway. It hissed as the acid ate into its husky skull. The other two crashed against the door close enough to splash acid on the remaining hands. All but the bottom hand receded. The door lurched forward under the reduced resistance.

I figured we had no more than seconds before new hands came forward to hold the door open. The gate was closing, but now the problem was the mass pressing in through the aperture. The door simply would not close against all those bodies.

I reached back in my pack for a large beaker wrapped in cloth. Our line fired off several shots in succession, but still had to retreat another ten feet.

I yelled at Hayner over the *Wooooooooooo* of the plant-men. "If I can hit the opening with this, we may have a chance to get the door closed, but it may blow the door right off the track! Do you want me to try?"

The vine burst into the shaft and latched around one of the machine guns. It tugged in a back-and-forth motion, ripping it off its mount. The vine shot back at our line. Utilizing the machine gun as a bludgeon, it connected with a soldier on Hayner's left, killing him instantly with a blow to the head.

The vine swung riotously, whipping the machine gun back and forth across our line. I dove for the floor just ahead of it and the gun whizzed past my head. The soldier to my right never saw it coming. It smashed him against the wall together with another man, and they both fell limp against the floor.

The vine came back for another pass at the line, whizzing over my head again. The hordes kept it from lowering the gun farther and the vine's attack impeded their progress against us, but we did not have time to spare. The door would be irrevocably breached soon, and I was pinned by the gun slamming back and forth.

Then the vine arched its tip over the last line of plant-men and started spiking the weapon downward like a scorpion's stinger. The gun clanked against the floor as it struck. It found one of the soldiers on the floor and impaled him in the back.

It was getting close to Hayner and to me. Our back lines fired on it to no avail. The bullets passed cleanly through the vine's flesh. They resumed their fire against the plant-men instead.

The vine was now three feet from Hayner and approaching. I grabbed Hayner's neck and pulled him close. "Order a cease-fire!" I screamed directly in his ear.

The vine smashed the gun down again a little closer. One of the soldiers from the back lines rushed at it with a knife. He succeeded in getting one arm around the vine, while stabbing it repeatedly with the knife. It coiled around him, gun and all, but left his knife hand free. The soldier switched to a cutting motion with the knife.

Sap oozed from a laceration where the knife had penetrated the vine's skin. It seemed the soldier might succeed in severing the thing, but it slammed him against the wall and dropped him lifeless on the floor. The knife rocketed off the wall, ricocheting into the horde where it clanged onto the floor.

I yelled at Hayner again as the vine made another pass over our heads with the machine gun, so close the butt of the gun parted my hair like wind through a field of ripe grain. "Order a cease-fire!"

The line behind us sent several more volleys into the Pflanzen-Kriegerin. I figured our ammunition had to be running low.

"What? Are you crazy, schoolboy?"

I showed Hayner the sealed beaker and made an exploding motion with my free hand.

His eyes lit up and he nodded. "Cease fire!"

German efficiency: even under the most adverse conditions, the soldiers obeyed.

The massive tendril whizzed overhead again, scraping my back with the gun. I signaled Falke to hit it with the flamethrower. Falke waited until it had crossed to the side, and he unleashed the flames in a quick burst so he wouldn't catch us all on fire. The heat was oppressive, but it did the trick. The vine shot out of the shaft, gun in tow.

I stood and lobbed the sealed beaker at the door as the horde resumed their charge now that the vine had left. I ducked next to Hayner, who ordered the back line to resume firing. Shots rang out as the beaker hit the ground outside the great iron gate.

The shockwave from the blast catapulted several bodies inward and leveled the mass of plant-men directly inside and outside the door. The mine shook, and I hoped the structure would hold. The iron gate wobbled back and forth inside its track with a sound of metallic thunder.

Another volley dropped more plant-men in front of us. Hayner stood and screeched at the top of his lungs for the door to close. Free from the mass of bodies, the door began sliding shut along its groove as soon as the wobbling ceased. It appeared to be unharmed. I hoped the plant-men couldn't react in time.

I lobbed three more vials of acid at the opening to deter more intruders. The vials burst open, spraying steaming acid across the aperture. The door was only open a foot now, and closing quickly.

Plant-men still filled the area inside the door. The enemy was close to breaching the encasement. I nudged Hayner and pointed. They had worked the iron plating open at the joint between the side and roof, and were violently shaking it back and forth, whipping their vines at the soldiers inside to keep them at bay. It would give before long.

Hayner ordered the back line to train their guns on the encasement. A volley fired and the attackers fell. The iron gate slammed shut. If we could reach it, we might get out of this.

I had one vial left and four shots in my pistol. There were still a horde of intruders inside the mine. I popped four rounds into the creatures directly ahead of me, and the rest of our skirmish line unloaded their weapons at will.

I waved Falke off. I didn't think the mine would catch fire, but we had to get to the door as soon as possible, and a burning mass of plant matter was not going to help. Already, some of the plant-men had reversed direction and were attempting to reopen the door. I doubted they could, but we didn't need to take the chance.

Most of our side was out of ammo, and the enemy sensed it. Men drew knives or crouched into fighting stances. The horde charged with renewed vigor, thorns exposed. Overhead, the flashing red light continued.

The most amazing thing from that point forward was Hayner. He was a one-man Pflanzen-Kriegerin destruction force. He rushed the line with a look of sheer joy on his face and engaged the plant-men in hand-to-hand combat.

His strength was astounding. Hayner squashed the head of the first plant-man he met simply by pressing it between his hands. Its head splattered him with pulp and fell limply to the floor. He hit the next one with a right cross so hard that the husk on its face snapped off its head.

A hand of thorns gashed Hayner's back, opening three grooves from his shoulder blade to his kidneys. Hayner screeched, wheeled around, and ripped the plant warrior's arm off. He threw the arm back at it like a spiked mace. It stuck in the thing's trap. Hayner lifted the plant-man off the floor, one hand behind its back, the other under its legs. He compressed it together, snapping it in two, like a celery stalk, and threw it at the line of invaders.

Hayner reared back with his arms in the air, muscles rippling. He emitted a bloodcurdling scream that stopped the horde in its tracks.

Our skirmish line, emboldened by Hayner's heroics, charged. A grisly fight ensued in the flashing red light of the alarm. The hand-to-hand combat favored the spiked invaders, though, and they inflicted heavy casualties on the soldiers.

Falke shed the flamethrower and trudged up beside Hayner, grabbing two plant- men by the head and lifting them off the ground, squeezing their heads until they exploded. This two-man vanguard was too much for the plant-men to handle and their line cracked. The invaders overflowed around the side of the line and confronted Gott, Rolf, and me.

An attacker a foot taller than me shot its vine at my head. I dodged to the left, pulled my dagger from my belt, and stuck it in the leg above the hawthorn leaves.

It did not react in pain. Instead, it exposed the thorns at the end of its arm and lashed at my head. The two-inch thorns would have penetrated my temple had I not ducked. As it was, the thorns raked across my head above my right ear, scratching my scalp from the side across to the top of my skull.

Its vine whipped out of its mouth and coiled around my neck. The trap in its midsection opened. It reared back its arms, thorns exposed, with the intent of spiking me in a pincher attack.

I leapt forward, thrusting my dagger upward, driving it in below the husk of its chin. I grabbed it with both hands and forced the blade through the pulpy head. Rotted sap ran from its head down the hilt of the dagger and onto my gloves, smothering them in a steamy thick juice that stunk like sewage. Its arms fell limp to its side.

The trap closed around my sides, the spikes on the outside of it reaching around me.

I sawed desperately and the blade ripped between the thing's eyes. The vine loosened and the creature fell backward, dead.

I should have trembled, but my body was awash with the rush of the Nachthaus. I stood as straight as Hayner.

Rolf called for help behind me. I turned to see a plant warrior with his vine wrapped around Rolf's left elbow. Rolf was trying to flee, but the vine was reeling him into its open trap.

I leapt on the plant-man's back and drove my dagger into the top of its head to the hilt. I fell from its back, clutching the blade as I did. It cleaved the husky skull in two down the back. It released its hold on Rolf.

The plant-men counterattacked around Hayner's and Falke's left and overpowered five of the soldiers with a coordinated vine and thorn thrust maneuver. The soldiers' screams were chilling as they were sucked into the traps. Hayner and Falke cornered the feasting plant-men between the wall and the remaining soldiers, and dispatched them.

At this, much of the horde fled for the door. I lobbed my last vial, which crashed against the wall where the iron door met the side of the mine. It bought us a little time. I slipped forward against the wall of the mine with the melee to my left and tore away two plant-men trying to work the iron plate off of the encasement.

I was trapped against the wall of the mine, surrounded by three more of them. They pressed in against me, vines whipping. One caught my left wrist, coiled so tightly I dropped my dagger. I sent my right fist into its face, but failed to do more than bruise its head on account of its height. A branch growing out of its face cut my arm right above the wrist.

Another vine caught my right arm, and one coiled around my neck. A trap opened in front of me and I was pulled toward it.

I fought against the vines, but they were too strong. A sappy substance formed on the pink flesh of the trap like saliva, and a clear fluid welled up from its gullet. This was how I would die, digested by a creature from a nightmare.

Pulp exploded onto my face and shoulders. Suddenly, the vines released me and I was free. Gott and Rolf stood behind the fallen plant warrior, both holding shovels. I worked my neck free of the coiled vine in a circular motion.

In front of me, Hayner stood atop a wall of dead plant-men. He was shirtless, his pants were ripped up both sides to the knees, and his muscles rippled like shockwaves. His arms were outstretched and covered with lacerations and blood. His face was maddened. He was a god of war, and Mars' red light flashed across his face. The black slugs were the size of pythons, circling around his neck, chest, waist, and legs. He let out another bloodcurdling war cry and leapt from the mound of dead plant-men onto a pack of cowering live ones.

With Hayner and Falke in the lead, we made quick work of the remaining horde. About ten were left backed up against the door. Their flesh was burning from the acid, but they seemed to prefer it to facing the advance of Falke and Hayner. In minutes, they too lay motionless upon the floor.

I stood like a savage, clutching a dagger and panting deeply. How had we survived? I fell to my knees, my mind swiftly shutting down. Death would've been a relief.

The mine was littered with the fallen of the forest. The Nachthaus was a greenhouse with no sun, stuffed with dead flora.

A lingering haze from my exploded vials hung in the air, along with smoke from Falke's flamethrower and the burnt-out husks of plant-men. The mine stunk like compost.

I bent to pick up a tattered German officer's jacket. Its leafy owner wriggled at the base of the great door, its torso nearly cut clean through. Through the vegetation on its head I saw its eyes staring back at me. They were vacant eyes, as if it were trying to remember but couldn't. The plant warrior looked almost human for a moment: the contour of its husky skull and its stem arms and legs had not completely finished their metamorphosis. Was there a touch of humanity left? Where had these things come from and what did they want with us? The Nachthaus didn't have the answers.

All around me, the surviving soldiers milled around as though nothing much had occurred. No one mourned over fallen comrades, no one showed curiosity in a mine full of strange creatures with human eyes and Nazi uniforms.

Hayner strolled over and squashed the thing's head with his boot.

11

That night I dreamt that the glory had departed from the mountain above the forest, as I had seen when I touched the face in the granite. The glory had departed and, in its place, the forest had decayed into a cistern of evil.

I marched through the forest to the base of the mountain and began to climb. The mountain was cloaked in perpetual darkness. As I ascended I entered the fog circling the mountain. Below me on the ground I could hear a foghorn and the tramping of monstrous feet, though I could not see through the fog. I climbed higher and happened upon a ridge that ran along the face of the mountain. I followed the ridge for a while until it ended abruptly at a cave.

The cave was lit by a fire, by which sat a bearded man cooking over the flame. He motioned for me to sit. "We get few travelers up these cliffs, my son," he said. "What brings you this way?"

"I think I'm dreaming," I said.

The man stirred a pot of stew hanging above the fire. "Is that so?"

I noticed his fire was low so I reached forward to adjust the wood under it. The fire was barely lit. I reached into my pocket, took out a vial, and poured it on the flames. The flames licked up and the stew began to boil.

"Thank you, son. It seems you have a talent for that." The man's eyes flashed momentarily at me, then he stirred the pot. "Now then, what makes you think you're dreaming?"

"This mountain, the forest, the Nachthaus, plant-men . . . certainly I'm dreaming, right?"

"Dreaming is seeing the world as it is not," the man said. "Did you smell the plant-men?"

"Yes," I said. "They were widerlich. Disgusting. Like dead and rotting foliage."

The man snatched a burning stick from the fire and held it up from the unlit end. "And you burned the gypsy girl, did you not?"

My head dropped. "I did."

"Then what is real and what is the dream? Did you ever recognize evil for what it was beneath your blue Austrian skies? And did you ever recognize who was evil while in the arms of your lovely Katia?"

"No, sir. I didn't. I read about it, but I never recognized it."

"Then that was the dream and this is the reality. It's only the recognition that counts."

Suddenly the cave was empty.

I exited the cave and resumed my climb. The way became impassible and I was caught on a ledge, afraid to go forward and afraid to descend. I was paralyzed.

A vine rose out of the fog and wrapped itself around me, lifting me off the ledge and away from the face of the mountain. Upward I sailed until I reached the ceiling of the sky. The mountain rose yet farther, but I could go no higher.

The mountain had a face and it peered at me. Then it began to quake, and a crack ran down its center. The rock exploded and the mountain transformed itself into Hayner.

He was standing upon mound upon mound of plant-men corpses and charred victims of Dante's inferno. He was naked and covered with the blood and soot of his victims. The slugs were pythons wrapped around his waist, writhing in full strength. The fog dissipated, the sky turned crimson, and the world beneath us turned to a raging torrent of fire.

Hayner cackled against the blood-red backdrop of the sky. He looked at me and his thin lips sneered as far as the taut skin around his face would allow. He took hold of the vine that held me. I saw his great muscles contract and the vine ripped in half. Hayner rubbed my face across his chest, smearing me with blood and soot.

Then he held me out and dropped me. I fell and fell and fell, ever closer to the torrent of flame below me. When I plunged into the flame, I awoke.

It was time to go to work.

12

I was already mixing chemicals, conducting experiments, and measuring results by the time Gott showed up in the lab that morning.

"Rolf's examining the bodies up front," he said. "He gets to decide which ones he can keep for research and which ones get incinerated. We have a lot of burning to do today."

Did no one here care where these things came from, what they were, how they were even alive? To be honest, it had slipped my mind too after the battle, but now that we were talking about them, it seemed odd.

Plant things with scraps of Nazi uniforms assaulting the door of the Reich's premier reclamation center ought to attract someone's inquisitiveness. The forgetfulness and lack of curiosity was almost as strange as the plant-men, giant vines, and giant-handed ape things.

"Good," I said. "I'm interested to see how the inferno performs with more bodies in it." I scribbled some notes on a pad and handed it to Gott. "Give this to Hayner."

Gott looked at the pad, but did not take it. "You might want to hand it over to him yourself. He ordered me to tell you to come up front."

Ten minutes later, Gott and I were watching Rolf sift through the bodies. The smell was even worse now that the bodies were truly dead. Rolf was poking at the bodies with a scalpel and making notes as he went along. I wondered about the extent of the carnage outside.

Hayner walked up and pulled me off to the side near the encasement. He was making an effort at civility and even handed me back my dagger, which I had dropped in the melee. Kindness, even feigned, fit strangely on him, like a coat three sizes too large. "Oberleutnant," he said, "nice work last night. We might not have made it without your quick thinking."

The plant-men would be using our heads for soccer balls by now, actually, I thought.

"Gott tells me the oven is enhanced," Hayner said.

"Seven times hotter." I watched Hayner's fingers tapping his crop.

"I thought I told you to develop the solvent first?"

"Working on it, sir. Here's a list of more chemicals I'll need and the quantities I'll need them in." I handed Hayner the pad.

He studied it for a moment like a dog reading Latin."How long?" Hayner asked.

"I'll have a preliminary solvent in a week. How long it takes to bore through those walls depends on how thick they are."

Hayner nodded. "Look over here." Hayner walked to a stack of plant-men by the front door. He pointed at one of them on the floor. It had a flowered badge on its uniform.

"Edelweiss badge," I said.

"Correct," Hayner said. "Hits pretty close to home for you, doesn't it?"

I thought of Katia, the blue Austrian sky, and the possibility that dreaming is seeing the world as it is not.

"Schoolboy, do you have any idea what is happening here?"

"I'm working on that part, sir." I pointed at the iron gate. "You should have that door reinforced. Did you hear the size of those footsteps yesterday? I think they'll eventually devise a way to start battering the door."

"You work on the solvent, schoolboy. Leave the forest to me. We killed almost one hundred and seventy-five plant-men last night, counting your bomb. I'll kill every one of them myself if I have to." The slugs popped out from Hayner's eyes.

I nodded. "Get my chemicals."

Around noon we endured the stench of sewage and stacked fifty plant warrior corpses in Dante's inferno and summoned the fire. The inferno incinerated the bodies as if they were straw, leaving nothing but fine ash.

It was as if the inferno had become self-aware and intent on its gruesome duty. I stood out front, as usual, while Gott and Rolf ran the controls. The glass slit eyes leered at me as it labored.

We burned seventy-five Pflanzen-Kriegerin on the next run, mostly trucked in on carts by Falke and the soldiers. The inferno grew increasingly hungry. I felt the glass slit eyes prying into my mind as the oven roared. It paced back and forth in my mind like a hungry lion in a cage.

The inferno would have its main course too. That afternoon, several transports—many were a similar make and model to the Nachthaus's trucks parked out front—from Ploiesti arrived with nearly one hundred prisoners. Evidently the forest had cleared its own dead outside, for none were discovered when the iron gate was opened.

The alcoves would be packed to capacity, and one of the soldiers' quarters was being refitted to handle the overflow. That probably meant Hayner would accelerate the incinerations. The prisoners were a variety of gypsies, seditionists, spies, Allied soldiers, and general enemies of the Reich. Hayner had called me up front when the transports had arrived because he had managed a last-minute addition of my chemicals to the transport, as well as additional soldiers. As usual, the forest let in, but didn't let out.

I observed the new prisoners with Hayner. He had them lined up against the wall of the mine under gunpoint. He strolled in front of them with his crop out. They would all be given a chance, he told them, to come clean to the Reich of their own volition. Those who would not had heard previously of the Nachthaus, no? Of its vaunted interrogation rooms? Of its death chamber in the belly of the mountain? Those who cooperated would be treated with kindness and respect, he said. Those who defied the Reich would have chosen the way of despair and agony.

Hayner gave the order and the soldiers marched the prisoners to the alcoves. I watched them pass: the blank stares, the bruised faces, the soulless walk of the condemned. Not one I saw was thinking *ex malo bonum* that I could tell.

My chemicals were precisely as ordered. I had Falke and Gott cart them to the lab. Rolf was occupied arranging his choice new specimens in the cooler. I think he may have packed forty of them in the cooler with his existing corpses.

At 1800 hours, we broke for dinner and then I spent the remainder of the evening working on solvent. I feared Hayner might be right that time was of the essence. I labored assiduously into the night, until the face began to speak.

13

It began as a low moan, which I initially associated with the groaning of the forest and mine. It continued for an hour or two before I started piecing together stray syllables and the cadence of speech, rather than incoherent groaning. I set my beakers aside and went into the hallway.

When I rounded the corner, Gott was down the corridor by the hallway leading to our rooms. Rolf was nowhere to be seen. Gott raised an index finger to his lips when he saw me. A low voice seemed to be emanating from the general direction of the inferno.

The voice was extremely deep, like the bass in a barber shop quartet, but very smooth. It was textured like velvet, as if you could touch it and feel the soft fibers under your fingertips.

The voice seemed to be repeating one word over and over in three-second intervals. It was garbled at first, but the more it droned the clearer the intonation and pronunciation became. Gott and I began to close on the voice, moving stealthily toward the center of the corridor in front of the oven door. By the time we were ten feet from it, I could see it was the granite face speaking, and it was clear what it was saying: *König, König, König...*

The face sprang to life in the rock. It shook itself, as if to wake up, and the 3D effect reached full force. The face protruded from the granite wall a foot at most, but moved in and out of the wall effortlessly. The tripartite brow furled, the nose lifted a bit above the lip, and the eyes locked on me. "You are König, no?"

I glanced at Gott, hoping for instructions. I received none. I spread my arms out to my sides, palms open and toward the face. "Ja, I am Sascha König."

"Ashes to ashes, König," the face said. The voice was a low droning, but it spoke soothingly, almost musically, not in a monotonous fashion. "You are the officer in charge of this monstrosity?" The face nodded toward the inferno.

"I am . . . I mean, I follow orders."

The face grimaced. "Much can be discerned about a man by whose orders he follows."

Gott protested. "We have no choice."

"Hmmmm, choice," the face said. "It is either obey or do not obey. Choice is an excuse. Either obey . . . or do not obey. It is times such as these that we see inside a man by what, or who, he obeys, or does not obey."

Gott took a step closer. "That's easy for you to say. You're on the wall there. No worries about being thrown in the inferno. Get out here and talk that way."

"Poor boy," the face said. "Do you genuinely think that what I would or would not do has anything to say about what's *true?*"

"But—"

I held up a palm. "He's right, Gott. *Argumentum ad hominem*, to be precise." I took a step closer to the face as well. "But he's not demonstrated his case, either. Us getting ourselves burned alive solves nothing. In fact, staying alive is the prudent course because at least then we would be able to help someone, rather than no one."

"Good is good; evil is evil," the face said. "Life, death, pain, choice, action—none of these change what is good and what is evil."

The closer I studied the face, the more benign it became. Its transformation from demon to dreamcaster to philosopher was astounding. And its presence in the Nachthaus was puzzling. Why was there such a distinct presence of good, or at least neutrality, in the heart of such evil? The Nachthaus had snuffed out the gypsy girl. Why not the face?

I had nearly concluded that the face was a potential ally when it dawned on me that evil by its nature is often clever and deceptive. Perhaps the face was a spokesman or an incantation for the Nachthaus. Maybe it was devising our ill through its counsel? Could we be sure? I didn't think so, and I reined in my desire to trust the face.

"But choice and action may determine good and evil," I said.

The face sighed. It was like the moaning of a great beast. "This is an idea popular at present," the face said. "The world is ever full of such confusion."

With that the face retreated into the wall. In its last moment before melding with the granite, it uttered a last thought. "God is concerned with your actions. He's already determined what's good and what's not. Align your doing with the good, as He has declared it. Leave the *ex malo bonum* to Him. For God and nature do not work together in vain."

The face solidified into the granite in a slightly different pose than before. I can't exactly explain it, but it was less threatening—less ominous. All in all, I felt better knowing the face was there.

Gott sidled up next to me and whispered. "What next, Sascha? What next?"

"Were I not a lover of the liberal arts, Gott, I'd say *The Road Less Traveled.*"

The next morning we met again for breakfast in the lab. I wanted to keep the face a secret from Rolf, but Gott blurted it out first thing after pouring the coffee.

Rolf fastened his goggles to get a better look at us. "The face came alive and spoke with you," he said. "So, what exactly did it have to say?" He looked like he thought we were playing a practical joke on him.

Gott noticed my disapproval, I'm sure, but it was too late not to trust Rolf with it now.

"Weird stuff." Gott spoke while chewing. "Philosophy. Morality."

I interrupted. "Nothing that your average face-that-shouldn't-be-there-in-the-first-place-much-less-talking wouldn't say. Same old stuff." I paused to study his face. "Why? You don't believe us?"

"What would you say?" Rolf asked.

"Listen up and I'll tell you." I leaned in and Gott and Rolf did the same. "Rolf, have you noticed what's going on around us?"

I held my hand in front of his goggles and counted fingers as I reeled off a list. "Plant-men. Cryptic writing on the wall. A talking face of stone that changed from a demon to a philosopher. The moaning forest that will let certain things in but lets nothing out that would help us, including certain radio transmissions or even handwritten messages. One hundred-plus-foot killer vines. My trances in the control room and while touching the face. Hayner and Falke."

I omitted the gypsy girl because I didn't think they had seen her eyes like I had. It didn't matter.

"I know," Rolf said. "I'm not supposed to admit such things as a scientist. No one's going to believe us without some empirical evidence, if we ever get out of here." Rolf sipped some coffee. He pushed my list-counting hand out of the way. "Look. I believe you, but there are some things that trouble me."

Rolf erected his own list-counting hand. "First, it bothers me that no one here seems afraid. With all the frightful things you mentioned, we should all be cowering in a corner somewhere. Instead, everyone goes about their business like it's the most natural thing in the world. Second, you know, Sascha, that that oven is not supposed to work like it does. You said it yourself: the engineering is shoddy and inefficient. Yet it burns and cools like clockwork. Like it has a life of its own."

Rolf seemed to be enjoying his newfound momentum. "Thirdly, I can't explain any of this scientifically. That bothers me too. The world is not supposed to act in that manner, nor be understood as such."

"There's more to understanding the world than science," I said.

I saw my reflection in Rolf's goggles. "So it would seem."

• • •

The alarms sounded around noon that day. I was in the lab testing what I had thought might be a successful solvent mixture, but I was having only limited results. At the sound of the klaxon I grabbed my knapsack and ran for the front of the mine.

Gott and Rolf were there when I arrived, as was the entire staff of the Nachthaus. The door was open but, as it was daytime, I was not concerned. I ran through the open door, glad to feel the sun on my face. Hayner stood by the opening of the mine, screeching. Every soldier had his gun drawn. I pushed through to the front around Falke.

Two soldiers had stolen one of the transport trucks and were idling about twenty yards from the Nachthaus entrance. They were partially covered by trees and brush, so it was difficult to get a good look at them, but the truck was visible and exhaust was fuming from the tailpipe. Its green canopy blended in with the forest.

Hayner screeched at them to return. He promised no penalty. That day I thought I heard Hayner pleading, as if he cared for the soldiers in the truck. He took a step forward, but a warning shot fired from inside the truck. He put out his hands in a peaceful manner, urging the soldiers at the top of his voice to forego their intentions to flee.

They fled anyway. Transmission gears ground and the truck lurched forward. It wheeled around and came right for us, then turned right in front of the Nachthaus entrance. We were caught in a cloud of dust and pelted with gravel pellets. It appeared the two soldiers were trying to flank the forest by following the mountain's base, rather than taking the main path out.

We stepped forward as a group to watch their escape. This was my first glimpse of normal, although misguided, behavior in response to the Nachthaus, and I'm sure most of us that day were proud that someone was giving it a shot, and perhaps that there might be a way out. Hope is sometimes short-lived.

The truck made it 50 yards along the base of the mountain before a boulder fell into its path. The driver swerved right and entered the tree line, out of view. A few seconds later the truck burst from the forest, heading back toward us, accelerating. I could see the driver through the truck's windshield. He was horrified.

Four vines were following the truck from the forest. They moved like serpents. The vines overtook the truck and entangled themselves around it. They halted the truck's progress, lifting the back wheels from the ground. The transmission whined and the back wheels spun. Another vine shot out and wrapped itself over, around, and under the cab of the truck, preventing the doors from opening.

Four more vines wrapped around the truck and the truck began to rise, rear end first. The passenger kicked the truck's windshield. He succeeded in shattering it after several kicks with both feet and, when the windshield gave way, we could hear their screams.

A soldier to Hayner's left aimed his rifle. Hayner placed his hand on the barrel of the gun and brought it down.

The passenger had made it onto the truck's dashboard in his quest to exit through the windshield, but the truck was now perpendicular to the ground. He fell through the windshield, skidded across the hood of truck, and plummeted toward the ground. A vine caught him halfway down, slipping around him like a tentacle.

The driver never moved. He remained behind the wheel, clutching it with a death grip, screaming. The vines lifted the truck until it was even with the tallest treetops in the forest. It hung there, bobbing like a cork.

The ground fissured beneath the truck, and we retreated a step toward the Nachthaus. The earth beneath the truck was opening in an oval pattern, the dirt piling up along its perimeter. It was forming a mouth.

Because of my angle of observation, I couldn't see all the way down inside the mouth, but it appeared to be hollowing out to a considerable depth. It belched out a putrid fog and its insides were molten, as if the mouth were a gateway to the bowels of the earth. Something tongue-like wormed out of the mouth and licked its dirt lips.

The vines released the truck. It plunged headlong toward the mouth. I saw the driver still clutching the wheel as he disappeared into the earth.

The passenger was still dangling by the green vines. They lowered him into the mouth like he was a last cherished morsel from a bag of chocolate. He was trying to scream, but the vines must have been wrapped too tightly around his midsection for him to get enough air through his larynx. The tongue licked him when he was about ten feet above the mouth. The vine released him, and he disappeared into the hole, finally able to scream. The earth closed up over him as quickly as it had opened.

A great moan arose from the forest and we heard the monstrous footsteps approaching us. We ran like Georgie Porgies into the Nachthaus. All except for Hayner, who lingered a while before joining us.

14

Following some idle conversation with Falke regarding the great iron gate guarding the entrance to the Nachthaus and the virtue of flamethrowers, I set out down the shaft toward the lab. Word had spread through the mine of the modified fire the oven now produced, and Falke had even referred to me by my new name: Nebuchadnezzar. Rumor had it I would have the solvent within days, or weeks at the latest, once the new shipment of chemicals arrived. Rumors are seldom neutral. Boldly optimistic or ruefully cruel critters they are.

As I passed through the shaft leading from the entrance, I noticed remnants of the great plant-man battle: scars on the floor where the vine had spiked the machine gun, traces of vegetation and pulp, scars in the walls from bullets, chemical burns from my vials.

It was the oddness of the aftermath that unsettled me. As I'd noted before, no one seemed to be aware of the abject wickedness surrounding us. There was no grief from the soldiers for their fallen bunkmates. We incinerated the human bodies in the inferno along with the plant-men, and the soldiers transporting the bodies down to the oven might as well have been carrying bags of trash.

Dreaming is seeing the world as it is not, the old man in my dream had said. I paused at the turn to the alcove passageway and leaned against the cool walls of the shaft. I turned my cheek to the wall and soaked in the chill. Am I seeing the world as it is not?

All the soldiers in the Nachthaus were caricatures of the plant-men. They went about their tasks perfunctorily, as if it were natural to see such horrors. I guessed they hadn't been in the Nachthaus long enough to be desensitized to its weirdness, but had they? I could feel it working on me—the walls of the mine closing in, the spirit of the forest reaching for me, the droning of the forest, the scratching, Hayner's insanity. They were a misty presence in my brain, circling like buzzards.

But it was the fire. The inferno that stared at me with orange slits for eyes. When it sprang to life with the whir of the fuel pumps and the *whoosh* of the pilot light igniting the jets, it was as if a demon had awoken in the heart of the mine. Perhaps *demon* was too light a word—it was a *devil.* The devil would roar with its flames.

It was growing hungrier. I could sense its desire for flesh, and I was its keeper. I was its Nebuchadnezzar. It was seven times hotter and seven times more ravenous. And it was calling me to feed it. Dreaming gave me alarms that appeared as ducks crashing through my door. The fire was the world as it really was, and I was being consumed.

A clanking from the alcove passage caught my attention. I pushed away from the wall and saw a tiny object land and roll to the wood plank floor. I glanced up and down the mine shaft. Nothing and nobody. Not on the outside of the alcoves anyway.

My boots thumped a hollow beat along the wooden pier. Hundreds of eyes stared from the darkness of the alcove cages as I walked. From what I could see in the dark of the alcoves, they were standing sardines.

Several arms reached out from between the iron bars. A wailing began from many of the captives, and others pleaded with me. A few pounded the gates with clenched fists. As I walked, the noise level increased. I looked over my shoulder to see if any of the soldiers were reacting to the hullabaloo. I couldn't tell. No one was coming down the passage.

An older man crammed his face between the iron bars. His head was shoved forward so far, I thought it might squirt through the bars. He reminded me of the gypsy girl's companion who had startled me into falling back into the puddle. Rust from the bars had marked his face as if he were wearing Indian war paint. The rust streaks ran parallel down his face with deep grooves from malnutrition.

He extended his arms through the gate. "I don't deserve this, son." He repeated the line as if it were a chant. "I don't deserve this, son. I don't deserve this, son. I don't deserve this, son."

I kept walking, boots pounding the pier, eyes focused on the item that had fallen out from the second-to-last alcove. The stench of humanity reeked from the alcoves. I tried to convince myself it wasn't their fault, but somehow I was arguing with myself. Which of these hadn't tortured an animal as a child?

Which hadn't been smug in his former life? Which hadn't been party to numerous evils? Which was not in league with the apparitions that had assaulted me in the furnace when I had fired up the inferno that first time? If the tables were turned, which one of these would let me out of an alcove once I had been reduced to stinking, nearly sub-human status? None, I reckoned.

The item was now to my left, almost to the pier. It had rolled through a puddle and caked itself with dust before coming to rest. I bent down and retrieved it from the floor. Taking off my gloves, I wiped it between the palms of my hands, noting their stench.

It was a marble, rather large, and the deep blue of a sky before dawn. I sacrificed my shirt to remove all the dust. It was worth it. The marble was exceedingly gorgeous. Its deep blue was swirling. Not as a maelstrom or a hurricane, but more like unleashed winds traveling the outer portion of the sphere. They set a counterclockwise course around the sphere, and the marble was cool to the touch. From the core of the sphere, a faint light began to emanate as a binary star. I sensed the gypsy girl's presence. Those pinpricks of light would prove themselves her eyes. Somehow I knew it.

I wanted more than anything to wait for the eyes to appear in full. I would have endured a Hayner beating if necessary, the miniature was that beautiful. But the globe went blank concurrently with a new sound coming from the alcove to my left. It was a woman's voice. The gypsy girl's eyes disappeared.

I turned to the alcove. A woman was pressed to the front with her arms above her head, grasping the bars. I dropped the marble into my trouser pocket, along with my gloves.

Her hair may have been dirty blond or it may have been brown. It was too matted and filthy to tell for sure. She was gaunt, from the trauma of her situation, I guessed. Her features were rigid and distinct, though, and removing her starved and harried condition, I imagined an elegance, rather than beauty. Her fingers, which were wrapped around the bars, tapered into manicured nails, albeit soiled. Her head was lifted, defiant in her captivity. A tattered blue dress draped almost down to her bare feet.

Above the din, her voice commanded me. "Set me loose."

I stuttered.

She repeated herself. "Set me loose."

"There's nowhere for you to go," I said.

Behind me I heard commands. I looked to my left. No one had made the turn at the corner yet from the front of the mine. They were coming, though.

I ran down the wooden pier into the heart of the mine. When I reached the dark of the decline leading down to the inferno, I stopped to listen. Guards were banging on the iron gates and threatening the captives to be quiet, and it sickened me to think of all the ways Hayner and his men could abuse a female prisoner.

The next morning we breakfasted again in the lab. Gott and Rolf sat across from me at a workbench, dressed in their lab gear. I had slept well for a man surrounded by human and inhuman monstrosities, a ravenous inferno, a wicked presence entombing us alive in the Nachthaus, a philosopher face on the wall, the moaning of the forest, the scratching of the door, and the pervasive evil seeping through the very cracks of the mine.

Evil is a nepenthe, a narcotic that makes some men high and others forgetful. It lulls men into a false sense of normalcy, thinking this is the way the world is or, more accurately, how the world was meant to be. It was as if men of the Nachthaus—and perhaps all men—had forgotten how to dream of a world with no evil. They accepted it as the status quo, the here and now. In some sense this had to be so, but in another it was all wrong.

Rolf was right: everyone in the Nachthaus was under the spell of the evil. It had drugged us somehow. It was a parasite in our mind, worming its way into our synapses, affecting our thoughts, poisoning our wills. But I thought he was a little short in his conclusion. I thought it was a spiritual problem. The evil had deadened us, desensitized us. It had sung us a horrid lullaby, and we had dozed to its chant. Dreaming is seeing the world as it is not.

I prayed silently that moment for God to awaken me to the reality that lay before me under the rock and granite of the mountain. I prayed that He awaken me before I fell deep asleep.

I poured myself a stiff cup of coffee. Black. Strong enough to stand on its own without a cup. "You think we'll ever leave this place?"

Rolf stared at me through his goggles. He was a hard read, that one. Gott shrugged.

"Wake up," I said. "Do you think we'll ever leave this place?"

They spoke at once, then fell silent. Gott motioned to Rolf to speak. I took a sip.

"Not likely," Rolf said. "And if we do, we'll die in the forest."

I fiddled with a fork, thinking of the two soldiers who had made a run for it in the truck. "You, Gott?"

"I think our lone chance is if an entire division comes marching through the forest to our doorstep. Even then, I'm not sure."

"What are we doing here, then?" I searched both men for traces of their souls. I saw nothing.

"Waiting to die," Rolf said. "And we're doing those poor folks a favor. One quick second in the flame and all is over."

Although I understood his intent, I doubted Rolf's assessment of the pain involved. I could imagine standing in the center of the inferno, hearing the great iron door descending. I could hear the jets and the whoosh of the pilot light. I could imagine the louvers opening and that one last second before the flames scorched the oven. That one instant between room temperature and a searing hell.

It was comforting to be in the lab. The Bunsen burners were like candles at our altar, the chemicals my holy water, the periodic table our articles of faith. Science and faith, those eternal bedfellows of truth, longing for each other in vain in this dark world.

"So we absolve our guilt by claiming to follow orders," I said, "offset a bit by helping these poor souls with a quick and relatively painless death. That it?"

Gott took a bite of bacon, cooked over open flame, another benefit of the Bunsens. He pointed his uneaten half-strip of bacon at me. It folded over limply. "Aren't you taking a bit of a risk talking to us so openly about all this, Oberleutnant?"

"You two are not standard-issue Nazis. I didn't need a field manual to figure that one out. And after you forgot to close the oven door our first time out, I realized you're not by-the-book models of German efficiency, either." I scoured the corners of their eyes and the nooks of their features. Still nothing.

"So why should we be free with you?" Gott flipped the remainder of his bacon strip in his mouth.

"Because I got too much Leibniz at Leipzig. Or because you're not idiots. Take your pick."

"Hayner would be very appreciative of this information," Rolf said.

He attempted to pass it off as a joke, but I figured I might take advantage of the comment. I kept close tabs on their eyes. "I don't think that option is open to you. The way I see it, we three are complicit in everything that goes on down here. Anything bad, at least. You know Hayner. He'll throw all of us in that oven with half an excuse, the snitch as well as the snitchee. If anything, he'll spare me alone because he thinks I can deliver a solvent to cut through that rock."

Gott pushed away from the table and leaned back in his chair. He balanced impeccably. "Odds are if you don't get that solvent, Oberleutnant, you'll be first in that oven."

"I'll be first given what I'm of a mind to do."

Gott leaned forward on his chair, not making a sound as the chair came to rest on the ground. Rolf adjusted his goggles and leaned in.

"There are at least one hundred prisoners here," I said. "They wouldn't miss one, would they?"

"Yes, they would," Rolf said. "Forget it."

"I can't. After the gypsy girl, I have to do something."

"I won't be a part of it," Rolf said. "Let's get that part clear up front."

I rested my elbows on the table and leaned my head on my hands, rubbing my fingers through my hair. "You rat me out, Rolf, and you'll go in the oven also."

"Maybe."

I felt a tremor in the walls of the mine as if the forest had moaned in unison at the door of the Nachthaus.

I sprung up from my chair, hands disentangling from my hair. I'm sure my hair was as wild as the scraggly man's we had burned with the gypsy girl. Gott retreated from the table and arrived behind his chair like a cat slinking around your calf. Rolf froze.

I seized his wrists under the cuffs of his lab coat. His eyes ballooned behind the goggles like a cartoon character. I muffled a squeal with a backhand to his cheek and then regained my hold on his wrist. I could feel his bones creaking under my grasp, and the weight and power of the mountain began to press in upon me as I pulled his hands to the flame of the lit Bunsen burner.

"No! No!" he screamed.

I slapped him again.

The Nachthaus coursed through my arteries like slushy fire. The rage burned, but it was a sweet burn, like a hot shower. The power was intoxicating. I craved more, and the mine yielded itself with vigor. I pulled Rolf's hands to the flame.

"Please, Oberleutnant, please." Rolf's goggles were fogging up. "Please."

"I'll give you a taste of the inferno!" My voice roared, reaching a crescendo in the last syllables.

The evil was all-consuming. Outside, the forest groaned and a deep-pitched pounding commenced on the great iron door at the front of the mine. The flame of the Bunsen burner was now a splendid and glorious light and my inward desire was to pull Rolf into it. To make him *see*. To *enlighten* him.

I enlightened him and he began screaming. His hands were over the flame, and I began the descent, forcing his hands downward, ever and resolutely downward into the glorious refulgence of the flame.

He was pleading with me, but they were the pleas of the soon-to-be converted. First, a moment of pain, then comes the promised land. Trial by fire. Baptism by fire. All the clichés were but shoddy surrogates of the beauty that lay before me, a dusty replica of an ancient and beautiful calling.

The evil called, and I pursued the calling. Rolf's hands dropped a bit lower. The protracted pace of the decline was exhilarating, and I cherished each moment until Rolf's cries were a distant howl far beyond the peak of the mountain where Hayner stood grinning.

The last thing I remembered was the beauty of the flame before something crashed and I fell into darkness.

15

I came to on my back with my head flat against the floor, staring at the ceiling of the lab, which resembled a barren landscape. It was dark, pitted, rough, and uneven, but without stalactites. I had no referent for it at the time. This place was nothing like my lush Bavaria, nor had I spent any time at night in the deserts of North Africa.

My eyes adjusted and it occurred again to me how austere the Nachthaus was. I raised a hand in the air and turned it, first palm down then palm up, to convince myself I wasn't dreaming. I wasn't, at least I didn't think so. My hand rotated against a backdrop of desolation.

The desolation of the mine was in stark contrast to the forest that surrounded it, and the lush green of my life back home. The forest teemed with life to the near eclipse of the noonday sun. The mine had no sun to eclipse. Its suns were flickering electric bulbs strung out at odd intervals. The mine was an aberration, a human incursion into the earth.

I was beginning to see, lying on my back in the lab, now beginning to sense a lump throbbing on my forehead, that the evil presence in the forest was somehow natural. It belonged there, or somewhere at least, as if it were organic in the sense that it was not out of place. Its evil was not a malevolence; it was not evil for the sake of being evil. It was more like anger. But even more to the point, it seemed as though the presence in the forest were responding to hurt or pain. The forest was *groaning*. With all its teeming life, it was groaning as if it had been wronged somehow, even subjected.

The Nachthaus was different. It was unnatural. It was an intruding evil. It was an evil that brought desolation with it. A wickedness that by its nature could not coexist with anything natural, and therefore must ultimately rot its host or be cast in to outer darkness.

Gott poked his head into my view of the ceiling. "Are you hurt, Oberleutnant?" He towered over me, appearing as a god of the desolation.

I didn't think I was injured, but I ran my hands up and down my torso anyway. I sat up and patted my forehead with one hand.

"What happened, Gott?" I asked.

I caught a glimpse of movement near the lab door and turned to see Rolf backing against it. He was holding a scalpel toward me as he backed. I pushed up against the floor and stood, a bit woozy. Gott steadied me.

"Come no closer!" Rolf backed against the door and startled a bit. "Come no closer!" His free hand searched for the door latch.

I motioned for Gott with my eyes under the hand on my forehead. "What's wrong with him?" I grabbed a stool and sat down at the workbench, head in hand.

Gott sat down next to me and recounted the story.

"So you're responsible for this bump and my headache," I said.

Gott put one hand up as if to say, *what else could I do?* Over by the door, Rolf still seemed undecided as to what he should do.

"Rolf," I said, "come have a seat. I've got something I want to show you, and it doesn't burn."

Rolf took a step toward the workbench and paused. "You won't grab me?" He slouched like a skittish dog.

"I promise, Rolf. I don't even remember what happened." In fact, I did remember, but I wasn't going to let Rolf know. "As a scientist, you'll want to see this." I pointed to my pocket.

I could see Rolf's mind arguing with itself. He went to the opposite side of the workbench and sat down, keeping his hands out of reach. He raised his voice a touch. "If you grab me again, I swear by Jes—"

Rolf caught himself in mid-sentence, eyes darting between Gott and me behind his goggles.

Gott rose and pointed at Rolf in one astoundingly fluid motion. "You're a—"

"Hang on, Gott," I said. I deflected his accusatory finger with one hand and retracted his arm with another. I guided it down to the workbench. If there were a better time to broach the subject, I couldn't imagine one. "You named the name of Christ, Rolf."

"I used it in vain, sir. Naming the name of Christ is against regulation, as you're well aware." Rolf sat stolid, except for the darting eyes.

"Did you now?" I smiled. Time for the gambit. "Rolf. Gott. I'm a Christian. Always have been, and the Hitler Youth was not enough to beat it out of me. I'm not proud of myself since coming here, but I am what I am and I've done what I've done, or not done, as the case may be. Forgive me, but that's the truth. That goes double for me pulling your hands into the flame, Rolf."

The two men sat at the workbench staring at me. The solitary sound was the moaning of the forest outside the mine. They exchanged glances, then Rolf broke the silence.

"I'm a scientist, sir, but I've always made a place for Christ in my heart. Took to the faith from my grandmother, and I've never seen a reason to give it up. It's been under a bushel since I got stuck with you military types. How about you, Gott? You planning to inform on us?"

Gott took Rolf's left hand and my right. He closed his eyes for a moment, and when he opened them, they seemed to be misty. "What are the odds," he asked, "that three Christians could find themselves together, isolated in this mine? What does it mean, and what are we to do about it?"

I've always found faith an amazing bridge over uncertainty, when one will walk over it in obedience. "What it means is Providence, my friends. God has us here for a reason, even if it means our lives, which it probably does."

We prayed a little, talked about our faith a little, and shared a bit of our past. I think each man was satisfied that the other two indeed were Christian. At least no one seemed to be concerned with being reported to Hayner. It was well-understood that one could not be Nazi and a Christian, and though none of us was proud of it, we had all hidden our lights under bushels. In this case, it was a monstrous and decidedly dark bushel called the Nachthaus.

I retrieved the marble I had picked up in the alcove detention cage and placed it on the table. It flashed to life, its clouds swirling faster and faster in the sea of dark blue. The light from the center of the marble increased in strength, and again they began to resemble the gypsy girl's eyes.

Faster and faster the clouds swirled in the increasing light until the marble faded away, leaving a growing sphere of light on the workbench. The sphere grew to a foot in height, and we backed away from the table in fright but with rapt awe. The light from the gypsy girl's eyes was beginning to suck the light away from all other sources in the room. The eyes emerged from the sphere and floated a foot over the rotating globe. The lab was now entirely dark except for the eyes. Even the lit Bunsen burners were flames writhing in darkness.

The eyes filled the lab with beauty, but most strikingly across the ceiling's desolation. Moments before it had been a wasteland; now it was a sea of diamonds, a luxuriant panorama of splendor. The ceiling twinkled in the darkness as the clearest night sky. Then the light shut off and she was there, hovering over the sphere.

The gypsy girl. She was as before: perfectly cut hair, blue dress, no burn marks or ill-effects from the inferno. It was impossible.

"Deus et natua non faciunt frusta." Her voice wrapped around me like a mother's love. I was so enthralled by those eyes, I never thought to see how Gott and Rolf were reacting to the vision.

Except as the gypsy girl began to speak, I realized this was no vision in my mind. Somehow, she was really there, floating above the sphere.

"God and nature do not work together in vain," she said. "It is no accident you three have been called to this place for such a time as this. You did well to realize this before I came, but make no mistake, the hand of Providence would have awakened you either way."

"I want to ask your for—"

"Not now, son of Adam." The eyes bore into me. At once they focused all their light and energy in my direction. "Your sin has been forgiven. Now is not the time to ask for forgiveness. It was a horrid thing you did, but out of evil comes good: *Ex malo bonum*. You meant it for evil, but God meant it for good. Now you also know what it is you must do. She waits for you in the alcove. Do not make the same mistake twice, son of Adam."

I fell to my knees before her, pleading with my hands. The stench of soot was overbearing. "But there's no way. Even if we do somehow manage it, there's nowhere to go and nowhere to hide. The forest will kill us outside or the Nazis will kill us inside. She'll end up dead either way."

"Son of Adam, do not ever kneel before me!" Her eyes burned with fire.

I rose.

"Yours is not to worry about consequences, but to be obedient. Out of this evil good shall come forth, and in the end you shall see and recognize it. Until then we both see through a glass darkly. And if you should refuse to be obedient, another will be charged to act in your stead. Even the rocks of this mine and mountain may cry out if need be. Now go, Sascha König."

The eyes lit up in one brilliant flash, like a supernova, and then the gypsy girl was gone, and the marble was back to its original state. I picked it up and put it back in my pocket.

"I'll do it by myself if I have to," I said. But one glance at Gott and Rolf and I knew I wouldn't have to.

16

The mine shaft was dark and deserted. Gott, Rolf, and I made our way toward the alcove. It was around two in the morning and we were dressed in gray fatigues. I felt as though the whole mine would smell my hands as I passed, so I inserted my hands into my gloves. It didn't help.

We crept past the intersection that led to Hayner's quarters, still with no signs of life. Up ahead there was some shuffling and stirring in the alcoves, but nothing else other than the constant buzz of the electric light bulbs and the groaning of the forest. The scratching at the front door was worse than normal, and I figured that helped with our chances in keeping the guards at the front gate occupied. The rest of the soldiers appeared to be in their quarters.

At the entrance to the alcove hallway I peeked around the corner. The passageway was clear, so I motioned for Gott.

He crossed the entire hallway over the wooden pier in what seemed to be three steps, the whole time making what we thought was the universal sign for *shhhhhhhhh*. It appeared to be working as there was not much commotion from the captives.

Gott reached the end of the alcove passage, leaned against the corner at the far side of the hallway, and gave us the all-clear signal. Rolf and I stepped out onto the wooden pier, me with my pack of chemicals, Rolf with a crowbar. We repeated Gott's universal signal, but the captives were beginning to get restless. One thing I could tell already: there would be no opening of just the one gate to free one woman. The captives wouldn't stand for it. It was written on their faces and the way in which they pressed up against the iron bars.

Gott held up a palm and we stopped in our tracks. The captives began to rattle with anticipation and uncertainty of what was happening, and my initial optimism waned. When Gott came bounding down the hall, it dissipated.

I turned to run and ran into Rolf. We tangled and fell in a heap as Gott sped past us, the vials in my pack jingling against each other. From the main hallway I could hear marching boots approaching, and they were nearing the alcoves.

We sprang up and raced after Gott in the direction of the lab, reaching the darkness of the shaft just as the squad of soldiers stepped onto the wooden pier. Their boots rattled in unison against the wooden planks, and from our concealment we could see them as they came into view at the intersection. They halted in front of the second-to-last alcove cave, where the woman we had come to rescue was held.

We were too late, and all I could think of was how the gypsy girl's eyes would look when she found out we had failed.

The squad leader barked out commands. Three of the squad members stepped forward. One detached a set of keys from his belt and unlocked the gate as the other two pulled out nightsticks. The remaining soldiers were armed with drawn pistols.

The lock clicked and the iron gate creaked open before the captives began to riot. The hallway erupted in a general tumult as the prisoners yelled at the guards. I discerned at least three separate languages.

I craned my head up and out for a better look. The guards had seized two male prisoners and dragged them out of the cage, forcing them back to the squad of soldiers. They were now attempting to pull the woman out of the cage.

The other captives resisted, and a tug of war over the woman ensued. The captives were trying to pull her back into the cell behind them. At first, they succeeded, and the woman lurched back inside the cage. The guards began swinging the clubs, and they connected with a vicious accuracy. One man fell with a broken arm, another with a blow that split his forehead open.

The captives fought undeterred until a shot rang out. The alcove went silent. The squad leader lifted a smoking gun. One man fell from the cage clutching his gut.

The woman held up her hands in submission and stepped from the cell. Her regal disposition never relented, though by this time she looked more gaunt and haggard than when I had first seen her, which had not been long before. Time and the Nachthaus danced a strange tango. She stepped into line inside the squad of soldiers with the two other captives, and the gate was locked back into place after a couple of well-placed club strikes on the prisoners.

The squad led the prisoners to the intersection past the alcove hallway and took a right down into the shaft leading in the opposite direction from Hayner's quarters. We slipped back into the shadows, noting the procession as it passed.

The soldiers, with the exception of the squad leader, were not any older than me. They appeared so young in the false light of the mine that, as they passed, I imagined them not much removed from playing ball back in our German homeland. What was it that had turned these young men from playful kids into apathetic killers? Their faces gave no indication that they cared what was going on here or what was about to happen to the three prisoners they were escorting deeper into the mine.

I whispered to Gott. "The torture rooms are that way, aren't they?"

He nodded. "There's a T junction about a hundred yards down. To the left are the officer's quarters and a mess hall. To the right are the enlisted men's quarters. Past the enlisted men's quarters are the rooms." Gott's face crinkled when he mentioned the *rooms*. It did not sound pleasant.

These soldiers, then, knew where they were taking the prisoners and what would take place there. They *knew*. They had probably done this several times and knew it had gone on for quite some time. Yet their faces were as stolid and unconcerned as if they were examining cucumbers at a local market. Rolf had been right, the Nachthaus had a way of desensitizing people. That, or it was something much, much worse, as I had begun to suspect, or both.

"Follow me." I ran down into the darkness in the direction of the lab as fast as I was able.

• • •

Minutes later we were creeping back through the shadows to the intersection in single file: Gott led, I followed, and Rolf brought up the rear. It was now 3:30 a.m. Sleep was not a bountiful commodity in the Nachthaus and the adrenaline I felt from this redirected mission meant I might not sleep at all this night, even if we made it through without getting caught. The adrenaline, however, was a sugar pill compared with the gypsy girl's eyes that compelled us forward.

The intersection appeared clear and Gott motioned us forward. We crept across the lit crossing and into the shaft that the squad of soldiers had taken with the prisoners. The shaft was ill-lit with one bulb about halfway down and another at the T junction one hundred yards ahead. The floor of this shaft was rough and uneven, littered with gravel that rattled in the wake of our steps. The hallway descended at enough of an angle to be noticeable as we crept along in the shadows.

We hugged the left wall of the mine as we descended. The wall had intermittent depressions and a few recesses along the way that we ducked in and out of as we progressed. We gained the halfway point, marked by the overhead lightbulb, and crossed through into the dark on the other side. The junction was well in view now, and only once did a soldier cross through the light at the junction. We pressed into one of the recesses and waited for him to pass, hoping he would be gone when we reached the end of the shaft.

While we waited for the soldier to clear out, Gott beckoned us to listen. "When we get to the end of the hall, we'll take a right and move as quickly as possible without making too much noise until we get past the soldiers' quarters," he said. "The quarters are mostly lit, so when we get past the light you'll know they're behind us. The torture rooms are 50 yards past the quarters and down a shaft to the left. It's dark that far in, so we should be able to hide once we get past the soldiers' rooms."

Rolf and I nodded.

I adjusted my pack, and then rested a hand on each man's shoulder. "Now's the time if you want out," I said. "Now's the time. The way forward is probable pain and death; the way back is the certain pain and death of conscience. Forward hurts much worse, but the pain is quick. The way back is a pain of the most enduring and exquisite kind."

"The gun or the cancer," Gott said.

"That's close," Rolf said, "but it's not it exactly. The way back is a cancer of the soul, and it's a cancer that may never kill. It leaves a man permanently sick, always near death, but not able to have it. The way forward may end with the gun. But then again, we might actually make it."

I tallied another victory for the liberal arts over science in Rolf's assessment. "Ahead is obedience, and behind are the gypsy girl's eyes," I said. "Take your pick."

We agreed. Ahead. When and if we saw the gypsy girl again, those eyes would be pleased. I recalled again my decision to face with courage whatever I would find. Now, perhaps, I could renew that vow. I felt in my pocket to make sure the marble was still there, even though I could feel it against my leg.

We pressed forward through the shaft, following Gott toward the junction. Rolf and I sounded as loud as a marching band compared to Gott's silence. He could sneak through the dark of these mines undetected all night, I figured. We allowed him to approach the junction alone.

Gott reached the T and peeked around the corner. He was now vulnerable in the light, but he waved us forward and we hurried to join him.

"Quickly," he whispered.

We set off down the right shaft in full light. Here the floor was cleaner. We were exposed, but moved quietly. After 25 yards, the entrances to the soldiers' quarters appeared. There were several doors along either side of the mine. These barracks cut into the rock held 20 soldiers apiece. We hurried past.

Fifty more yards brought us to a left turn into the shaft leading to the torture rooms. Gott paused at the turn, checking for a sentry. Again, he waved us forward. There were three doors along the right-hand side of the shaft. The hallway was dark except for a wavering light coming from the crack under the last door. I unzipped my pack as we crept toward it.

At the door we were met by a sickening odor of ozone that was almost as strong as the odor of my gloved hands. A hum of electrodes came from the room, along with shrieks of agony. Between the hums and the shimmering light, there were commands in German, followed by pleading. I did not hear a female voice. I hoped she wasn't already dead.

Above and below the shrieks was another distinct sound. The soldiers were laughing. And between laughs came more shrieks, punctuated by taunting and joking. The laughing was more disgusting than the shrieks. It was inhuman.

I glanced at Rolf and Gott. They were staring at the floor of the mine. Rolf doodled in the dust as if he were trying to forget and remember at the same time, as if he were trying to be incensed at the torture but was struggling to be outraged.

I understood. The Nachthaus must have sensed us prodding at its foundation with blunt spades. Though it knew we couldn't hurt it, I thought it would not tolerate any incursion of light within its depths. It was trying to cloud our minds again, and it was using our sin against us.

My mind filled with the oven's glaring orange eyes. They peered inside me, reminding me of my complicity in the gypsy girl's death. I had stood there watching as the oven had fired up, sealing her fate. The oven's eyes shone on Hayner's face and he was again smiling at me. My inaction was action.

Maybe it was worse for Gott and Rolf, because they had primed the oven and thrown the switch. I wasn't sure, but another glance told me they were feeling the weight of conscience.

It would be so much easier to sleep. To forget. To rationalize. To let time heal all ills and wounds. To let the haze and the darkness cloud out the hurt.

The Nachthaus was calling to me. It was a lullaby of evil, but it was a sweet melody that called me.

Sleep, my Adam, in the arms of your love.

I fought at first, but it was as if I had carried a burden of ages across a desolate land. Sleep was a sweet elixir held out in a golden chalice to a thirsty and tired man.

Sleep, my Adam, in the arms of your love.

To drink deep the elixir of sleep—all my warts, all the rotting and stinking of my flesh, the pains of conscience, the remorse of my failings, the disgust of the sin at large in the world, the evil around me and within me—to drink the elixir of sleep would remove them once and for all. Perhaps they would be banished to a deep, dark place, a Tartarus, perhaps, never to torment me again.

It was a beautiful lullaby, and its melody caressed me. Its tones curled around my neck like a warm scarf.

In the arms of your love there is solace and bliss.

Yes, I could feel it. To sleep. To rid myself of the ills of this life. The darkness was sweet solace.

A cry from behind the door to the torture room shook me out of my daze. I looked at Gott and Rolf. They were entranced.

How could I find solace when there is pain in the world?

The Nachthaus wormed its way into my thoughts. It was as careful as it entered as a child sneaking in the dark of its parents' house, but I could tell it was great power under great restraint, like a father stepping around his child's tower of blocks that would fall at the least disturbance.

"It hurts to look at the sun," the Nachthaus said. "It blinds, does it not?"

True. I gave myself a moment. "But we don't look directly at the sun. We look at the things it lights, and it allows us to see them clearly. Without the light, we can't see."

The Nachthaus wasted no time. "Does it? The light shows you things as they are not. A rose is not red; it retains some of the light and reflects other parts of the light, thereby deceiving you that it is red. Thus, the light always deceives. In the dark we see things as they truly are, for the dark does not attempt to color."

Sleep, my Adam, in the arms of your love.

Another cry from the torture room jostled me. There was another buzz of electricity followed by coarse humor.

"How could I sleep with all that going on?" I asked.

The Nachthaus didn't miss a beat, as if this were well-trodden ground. "Do you think that any goodness would stand by idly if it cared or had any power to stop it? Do you think it would sit here watching this like a bystander or, worse, a *voyeur*, if it cared? Sascha, think! Would a God send *you* to stop this, as if you *could* stop it? Why wouldn't He do it Himself if He cared?"

Your love awaits you in the dark, my Adam.
In the dark is where love is made.

17

Sleep, my Adam, in the arms of your love.

    In the arms of your love there is solace and bliss.

Your love awaits you in the dark, my Adam.

    In the dark is where love is made.

Why *would* God send a man like me for a task such as this? The Nachthaus was beckoning, and I could feel myself drifting. It wasn't a sleepy drift. It was a dreamy sensation, as if everything around me were starting to look and feel less real. It was more a hypnosis than a slumber.

    Gott and Rolf were along for the ride as well. They were staring at the floor of the mine, Rolf still doodling in the dust. He was writing something but I couldn't make out what it was.

The light was still emerging from the crack under the door to the torture room, and the intermittent buzzing continued with all the attendant screaming and joking. Somehow, it didn't seem quite as horrific as it had moments before.

Or was it moments? Time and the Nachthaus had resumed their eerie tango, and I was unsure how long we had paused at the foot of the door. It didn't seem to matter.

Another shriek came from the torture room. This time it was a woman's voice.

I imagined her strapped to a rack, her torturers armed with electric prods. Her two companions would be worn out by now, cast against a back wall in shock from the pain. Perhaps one of the soldiers was taunting them with a red-hot poker, balancing it right at eye level and moving it closer and closer.

The captives should have revealed whatever they knew so we could be done with this business. We didn't like it any more than they, but business was business and all was fair in love and war. Why didn't they spill what they knew instead of being obstinate? They knew we had orders to follow.

Did they think we would disobey and end up receiving the same treatment from our own fellows? Did they think we should let them be when their information was vital to our friends on the front line? Their silence would cause the deaths of several of our fellow soldiers. Why was it so fair and right to allow them to withhold that information? After all, it was their armies attempting to kill us.

The joking must have been advanced interrogation techniques, not the outworking of wicked hearts. It was the captives' fault for what was happening; we had every right to do what we were doing.

A burning sensation erupted right below my hip on the outside of my right upper thigh. It burned like I was the one being stuck with a hot poker. As I wriggled around, it felt like the poker was being twisted inside of my flesh.

I reached into my pocket right above the burning sensation. My gloved hand grazed against the marble and then I grabbed it. It was a fiery globe and it was causing the pain.

I had to get it out of my pocket to stop the burning within my thigh. I pulled the marble up with a gloved fist balled around it, and the pain transferred from my leg to my palm. My balled up hand caught in the pocket opening, flesh boiling inside my fist. I yanked with so much force I ripped a hole in my pants.

Suddenly, the marble was cool again, and instead of throwing the marble against the side of the mine to relieve the burning, I opened my clenched fist in front of me. The marble was swirling again in the black fabric of my glove. There was the pre-dawn blue and the hint of the gypsy girl's eyes. Those eyes reminded me that I would have to face the gypsy girl again. I heard the words of the philosopher-face-on-the-wall in conjunction with the gypsy girl's eyes and the marble I held in my hand: *It is times such as these that we see inside a man by what he obeys or does not obey.*

My hand was open again, and the marble rested directly on my palm now through a perfect circle cut into the glove by the marble's heat. The pain had ceased. I was afraid that the marble had fused into my palm, but it wasn't so. I lifted it out with my other hand, dropping it and my gloves into my other pocket. I muttered a quick prayer of thanks and then studied the brand in the center of my palm the marble had left. It was a perfect circle.

• • •

"Gott." I shook him by his shoulders.

He was on his knees by the door, staring at the wall of the mine. He came to and gazed up at me with hollow eyes, pupils adjusting as he became cognizant of his surroundings. "How long?" He looked over at Rolf, who was still doodling.

But now the doodling was an overwritten jumbled mess, but I thought I could still make out the letters *eam*. I kicked a heel through Rolf's doodling, and his eyes tracked the heel of my boot, up my leg, and then to my face.

"How long?" Gott asked. This time I detected urgency in his voice.

"I don't know," I said. "Too long." I traced the circle on my palm. The flesh was cool, but not cauterized. I couldn't feel the brand—it wasn't scar tissue—but the circle was there. "Get Rolf up and take him back to the lab, Gott. As fast as you can."

Gott began his protest, as I knew he would. I cut him off. "Now, Gott. That's an order." It had been way too long and now every moment was precious.

"I understand, Oberleutnant." Gott's grace had returned, and he was down the hall with Rolf before I could get my pack opened.

I was hoping there was enough time left. It must have been around 4:00 a.m. by the time we'd first arrived outside the torture room. How long *had* we been out? Thirty minutes? I couldn't tell for sure, but at any time now the guard could be changing for the morning. Or, any moment now the torture session could be over and the door would open, leaving me kneeling in front of armed guards.

Gott disappeared around the corner with Rolf in tow. I riveted my attention on the pack and the task at hand. The idea of time was beyond me now. Either there would be enough or there would not be enough. The face had been right: it was indeed in times like these that we learn about a man.

From the pack, I extracted two sealed beakers, a rather large open one, and a cork with a three-foot tube that ran through the cork. Inside the torture room, the woman's cries spurred me on. There might not be enough time to pull this off, but there was enough time to end her pain.

In the corridor behind me, no sounds interrupted my concentration on the contents of my pack. Gott must have gotten through, at least past the barracks and into the T junction. If time ran out, it might only be me who was apprehended.

I reached into the pack again, took out a gas mask, and strapped it on. I righted the large beaker on the floor of the mine and unsealed the other two beakers, pouring their contents into the third beaker until they were empty. The chemicals in the large beaker began to react.

As quickly as I could manage, I set the empty beakers down and thrust the cork with the tubing into the large beaker. The reaction was accelerating, and gas began to pressurize and flow through the tubing. I forced the tubing underneath the door and waited.

Perhaps Jekyll would have been a better name for me than Nebuchadnezzar.

I shook the large beaker a bit to hurry the reaction, but it wasn't necessary. The chemicals were working in accordance with natural law, as predicted. *Deus et natua non faciunt frusta*, I thought.

"It's a grave error on your part, this thing you now do." The Nachthaus was back and reaching for me.

"You can learn a lot about a man in times such as these." It was not a verbatim recounting of the philosopher's words, but it was close enough. I was muttering to a mine shaft wall. "Why don't you stop me, then?"

"Don't you realize I could shake everyone awake?"

Good question, I thought. But better questions came to me: if the Nachthaus *can* manifest physical events such as earthquakes, why hasn't it already? Better question: why am I no longer scared?

A definitive answer to the first question came through the voice of the philosopher-face. *If the Nachthaus could—or, better, if it were allowed to—don't you think it would have done so already? And if it could, why wouldn't it do something more direct, such as drop a 300-pound section of rock on your head from the roof? Much cleaner that way and no chance of human error.*

That much was clear. The Nachthaus was not going to intervene. It was restrained in some fashion, held back by a greater power, perhaps. The Nachthaus didn't respond.

The second question was trickier. Why was I not afraid? The philosopher-face answered. *It is the first step men are fearful of, Sascha. After the first footsteps forward, the other naturally follows, and each subsequent step is less fearful. It's the spiritual economy of God's universe, and also why intimacy with God comes through obedience.*

The chemicals in the beaker were spent, having converted into gas and entered the torture room. It was quiet behind the door, and I supposed I could enter safely. I didn't have much choice either way. It had to be now.

I put the equipment back in my pack, with the exception of my gas mask, which I left on. I stood and opened the door, slowly at first, trying to see through the crack before I opened it enough to walk through.

The room was a harbor of malevolence. It was a killing floor.

It was a little more than thirty feet square, with an island bar running down the center, from about three feet from the door to the halfway point of the room. The bar had a slate countertop about three or four feet across, and there were three large cages on the bar. Countertops and shelving ran along both outer walls.

The sides, ceiling, and back walls were roughly hewn, and a single bulb suspended from the center of the ceiling cast a dim light. Three soldiers were at the end of the bar, facing the back of the room away from me and standing in front of the woman, who was harnessed to a metal framework in a spread-eagle position.

The lingering smell of electricity hung in the air, mixed with a nauseating compost odor, and I noticed several batteries connected to a machine from which electrodes passed into the cage. One hung freely with an applicator that appeared to be a prod of some sort.

The two male prisoners were already dead. They lay against the back wall, naked, with burns from the electric prod across their chest and legs. Their faces had been stripped away, and they stared up into space with empty eye sockets. Their hair clumped to the sides of their heads like wet seaweed.

The woman was screaming. I stepped into the room and closed the door without making noise, hoping to avoid arousing the barracks. I crept forward, wondering again how much time I had.

The gas had dissipated the moment it entered the room and had had no effect on any of the room's occupants, except a guard stationed by the door, who was slumped over in a chair, asleep. Thank God for small miracles, as well as the large. He would have knocked me unconscious before I'd even seen him.

I breathed heavier through the mask. I saw now why the Nachthaus was feared above all other camps in the Reich.

The first cage on the bar still had an occupant. The cage was four feet wide and three feet tall, and I passed it from the right of the island bar, hesitating next to it to peer inside.

In the dim light of the bulb, I could see some form of monstrous vermin in the cage. Its mandibles clicked open and shut like a large pair of salad tongs. The creature was a cockroach with the jaws of a beetle. It was lightly armored and appeared sleek and fast. Its legs pistoned up and down in the cage as if it were wanting out. The back of each leg was barbed from the thing's thorax down to a razor-like talon at the end of the leg. The talons clicked against the slate countertop like a manual typewriter. A filmy slime oozed from its mouth and a pair of antennae pivoted back and forth with great interest in the proceedings ahead. It must have been three feet long.

The two cages in front of it were empty. I froze, trying to rid myself of the creeping feeling that something from one of the empty cages was slithering up the top of my shoes. Scattered along the bar between the cages were scalpels, hooks, and other assorted gruesome implements. They were soiled with use. One blade in particular was awash in blood, and shrouded by a thick flap of severed flesh. The flesh was supple and moist, as if it had been recently slashed from its owner.

I looked toward the back of the room and saw one of the roaches on the torso of one of the dead prisoners. That explained why the prisoner's face and eyes were gone, and now the bug was going to work on his chest. Its jaws clicked greedily, and the antennae slid along the dead man's neck.

Next to the other dead prisoner, a plant-man was caged. It was reaching through the bars of the cage and caressing the dead man with one of its hawthorn-covered stalk arms.

The soldiers, who were standing shoulder to shoulder at the end of the bar, wore thick gloves that covered their hands and arms up to the shoulders. They looked like extended falconer's gloves. The two men on the right held six-foot-long poles that tapered down to a sharp metal gig. These were positioned in the general direction of the bug on the dead man's torso. The other, on the left, held the second bug by its midsection in his gloves. He was moving it toward the woman's face.

I looked at that proud, defiant woman. Her elegance was nearly gone, here in this room. And the last vestige of her regal look evaporated as the bug was moved closer to her. Its mandibles snapped, and slime dripped from its mouth and splattered on the floor. She screamed and kicked at the soldiers while pulling against the restraints that held her wrists.

The soldier stepped back to dodge the kicks, and he thrust the bug forward again as if he were taunting her. The soldiers were laughing.

I must have looked insectile myself, with the gas mask still on. The woman saw me over the bug's armor-plated head and back, and screamed for help.

The soldiers wheeled around in unison, and several things happened at once.

The bug scavenging the dead captive reacted as if it had intuited an unusual opening. It rotated around the dead man's torso, managing to raise up on its back four legs against the corpse. It opened its jaws and hissed at me.

The plant-man retracted its arm from the other dead captive and pressed to the front of its cage, grasping the bars and rocking back and forth. The seaweed covering its face parted, revealing a sunken face with a swastika tattooed on its forehead. It howled: *Woooooooooo!*

The soldier on the right dropped his gig and reached for a pistol holstered at his side. Had he not fumbled with the holster cover drawing the gun, he would have shot me. The soldier in the middle brought his gig to bear on me with an overhead motion, so as to maneuver the gig in my direction without hitting the two soldiers flanking his side.

The remaining soldier turned with the bug still in hand, but instead of wheeling to the outside of their line, he swiveled toward the inside. That left the middle soldier's flank open to the roach as he turned.

The roach clamped down on the middle soldier's shoulder with its jaws. The point of each jaw sunk into the soldier's flesh as if it were a cheese log. The soldier yelped in pain, and the gig he was swinging overhead veered off-course and burst the solitary light bulb suspended from the ceiling. The room went dark.

The impression burned into my mind as the light went out was the pistol leveling at my chest, the middle soldier falling to the floor with the roach on top of him, and the second roach leaping into action off the corpse in the back of the room.

18

I hit the floor in anticipation of the gunshots, but they never came. I thought I heard the gun hit the floor, perhaps caused by the bug pouncing on the soldier. I crawled like an insect toward the door, feeling the bar to my right to make my way through the dark. The room was a free-for-all and I wanted out. I jerked the gas mask off my head and flung it toward the door.

I could hear the death struggle in the back of the room. The soldiers hurled German curses and pleaded for help. One cried to his fellows to get the thing off him, and then his words blurred into a gurgling sound before falling silent under the hiss of the roach. I could see it on top of him in my mind: its talons anchoring in his chest before it descended upon his face with clicking mandibles and oozing digestive juices.

The plant-man's howls increased as if it were enjoying the show and wishing to participate. Its cage rocked back and forth.

The woman shrieked again. One other soldier must have been grappling with the second bug because I could hear them rolling on the floor. Something crashed into the electrical unit then. There was a brief flash of light and the room went dark again.

The dread feeling of insects crawling up my legs resurfaced in the dark. I could feel the tingling, and I anticipated the bite at any moment. I crawled faster for the door and felt the end of the bar. I might make it before the bugs finished with the soldiers and turned on me.

The sphere in my pocket began to heat up. I knew it was at a warning temperature, waiting to see what I was going to do.

Lord, it's dark. I cannot crawl back there with those things waiting. I won't crawl back there. Ask anything else and I'll do it. Not that, though. Please.

The sphere warmed a bit more.

Lord, she's a goner by now. Even if I went back, I couldn't save her. We'd both die.

The room fell silent except for intermittent insect chatter at the back of the room, and clicking. I sat still and quiet, crouched at the front of the bar. Above me, the caged roach clattered in its cage.

Lord, I can leave here now and get away. I'll live to do Your will if You would see me out of this hellhole. Isn't that what You want?

The sphere began to burn. I was certain that wasn't what He wanted. He wanted me to go to the woman. All I could see were the gypsy girl's eyes, their brilliant flash inside the oven, and then flames everywhere. Flames in the darkness, shining through the oven's orange eyes.

I crawled to the edge of the bar and turned the corner toward the back of the room. The heat on my leg subsided. I shimmied forward a few feet and stopped. The room was now silent. The bugs sensed my approach. I was certain of it.

Lord, I cannot do this. This is too much for You to ask of me.

The Nachthaus shuddered its cavernous frame. "Ah, yes, Adam. Even through my sickness, even in my weakness, even in my distress, it is I who offers you what I have. It is I who offers you forgetfulness. It is I who offers sleep. It is I who offers you what peace can be had in your tenement of clay."

"You offer Hayner and death and evil and senselessness," I said.

The woman moaned anemically. She sounded unconscious.

Time. How much time was left?

The Nachthaus shuddered again, as if it were trying to break loose of a bear hug. "Did I cause all this, Adam? Was it my will to be thus? Or did you thrust it upon me? Did you not recreate me in your own image?"

"I wasn't there."

The bugs chattered from the back of the room.

"Ah, but you were, Adam. I was there, and I remember you. Your poets did not say *In Adam we sinned all* in vain. You were there, and you're the reason I am as I am. I swelled with lush fruit and beauty before you defiled me. Come now, return to me and sleep. I am groaning."

"You're evil."

"No, Adam. I am fallen. I am barren. I am fruitless. It is you who are evil. I am but your host. You are the parasite."

The plant-man howled into the darkness. I clenched my fists and hit the floor, my face wallowing in the dust of the mine.

"Dust to dust," the Nachthaus said. "Come back to me. I offer you sleep against the horrors. What has your God done about this earthly asylum? Has He lifted a finger against the evil? Has He not seen? Has He not heard? Could He not prevent it?"

"*Deus et natua non faciunt frusta. Ex malo bonum,*" I said. I was muttering into the dirt of the floor, my hands splayed in front of me in the darkness. "God and nature do not work together in vain. Out of evil, comes good. If it is as you say, I deserve whatever happens to me. If I had a hand in this monstrosity that is the world, how could I complain, whatever befalls me?"

I felt a tepid and pus-like juice drip on my hands. It was sticky like saliva, and it burned. Feelers caressed my fingers. The antennae moved up the backs of my hands, over my wrists, and up my arms, almost to my elbows. It tickled the hairs of my arm as it passed. There were now two sets of feelers, and they passed up along my shoulders and across my cheeks. They tickled my ears, running through my hair and down the back of my neck. I compressed my toes and my fingers into balls to resist the urge to flee and the urge to jettison my mind from my skull.

Lord, how resolutely You direct each man to his end. It is the end of his days, the end of a professed faith in You or the end of his lack of trust in Your goodness and graciousness, even in this dark world. I see the choice in front of me: I may either live or die whichever way I choose, but I must either now kill my faith or allow it to be faith. There is no other way. As for me, though You slay me, yet will I trust in Thee.

I began to crawl, inch by inch at first, dreading the pain of the razor talons anchoring in my back and the jaws sinking into my neck. I loathed the thought of lying here dead in the dark, beneath the mountain, consumed a bite at a time by these hideous vermin. I pulled at the dust of the mine, my cheek scraping across the floor of the room. Dust filled my throat and lungs, but I crawled nonetheless. There was no other way.

A crash erupted from the opposite side of the bar. It sounded as though the third bug had managed to jostle its cage off the bar. The fall must have dislodged the cage's latch, because I heard the bug scrambling out of the cage and onto the floor, where it clicked feverishly in the darkness. Now there were three of the monstrosities looming in the dark. I kept crawling, inch by tedious inch, wishing the bugs would get on with it.

Then a thought came to me: all is not darkness. The world is bad, no doubt, but it's not as bad as it *could* be. There are some rather fine things. My Katia in the lush green of my Bavarian home was just one example, but it seemed enough. There *was* love in the world, even if it was a strained and fallen love. And the greenness of Bavaria . . . it was a cultivated greenness, not the unruly hue of the forest surrounding the Nachthaus. There were isolated camps of goodness in the world. Rebel outposts of goodness, perhaps.

Dreaming is seeing the world as it is not.

I kept crawling, sensing the bug's weight upon my back. I clung to the thought that even in the Nachthaus, there was some goodness. Didn't I somehow find myself in the immediate presence of two relatively good men, the philosopher-face, and the gypsy girl? How was I to explain that coincidence? Sheer luck? Mere happenstance? All was not darkness. There were two opposite and equal errors here: seeing no objective evil in the world and seeing only evil in the world.

Dreaming is seeing the world as it is not.

My hands, still spread in front of me, brushed against scurrying insect feet. The third bug was in front of me, and it had to be hungry. A glob of the pus-like saliva dropped to the floor in between my arms and splattered. It stank like a latrine in July. I raised my head, feeling for the jaws, which had to be inches from my face. The bug chattered, clicked its legs, and hissed. A pair of antennae brushed my cheeks, running down across my lips and chin, and then back up the bridge of my nose to my forehead.

I pulled my left hand back along the floor toward me and through the pool of saliva. It was disgusting but I dared not shake it off with the bug's jaws inches from my face. I managed to bring my hand back behind my shoulder without disturbing the bug, and found my pants pocket. I pulled the sphere out.

No longer worrying about disturbing the bugs, I thrust the sphere into the air. It was faith-proving time.

The sphere burst into a galaxy of light, suspended in the dark void of the room. I was a traveler beholding the beauty and mystery of a new world. The light rotated around the room, a billion stars orbiting their course across the rough hewn wall of the cave.

The roaches did what all roaches do when light is shined in the darkness.

I stood in amazement, but only for a moment, knowing I had minutes left, if that. The woman was passed out, still strapped to the torture rack. I rushed to her, holding the sphere out in front of me with my left hand.

The restraints consisted of buckles that operated much as a dog's collar did. I had them undone in seconds, and I hoisted the woman across my shoulder in a fireman's carry. I made for the door and opened it, looking back for the bugs. They must have been hiding. I stopped long enough to gather the contents of my pack. I slung it across my other shoulder, dropped the sphere into my pocket, and headed down the hallway, hoping there was enough time left.

I peeked around the corner at the end of the hall, seeing no one in the vicinity of the barracks. One lone sentry approached the opening of the T junction that led back to the lab. He exited a shadow from beyond the junction, halted under the light at the junction, and then performed an about-face and disappeared back into the shadow.

I could not remember what Gott had said was down that hallway, if he had mentioned it at all. Worse, I didn't know how long it would take the sentry to reach the end, turn about, and return in my direction. As soon as he made the turn, he would be able to see the hallway in its entirety. I had to carry the woman and the pack, which slowed me, but I had no choice but to risk it. I could sense the time now. The mine would be a bustle of activity at any second.

I loped into the hallway as fast as possible, carrying the woman. The pack swung and the strap began to edge toward the end of my shoulder where it could fall off. By the time I reached the first barracks door, I felt the first pangs of fatigue in my thighs. By the end of the hallway they would be burning.

I passed the second barracks door and the pack jostled off my shoulder. The strap dropped all the way to my wrist. It was now swinging back and forth, pounding against my knee. I pressed on, trying to reach the relative safety of the junction before the mine woke up. I had almost made it when the soldier emerged from the shadows ahead.

It was Gott. Thank God for small miracles, as well as the large. We ducked into the junction.

"We've got about two minutes," Gott said. "Give me the girl."

I transferred the woman to him, reshouldered my pack, and followed him on at a brisk pace. He floated down the hall ahead of me and I knew I never would have made it on my own. We traversed the junction passageway and, just as the mine woke up, made it into the tunnel that led to the lab.

Minutes later we laid the woman on a table in the lab. Despite her ordeal, she looked much like a princess waiting for someone to awaken her with a kiss.

19

The beady-eyed man with thick glasses, my primary interrogator, reached over the table and struck my cheek with an open hand.

I felt sorry for him. It appeared he had invested himself in the slap, but it was rather womanly. I chuckled.

The bravado he'd showed as he'd slapped me snuck away like a child hiding behind a mother's skirt. He adjusted his glasses and nodded to the two women who flanked him at the table.

They stood, marched to my side of the table and hovered over me like harpies. They were still heartless, despite my narrative. I could tell from the corners of their eyes.

One woman thrust her fist into my left kidney. It felt as though she had burrowed inside my skin and pulled out my pancreas. The other brought her hand down on my right wrist with some specialized karate chop. The effect of both strikes leveled me. I collapsed to the table, my chest heaving.

"Mr. König, we will have answers," the beady-eyed man said.

A general concurrence came from the onlookers lining the walls of the room.

I lifted my eyes from the table to the women. "You are noble, beating an old man." I deliberately infused a hint of German into my next words. I directed the pain in my midsection and wrist at the beady-eyed man through my eyes. "Ya zend de vemen to do ze verk off da man, nein?"

It's debatable whether the spite was worth it or not. Da vemen alternated: the one on the right now struck my kidney on her side and the other brought her hand down on my left wrist. I wanted to vomit my midsection onto the table, anything to get that feeling out of me. A second round of spite would not be worth it.

De vemen lifted my head from the table, driving me back against the chair with my forehead. One of de vemen put a knife to my throat. It was a huge knife, tapered and sharp, like an oversized roach talon. The blade scraped up and down against the whiskery gristle on my neck.

"Go ahead and kill me," I said. "I wish you would. I've been reliving that nightmare every day for decades now. Go ahead and send me home. You'll be doing me a favor." I pressed forward as best I could against the knife. Rolf's words about doing the captives a favor in the oven came back to me across the years.

The beady-eyed man waved off de vemen, and I collapsed back to the table. I had hated the Nachthaus, but as I was coming to realize, it wasn't the Nachthaus so much as it was the management. I'm not sure Hayner ever beat me as efficiently as de vemen, nor am I certain who enjoyed it most. All I can say for sure is who enjoyed it least.

A line from a rock song occurred to me then. I didn't know it perfectly but it was something like, "When you meet the new boss you will find he is much the same as the old boss." I thought it was from a Who song. I could hear Roger Daltry belting out the frenzied line in "Won't Get Fooled Again."

But in fact we had, hadn't we? We had been fooled yet again. We had daydreamed in the days since that war, and the world had turned over as it had before. People lived, people died, and the world went on as if we had not learned our lesson.

The daydream had appeared in a new form—that a horizon loomed ahead offering the promise of light, a new dawn where the management was good and the occupants of the Nachthaus would live in peace and prosperity.

But the truth is that there are no horizons, neither dawn nor dusk. It has been noon since the world began, and the world's true management—a sole proprietor—has resided at twelve o'clock high since the beginning. It's not that the light isn't there; it's that daydreaming occurs during the day.

The world of man is a Nachthaus and we are fish with atrophied eyes. Having lost our sight through disuse, through daydreaming, we inhabit the cave of this world.

The beady-eyed man pushed back in his chair, crossed his legs, folded his hands over his lap, and spoke four words. "Fire up the oven."

When you meet the new boss you will find he is much the same as the old boss.

Two attendants left from the back of the room. Could it be that the inferno had one last burn left in it after all these years?

"Names, dates, historical data," the beady-eyed man said. "If you cooperate, things will be much easier for you."

How rich the irony. I *had* been cooperating, but they didn't believe my narrative. Now my old nemesis was warming up. Its orange-slit eyes would be gleaming in anticipation. I sensed the iron door rising outside, and I could feel the Nachthaus awakening. Its hunger for dissidents of the Reich had been one thing. Its hunger for special treats was another. The gypsy girl was special, and the inferno had flared with great desire and greed. I would be special, as well, and the new management seemed to appreciate that as much as Hayner had.

I had been cooperating. But the Nachthaus simply had a narrative of its own. It was called a daydream.

20

Gott, Rolf, and I rested the woman on one of the tables in the lab. It reminded me of the plant warrior corpse that had come to life my first day at the Nachthaus. I was now hoping the same for her. Indeed, she seemed to be coming to. A soft moan escaped her lips, and I thought of my Katia.

In the sterile and desolate landscape of the Nachthaus, a flower had bloomed. I wasn't sure from whence it was drawing its life or how it could take root in the rock. Nevertheless, it had found a crevasse and blossomed. Through the grime of captivity, I smelled a distant and pleasant scent in her hair. I shuddered like the Nachthaus and feared for my Katia. So far away. She seemed as a dream.

I dispatched Gott to reconnoiter the general tenor of the mine. Rolf sidled up to the table and examined the woman for injuries. I rubbed her cheek and her lips pursed.

Her neck arched up and her eyes opened like louvers on a window blind. They fluttered a time or two before opening widely. "You saved me from the vermin?"

I brushed the hair from her forehead with a clumsy arc of my hand. "I did. I've never seen anything quite like them. Those antennae."

"You misunderstand," she said. "I meant the Germans." Her mouth curled at the corners, and the Nachthaus became as Bavaria to me.

Her ordeal had created a disguise almost worthy of Charles Graves. I had noticed her regal appearance in the alcoves, but it had been masked by the dim light and the fact that she had been in captivity for quite some time. Now that she was safe for the moment in the lab, it began to shine through.

She was not beautiful in a pin-up girl manner, but in a way that arose from her demeanor. It screamed *I am here and you will notice me.* It was the way her eyes demanded attention. It was how her chin lifted as she spoke. It was the way she carried herself: knowing that she had been dehumanized by the Nazis, yet expecting we three men conduct ourselves as if there were a queen in the room, even one with snarled hair and dirt on her nose.

Gott burst into the room. "Hayner's on his way. You've got two minutes at best!"

We stood at attention under the philosopher-face, Gott on my left and Rolf on my right. Hayner paced in front of us, riding crop on full display. A squad of soldiers flanked us on either side. Falke lingered around the door that led outside. The oven overlooked Hayner, its eyes drab slits.

"You look somewhat tired this morning, König," Hayner said. His pacing ended abruptly in front of me. He tapped the crop on his shoulder. "Were the night's solvent efforts taxing?" The two veins on Hayner's head were pounding. For a moment his eyes were aligned with the oven's eyes behind him. "I said, were the night's solvent—"

"I heard what you sa—"

Hayner brought the crop against my cheekbone so fast and hard that I couldn't process what had happened. The strike was utterly disorienting. Hayner had me on the floor with a fist to the gut and an elbow to the back of my neck before I realized what he was doing.

I ignored the dust I inhaled from the floor. "Said."

"What did you say?" Hayner towered over me.

"Said. I said, *said*." I pushed myself up to my knees. "I intend to finish my sentences from here on out, Hayner."

Hayner slipped a hand under my jawbone and lifted me up. He kept pressure around my windpipe, and I knew he could crush it with little effort. He held the gas mask I had forgotten in the torture room in his other hand. He shoved it in my face. "How do you intend to explain this!"

Despite the force under my jawbone, I managed a smirk. "It appears to be a gas mask."

Hayner's face parted in unbelief like the Red Sea. The hand around my throat tightened. "What was your mask doing in the torture room, Sascha?"

"Mine's . . . in . . . the . . . lab." I winked at Hayner.

Hayner's pythons exploded out of his ears and hissed, their tongues licking at my face. He thrust me back against the wall.

The back of my head must have connected with the philosopher-face because without warning *Hayner and I* were in a desert at night. He must have been receiving the vision too, his hand being connected to the wall through my head. I could tell he was seeing it, because he was looking around at the desert in disbelief.

He looked back at me with a quizzical look. The desert surrounded us as far as the eye could see through the darkness. The terrain was rocky and desolate. It was uninhabited as far as I could tell, and there were no paths readily apparent to the eye. We stood on a rim of hills that appeared more or less circular. From every direction, the hills sloped into a central valley.

Our attention fixed on one lone crag in the center of the valley that lay before us. It rose perpendicular from the valley floor, and was the sole point of elevation visible in the valley. It rose above the height of the ring of hills surrounding the valley to the point where we were looking up at the top of it.

At the peak of the spire was a light, and it functioned as a lighthouse. The desert and valley were dependent on the star for whatever light was to be had, and it was not much. The light may have been severely luminous, but the top of the crag was shrouded with black ether that prevented much of the light from illuminating the valley and hills.

We started down the slope of the hill toward the valley floor without a word between us. I led. Hayner followed. The way was slippery on account of a loose stone composition that covered a slick slate forming the sides of the hills. We felt our way down until I stopped to ask Hayner his impression of the landscape before us.

We fell together as he tried to respond, and we rode down the remaining portion of the slope like a two-man bobsled team. We came to rest at the base of the slope. Without a moment's hesitation, Hayner attempted to claw his way back up the hill. He made it about six feet before sliding back down, face full of dust and dirt. He tried once more before ceasing his efforts. With all of his strength, he was not able to make it ten feet up the grade. In fact, his strength worked against him as the weight of his own body pulled him back down the slope. I was reminded of the biblical passage, "In due time their feet shall slip."

I tried as well, with the same result. It was hopeless. Even Hayner's pythons could not help him scale the hill. We set out along the perimeter of the valley searching for a foothold that might allow us to climb. None was to be found, and at length I asked Hayner why we would be so decided on climbing back up when we had wanted to come down initially.

Hayner eyed me with a look of uncertainty on his face. "You don't feel it?"

He was right. There was an unmistakable dread in the valley—an overwhelming sense that something was watching us through the black ether and that what it was observing was not pleasant. "I feel it."

We took a few steps toward the heart of the valley and it was clear to me what the cause of the ominous sense was. The valley before us was littered with humanity.

I stopped at the foot of a corpse. I thought: am I now daydreaming? Is this seeing the world as it is not, or as it is?

The corpse was lying on its back with its mouth agape. Its body was shriveled. Its stomach distended. Its face covered with flies.

The earth beneath it was a loamy, rich topsoil that, judging by the impression my feet made in it, would make for the best farming. Next to the corpse's head was a field of thick cornstalks in full bloom. The corn was ripe on the stalk, and each ear was fuller than the next. The corpse's mouth did not move, but I heard it whispering: "I hunger." It repeated the line over and over until we were out of earshot.

Hayner followed me as we progressed toward the crag. We came upon another corpse, this one shriveled and chafed. Its mouth was agape, as with the starving corpse, except that its head was cocked toward the purest stream of water I've seen. This water was purer and more enticing than the snow-melt runoff from my home. My dry mouth, full of the dust of the mine where Hayner had beaten me to the floor, craved it.

I bent down to drink, and as I knelt next to the corpse, it whispered to me: "I thirst." The water was sparkling, and I could not resist. I forced the corpse's image from my mind and drank deeply. The water delivered as advertised. Hayner slurped next to me on all fours, and the thought occurred to me that there was plenty to go around. I had needed to refresh myself before I could tend to the needs of others. I cradled some water from the stream in my cupped palms and turned to the corpse, but it had disintegrated to ashes.

Hayner stood me up and pulled me toward the crag. There's no need to tell you what we passed on the way: shivering corpses next to palatial homes, lonely corpses next to crowds, poor corpses lamenting opulence, diseased corpses dead next to stores of medical supplies. The valley of life was disgusting, and overhead the sense of foreboding grew as the light shone through the darkness in anger.

As we approached the crag, Hayner muttered a phrase to himself. "There's a reason for this . . . there's a reason for this . . . there's a reason for this." Interspersed within this phrase, Hayner would interject a terse "They lacked discipline" or "They were inferior races." By the time we reached the foot of the crag, he was babbling—and smiling sickly through his babbles.

The phrase stuck with me, though. There is a reason for this, I thought. I looked up at the light shining through the darkness from the peak of the crag. There is a reason for this, and it's me. That's all I need to know. There's more to it, but that's all I need to know.

"God has a morally sufficient reason for allowing this, Hayner. Until the time that He steps in to sort this out, it's up to us to do something about it and cooperate with Him where we see Him working."

Hayner quit his babbling upon hearing my proposition. He seemed to regain some of his swagger before responding. "This proves there is no God."

I looked Hayner over carefully, and the disparity between the two views was never clearer to me. With God, evil could make sense, ultimately. Without Him, we are all merely daydreamers.

"Let's climb," I said.

Hayner was ten feet up the crag before I could get a good foothold. The sinews in his muscles flowed in rhythm, endowed with the confidence of man.

I struggled, finding a precarious grip here, a tenuous foothold there. The climb was exhausting, and the tower's height was dizzying. After an hour I was 40 feet off the ground, depleted of energy. I would never scale the crag.

At 55 feet, I reached Hayner. He writhed against the crag, unable to proceed higher, his face a whirlpool of uncertainty. "I can't move," he said. "I can't move."

Hayner's hindrance was his pythons. They had sunk their fangs into the ground at the base of the crag. As strong as Hayner was, he was not capable of dislodging them an inch from their hold on the valley floor. I climbed past him.

"Don't leave me here." He pleaded with me, all along struggling in vain against the pythons.

I left him and made it ten more feet before the weight of my own soul prevented me from climbing any higher. It now took everything I had just to hang on to the crag. Above me, the crag continued seemingly forever until it reached the ether. The light shone down from above through the blackness.

"We have to let go, Hayner."

"You're a fool." He looked up at me with disgust but nevertheless began the descent to the valley floor. He appeared rejuvenated and descended rapidly.

I followed him a foot or two. The descent was in fact rejuvenating. I descended another foot or two and could feel the weight of my soul decreasing. The footholds and handholds were easier, my breath was returning, and even the burning in my muscles was subsiding.

You have to let go, Sascha.

The view to the valley floor was dizzying, but I let go.

The weight of my soul propelled me down faster than what gravity alone would do. I fell as if I had been at a height of 5,000 feet instead of 50. Below me the valley floor approached, and before I hit, I saw Hayner engulfed in a sea of corpses.

I landed in a pool of water clearer and sweeter than the stream I had drunk from earlier. The water was cool and soft as a feather bed.

I stood up, thoroughly soaked. Somehow I had fallen down but ended up higher than where I'd let go. I was standing in a pool six inches deep at the summit of the crag. The light, now unimpeded by the ether, was both unspeakably glorious and utterly holy.

21

Hayner and I awoke sprawled out on the floor of the mine in front of the oven door. Gott later told me that he had knocked us off the wall almost instantly after he saw us connect with the philosopher's face—and had received a crack in the back of the head from one of the soldiers for his trouble.

Without hesitation, Hayner resumed command. He stood, brushed himself off, and screeched at the squad of soldiers on our left. "Search this entire sector of the mine!"

I got to my feet and faced him. I knew the situation would be disintegrating quickly now. Lines had been drawn and choices would be made.

"We will find the girl, Sascha." Hayner said. "We will find her, and when we do, you'll make another trip to the torture room. This time under less pleasant circumstances." He kicked the gas mask across the floor. It struck the wall under the philosopher's face and came to rest, face up.

"If you're blaming me for—"

"Silence!" Hayner cupped a hand around the back of my neck and led me off to one side, a few steps toward the lab. I could hear the soldiers ransacking the lab, looking for the girl. "Sascha, there's still time for you to prove yourself. In a moment, we will test your progress on the solvent. If it shows signs of promise, you will still have value. If, that is, you produce the girl before we find her. If not, well, I'm sure the Reich can find another chemist."

"I—"

"Hup. The time for talk is passed. Produce the girl." Hayner squeezed the back of my neck.

I said nothing.

"I see," Hayner said. "Sascha, that hocus pocus you pulled back there means *nichts*. I don't know what you did, what chemical you used, or how you delivered it, but I'm no fool, Sascha. We're not in any mythical mountain meadow. We're back in the Nachthaus, and the time for talking has passed. Go get your solvent."

Hayner released me and followed me to the lab. The soldiers had gone through every drawer, cabinet, storage bin, and closet. Now they were instructing Rolf to open the cold storage room. Rolf unlocked the door and swung it open. A blast of cold air escaped in a fog, and we beheld 100 plant-men packed into the room.

"They may awaken at any moment," Rolf said. "The warm air revives them."

The soldiers motioned to shut the door, but Hayner screeched. "Every one of them. Every last one of them must be checked."

It took fifteen minutes to clear a walk space into the cold storage room. Rolf, Gott, and the soldiers extracted body after body from the middle of the room, stacking them on the floor of the lab.

The woman was about ten bodies in, disguised in a tattered soldier's uniform. Rolf had scalped one of the plant-men from the table and covered her head and face with its bushy mane. If the makeshift wig held in place, it might work. Her face was mostly covered by the wig. But to complete the disguise Rolf had covered her face with blood and gelatin from the lab's supplies.

If I had not been out too long touching the philosopher's face, she wouldn't have been harmed by the cold yet. She had accepted the scalp and blood willingly. After captivity and the torture room, it was the easiest thing she had done recently. Her moxie under this severe duress was evident. Again I worried for my Katia—what would she think of my burgeoning fondness for this woman?

Gott placed her facedown in the crease between two other Pflanzen-Kriegerin. It was obvious that she was smaller and less stout than the other plant-men, but the soldiers must have approached the search of the cold storage room with some reluctance, or else a disbelief that anyone would be hiding there. They prodded a few of the plant-men, including the woman, but paid little real attention to the bodies on the floor. More thorough attention was given to the bodies remaining in the cold storage room.

Hayner personally inspected the interior of the room, and then ordered a search of the rest of the rooms, our living quarters, and the storage rooms. Meanwhile, Gott, Rolf, and I returned the bodies to the storage room. Rolf turned down the room's cooler a bit. She would be fine as long as the Nazis didn't take too long or the plant-men didn't awaken.

An hour later, Hayner's men completed their search and stood at attention in front of the oven door. Hayner summoned me, screeching. I left Gott and Rolf in the lab and went to Hayner with a pack of chemicals.

Hayner eyed me like a bird of prey. "Let's step out and see how fruitful you've been, Leutnant."

I exited the lab complex behind half of the soldiers and ahead of the other half. Hayner walked beside me and pointed to the mine shaft terminus once we had made it through the door. Falke had erected some lighting that pointed at the rubble at the mine's end.

Every shaft terminated in piles of rubble where the digging and drilling had ceased to be possible due to cave-ins. I selected a medium-sized rock at the base of the pile and approached it with my pack. I felt Hayner's eyes darting with anticipation.

The idea of utilizing a solvent to bore through the rock was a practical fantasy. It could succeed, given enough time, money, and effort, but a solvent would be even more unstable than blasting, regardless of the size of the blasting. There would be no control over dispersion or breakdown rates in any large-scale solvent process, and caustic fumes caused by the solvent process would be a constant threat. They would've been better off trying to dig, or perhaps using a water cannon, but their experience with the cave-ins had convinced them otherwise.

Maybe the Nachthaus had taken an active role in preventing the digging. I don't know for sure, but that's what I suspected. All I knew was that the Nazis wanted a solvent, and I had to let them think I could provide one if I wished to stay alive. So I went to work convincing them.

I extracted a large beaker from the pack and turned to Hayner. "You'd better get your men back. This will be unpleasant."

When they had retreated a few steps, I poured my solution over the rock at the base of the pile. The solution fizzed, and I stepped back from the fumes that rose into the air.

The jagged protrusions at the top of the rock began to flatten, then they melted. The top of the rock had dissolved about a half inch and the solvent had created what looked like a flattop haircut on the rock. A few light channels had been dredged into the side of the rock where the solvent had trickled down. Now it was sales-pitch time.

"That's it?" Hayner said.

I studied Hayner before responding. My next words were going to determine whether I would spend the night in the lab or the torture room. Hayner's eyes looked greedy to me. Greedy as a man who wanted more of what he had seen, but was attempting to conceal it. I had seen that look in the eyes of children before.

I pointed at the flat surface of the rock. "You see what it can do. It melted the very rock, Standartenführer. Is that not what you wanted? It'll take some time and a lot of chemicals. A *lot* of chemicals. But it will work. Go ahead and get as much as you can of the last order and keep it coming."

Hayner was nodding. As far as this sale, I was an order-taker, not a closer. It was easy. These men wanted out and would believe anything that hinted they might be able to . . . except the truth, of course. I tapped into their need and let the daydream do the rest. Another victory for the arts, I supposed.

"We'll also need ventilation," I said. "These little fumes here are nothing compared with what we'll be dealing with on a large scale. See what you can have brought in."

Hayner was almost giddy and began screeching orders. The soldiers scrambled, and Falke began lumbering toward the lighting in his unique way.

Hayner stepped toward me, placing his hands on my shoulders. "Can you do it, Sascha?" His eyes maintained the greediness, but they were also tinged with a child's hope. I've often thought about that moment, how even the worst of us remain filled with the image of God, even if it's repressed or banished to the depths of our own personal Nachthaus, deep down a rocky labyrinth in the torture chamber of a stony heart. No doubt Hayner was thinking of a lush Bavaria of his own, perhaps a Katia, or a stout ale enjoyed in the cool breeze of a peaceful evening.

Sharing the gospel could be quite the experience. What was I to do at this moment? The lights played along Hayner's face as Falke dismantled the tripod upon which the first lamp set. The vulnerability was there, it appeared, in Hayner.

We had attempted to climb the mountain together. Would he be open to hearing the truth about the Nachthaus, the good news, our ultimate means of escape from and understanding of this world?

And what about Rolf, Gott, and the woman? If Hayner flew off the handle, they would all be jeopardized as well as me. Was there a right and wrong time to talk about such things? Would God want me to share this now, knowing that Hayner would kill me for it? Wouldn't God have a better way of sharing it if He'd wanted Hayner to see it?

My confusion in the fog of war won out, and I lied. "I think I can with enough time, sir, depending on where we bore. A plat of the mine might help, if you have one."

Hayner seemed revived at the news. The childlike hope in his eyes was overcome by the greed. He patted my shoulders. "You might make a Nazi after all, schoolboy." He patted me again and left for the front of the mine just as Falke switched out the lights.

Even now I wonder what might have happened if I had told Hayner the truth. Not about the boring with solvents, but about the Nachthaus, the world, the people in it, and the good news of the gospel. I wonder about having to explain my lie to my Maker.

And I wonder if we'll even spend much time discussing my lie, given what came next.

22

She was indeed a flower taken root in the waste of the Nachthaus. I laid her down on a pallet Gott had constructed in the back corner of the inferno fuel storage room next to the lab. Gott had carved out a section in the back that remained concealed from the door by the 55-gallon drums.

It was now around two in the afternoon, not that time in the Nachthaus was that pressing. We had been up all night and the cool and quiet of the storage room was intoxicating.

My hand was still cupped behind her head where I'd laid her down, and she smiled up at me. Gott and Rolf had cleaned her in the lab and she lay clothed in a spare lab coat, having refused one of Gott's extra Nazi uniforms.

Her features had emerged from beneath the dirt and grime of captivity like the sun from behind a thundercloud. Her cheeks rose high upon her face with the beauty of carved and polished marble. She was a rock, as stately as my Bavarian mountains, and as enduring. I imagined her on a museum pedestal a thousand years from now.

I could no longer see Katia or feel her in my heart. I knew I was in trouble. There was a new presence there, and the thrill of a budding connection with this woman was mixed with a loathing guilt. I needed to gaze at Katia's picture again.

Was it the Nachthaus's influence? Were we bound to our desires for self, for what was here and now, rather than the promise made? The frailty and grandeur of man: to know both the good and the pain of not being good.

"I know I thanked you earlier, but I want to thank you again." She ran her hand along my cheek. "I come from a powerful family back in the Ukraine, and when this war is over, I'll be able to repay you."

Quid pro quo. Even in the tenderest of moments we retain our humanness. "Maybe. That part is not clear yet. I doubt we will make it out of here."

Her breath stopped for a moment, and the rhythmic ocean swell of her chest lost its sway over me for a moment. "Then why did you help me?" The question seemed genuine.

I thought of the gypsy girl's eyes. As beautiful as the eyes below me were, they were rotted orbs when compared with the gypsy girl. "You wouldn't believe it."

"I had the jaws of a three-foot-long roach inches from my face. I'll believe whatever you tell me."

"Miss K—"

"Call me Mirka."

I did, and I proceeded with the entire state of affairs since leaving Germany for the Nachthaus, with the exception of Katia. I wondered if she filled in the blanks. Then I told her about the events since I had come to the Nachthaus, the plant-men battles, and the gypsy girl.

She seemed oddly accepting of it all. Perhaps what she had seen in the torture room had carved out space in her mind to believe just about anything.

"Can you save the rest of the people in those cages?" she asked. "Some of them are my friends and family."

"How would you propose that I do that?"

The hope deflated out of her face, and I wished we were far away. I wished we were alone. I wished that love could be pure, untainted by the Nachthaus. But even there I was daydreaming. Even something as good and pure as love was blemished.

Gott burst through the door. "Hayner's on the way with a load of captives for the oven! Mach schnell!"

I leapt to my feet.

When Hayner arrived 30 minutes later, I was in my place between the philosopher's face and the inferno.

Hayner plowed through the doorway from the mine with a contingent of armed soldiers behind him. He was dressed to the hilt in his formal Nazi grays: starched jacket adorned with the iron cross and a compliment of medals; sleeves jacketed with red swastika patches; a gray cap with a black visor and an eagle on the brim, and black, polished jackboots. He held the crop in his right hand and strutted with it cradled in the crook of his elbow, the ruby eyes of the skull mounted on the handle gleaming.

The soldiers goose-stepped behind him, rifles held across their chests. A snare drum rattled from somewhere behind the procession still out in the mine shaft. Its rat-a-tat coincided with the march, and it increased in volume as it approached.

Hayner halted in front of me and rotated mechanically to face me, his back to the iron door of the inferno. Gott stood to my left and Rolf to my right. The first contingent of soldiers passed behind him and halted at the end of the corridor. Two soldiers with snare drums entered the doorway, and the sound of the drums filled every crook of the corridor. The drummers marched until they reached the first group of soldiers, then marched in place while drumming. The drums pounded my ears. It was a mesmerizing cadence.

Behind the drummers was a second group of soldiers escorting about twenty prisoners in chains. There were men, women, and children: beaten, filthy, and ragged. Their eyes lacked the steadfast resoluteness that had been displayed by the gypsy girl in the oven. They were forlorn eyes, filled with dread and tears. There was wailing from the train of captives. More than one of them, the children mostly, pleaded with the Nazis to be set free.

The flank of the Nazi escort responded to the pleas, not with mercy but with whips. I could see the lash marks on their arms. On their cheeks. One man looked like a barber's pole. When they spied the oven, the men in the front of the train fell to their knees, their cuffed arms outstretched before Hayner.

Hayner never took his eyes off me. Instead, the escort lashed out at the men who appeared to prefer the whips to the oven.

Behind the captive train, the rearguard filed through the door, followed at last by Falke, who shut the door. The snare drums went quiet. An eerie calm fell over the corridor. For a moment, the captives must have felt a spark of hope even in the face of the terror before them. The wailing ceased and the men on their knees at the front extended their hands out once more toward Hayner. The chains between their wrists jingled.

Hayner screeched. "Enemies of the Reich, behold!"

Two of the armed guards shouldered their rifles and marched to the oven door. They twisted the wheels, lifting the door along its track.

The lifting mechanism groaned with the weight of the door, and the oven seemed to speak as if it was beckoning all of us inside. The Nachthaus was the world, and the world had a hell at its core. A hell that beckoned us all. A ravenous hell in which we sank under the curse of our own weight, as certain as an axe head in a pool of water.

"Obergrenadier Moench! Herr Waechter! To your stations!" Hayner's command was unwavering.

Gott and Rolf stood motionless.

"The Standartenführer has given an order," I said.

From the corner of my eye I saw Gott turn to me with unbelief. "Oberleu—"

"Standartenführer Hayner has given an order. Orders are to be followed, Obergrenadier."

"But Oberleutnant, we—"

"Now, Obergrenadier, or you will find yourself in the inferno, I'm certain." The words exited my mouth sternly, but almost as a whisper, as if I were speaking in a dream. I detected the traces of a smile on Hayner's lips, and I hated him for it.

Gott and Rolf trudged into the oven and disappeared from view. Seconds later we heard the control room door open and close.

"The prisoners will now step forward!" Hayner performed an about-face as he gave the order. The snare drums resumed their cadence.

I wished Gott and Rolf would fire the oven with the door still open. It would kill me, but the monster Hayner would go up in flames as well. Would another take his place? I thought so. When you meet the new boss you will find he is much the same as the old boss.

The men at the head of the captive train pleaded for their lives and the lives of their friends and families. The flank escort loosened their whips again. The ensuing cracks were sickening, but the men did not budge. Hayner motioned to the guards at the door of the oven. They marched to the lead captives, grasped them by the hair, and dragged them to the inferno.

One by one the prisoners were forced into the oven. Women clutched their children. Men sank against the walls of the oven or tried in vain to fight their way out. One of the men managed to get the chain between his wrists around the neck of one of the guards. Hayner kicked both of them into the oven. The guard got free and returned to ranks. The snares rang on. Hayner ordered the inferno door closed.

The door began to descend.

The slow descent of the door was the closing of one world and the opening of another. The captives froze when the door started moving, all eyes glued on this massive iron divider. It made it almost a quarter of the way down before the first captive rushed the door.

He was met with a rifle butt to the face, and staggered backwards into the oven, bleeding from the nose. Another rose to take his place and was repelled in like fashion.

The door made it halfway down, and a rush at the decreasing aperture ensued. Hayner and five soldiers repelled ten captives attempting to force their way out. The descending door produced an advantage for Hayner and the soldiers, and they had little trouble defending the opening from the famished captives. Regardless, one of the soldiers shot a man in the chest. The gunshot propelled the man backward into the oven, where he collapsed onto the floor, motionless.

The door continued to drop and was now down to about a foot's worth of clearance to the floor. Hayner and the soldiers stomped on the hands and arms reaching for their feet from under the door. It reminded me of the hands that had grabbed the great iron door at the entrance to the Nachthaus and how they had retreated back outside when I'd hit them with the acid. When the door reached a few inches from the floor, there was one hand remaining. One of the soldiers forced it back inside with his rifle, and the door shut.

With the door closed and the snares blaring, the cry from inside the oven was gone. Through the glass slits I could barely make out nebulous forms inside. The slits were lifeless for the moment. Soon the jets would fire and the inferno would roar to life.

Hayner was pointing at the floor where the soldier had pushed the last hand back into the oven, giving instructions to the soldier. I backed up and felt for the philosopher- face behind me.

As soon as I touched it, I was outside myself, surveying the scene from somewhere beneath the ceiling. Hayner was still lecturing the guard, but his body had dissolved into near nothingness. I could make out the wispy outline of a man in length, width, and height, but it was as a faint border in a haze of light gray smoke. It reminded me of a murder scene chalk outline of a victim that had been propped upright. It strained to retain its form.

A black silhouette teetered around and across Hayner's outline, every now and then contouring to his shape. I surmised it might be the thing I had seen around his eyes at times. The pythons darted in and around the ethereal black mass, their tongues tasting the air. For a moment, they detected my presence. They leapt to the ceiling, hovering a foot from my face. Their tongues slithered at the air in front of my chin, then the pythons retreated to Hayner.

"How does it seem to you?" The philosopher-face had animated and was repositioning its considerable bulk to face me. The husky but velvety timbre of his voice was soothing, yet it was stern.

"It seems as I always pictured Hayner," I said. "He's an evil man. But where is he, exactly?"

The face rotated as a boulder might turn. It nodded toward Hayner's form. "He's there, certain enough."

"It's hideous."

"Sin is never picturesque in its essence, as it is often dreamed." The face rotated back toward me with a look of grim compassion. "Sin's easy to see in others. Have you the stomach to see it in yourself?"

I froze, fixated on Hayner's form. I had considered my sin, had confessed and repented. It couldn't be all that bad, could it? Yet I didn't wish to look. "What will I see?"

The face maintained its look of stern mercy. "That all depends upon how honestly you will look."

I considered his words. Did I want to see myself? Impressions of the Nachthaus cascaded through my mind. The butchery. The cruelty. The endless waltz with evil. How would I appear? I thought of myself as a human regular: better than most, not as good as some.

I looked down at myself, and felt my stomach heave. I saw myself as others see me, but worse . . . as I might be in reality.

My teeth shown through a black mask of rotting flesh covered with the same misty black gunk that hovered around Hayner's outline. The teeth were a bright enamel smile set against the blackness of the face.

My form was solid, but charred. It appeared as the scorched body of the old man we had burned with the gypsy girl. My nose had disappeared and my eyes shown through the blackness as if I were a wearing a wrestler's mask. From top to bottom my clothes hung off the decrepit form like the tattered remains of a uniform on a plant-man.

I convulsed at the sight. Seeing myself like this churned my gut as an acute case of food poisoning from which I could not relieve myself. The teeth grinned back at me sardonically.

"It can't be. Is that how others see me?" As the words escaped, I lamented their self-referential import.

"Of course not," the face said, "though they detect its concealed presence often, and in ways that are difficult for you to see in yourself." The face worked its way into a more reassuring posture. It must have sensed how horrid the experience was for me. "You've been given a wonderful gift, Sascha, seeing yourself how you once were, much like Hayner is."

"But Hayner's nearly all gone." I glanced at his outline. The oven stared through it.

The philosopher's face dropped its eyes. "There are some given over to their nature, Sascha."

Suddenly I pitied Hayner. I chastised myself for not connecting the thoughts previously. The nausea snapped me back to my horrid form.

"Then," I asked, pausing, "what do I look like now? You said *once were*."

The face nodded and pursed his lips, seemingly lifting the entire wall of the mine to do so, rearranging the granite around his mouth. A blinding white light escaped from the corners of his mouth and he blew on the darkness of my form.

My body radiated with the blinding light, as if a thousand stars burned within my outline. The starlight spilled over and through the outline of my body, pulsating with a radiance purer than the hottest furnace. It consumed the gloom of the Nachthaus around it, banishing the darkness to the nether reaches of the mine. The light swirled in great eddies through my body, like the clouds of Jupiter accelerated 100 times. I glowed. I glowed with a light rivaling the gypsy girl's eyes. In the twinkling of an eye, I had hope.

"That is how you are now, Sascha König. The light you see is not your own. You are filled with the King's fire." The face paused, his great eyes narrowing, brow furling. "One last thing, Sascha. One last thing before your looming choice."

I saw a great chain clasp around my ankle. The chain gleamed as the finest chromium and sparkled in the light of a thousand suns. At the other end of the chain was a corpse. It was my black corpse with the shining teeth and eyes peering through the charred wrestler's mask of a face. The great chrome chain clasped around the corpse's ankle.

I wept. Was I to be chained to that beast forever? Who would deliver me from this body of death?

The corpse rose, peeled back its putrid lips in a sneer, and pounced upon the back of my radiant new man, digging its filth into the glowing outline. The two wrestled, and my consciousness returned to Hayner, the Nachthaus, the oven, the snare drums, and the looming mass execution while the battle between old and new wore on.

23

The whoosh of the pilot light came sooner than I expected, and it left me less time than I wished. The louvers creaked open and the oven was ready to fire. Gott and Rolf would be in the control room awaiting the command to fire the oven.

In front of the oven door, I stood facing Hayner. Through the eye slits of the oven I saw over Hayner's shoulder a few of the condemned milling about. There was a faint moaning escaping from behind the oven's walls. Outside the Nachthaus, the forest groaned, and I detected a faint shudder from the walls of the mine.

Hayner stood fixated on me. "Leutnant, you may give the order when ready." His glee was palpable. "Or should I call you Nebuchadnezzar?" I saw my nickname had made it to the top.

The wrestling match inside me escalated to all-out war. Was this the time to fight or to live to fight another day? Discretion and valor, looking and leaping, hesitating and losing—they all passed through my mind and were meaningless, as clichés usually are. The salient dichotomy was to obey or not obey. But what course of action under the *obey* alternative was left to me?

No, the war inside me was to resist Hayner or go along with the program. What possible good was found in resisting? There would be some personal satisfaction, perhaps, but little good for what would be much misfortune. Certainly it would not save these people. Still, I couldn't resist.

"I'll not give the order, Hayner." I was already staggering from my internal battle, but I forced myself to stand at attention before Hayner. I held my hands out to him, palms up, which I later realized was a sign of weakness. "I've made your solvent, I've killed plant-men assailing the front gate, I've saved your life and the lives of every soldier here, and I've made your oven seven times hotter. But I'll not order an incineration of living beings. I'll not do it."

I forced my face to remain stolid, expecting the backlash of Hayner's crop across my cheek. Inside, I felt the wrestling match had almost been won.

"Chemists," Hayner said. He laughed and turned to one of his underlings. "Give Obergrenadier Moench the order to proceed."

The underling strode to the communication console and delivered the order to Gott.

The snares blared. In one of the oven's slit eyes, someone was beating on the glass. It looked like a pupil in one of the oven's eyes. A moment later he would be incinerated in the inferno. I longed for the philosopher-face's company, but I knew in advance what he would say: obey or do not obey. It is not the circumstance a man finds himself in that counts in the end, but what he does in that circumstance.

The oven fired. The Nachthaus shook as if a god of the underworld was rising. The oven was a flaming skull, its orange eyes glistening with cruelty. In its left eye, the man beating on the glass dissolved before me. His arms and head flashed as if the oven had a gleam in its eye, and then he was gone.

An hour later, the oven's cool-down system had decreased the temperature to normal levels. Gott's voice came over the intercom, and I opened the iron door. The soldiers had long since departed, marching away to the cadence of the snares, leaving the clean-up to the three of us. I had the door up about a foot when Hayner entered through the doorway to the mine. He must have noticed me struggling against the door, because he went straight to the second wheel and assisted me.

With the door opened, we stepped into the oven with handkerchiefs tied across our faces to combat the lingering particulate in the air. The cooling system had worked well, and now it was barely warmer inside the oven as it was outside. Gott and Rolf emerged from the control room, stepped through the ash, and left for the supply room to get cleaning supplies.

I walked about five feet into the oven and scraped my foot into the ash in a half-moon shaped pattern. There was a considerable amount of charred remains intact in the ash, which disappointed me, as far as the technical heat of the oven was concerned. On the third or fourth half-moon shaped arc, my foot found was it was searching for. I felt a piece of metal between my foot and the floor. I bent, sifting through the ash and charred remains, and picked it up, noting the stench of my hands.

How would I live a life with these stinking hands? I saw myself at dinner, reaching across the table for a salt shaker, my guests at the table covering their faces with napkins. I saw myself at my daughter's wedding—were I ever to leave this place and have a daughter—giving away the bride, the groom and minister nauseated. I saw myself trying to conduct business transactions in which no one was willing to shake my hand. And I saw myself trying to hold this new woman in my life, and saw her repulsed by the smell. These hands . . .

I rubbed the piece of metal I had found against my shirt to clean the ash from it. It was the slug that had killed the captive trying to escape through the oven door. I handed it to Hayner. "A souvenir of your cruelty."

Hayner held the slug in front of his face, rolling it in his fingers as a child might admire a shiny coin. "You're weak, Sascha. So much to be expected from schoolboys. We're in the service of a greater good, you and I. The greater good is not left to the weak. Were it, it would be trampled underfoot."

Rarely have I seen someone as self-assured as Hayner was that day. When I have, it's almost always been when they thought they were doing what was right.

"I'll have another execution today," he said, "two more tomorrow, and one the following day. That will have us ready for the next load of war criminals."

"You mean victims."

Hayner ignored me, admiring the bullet.

I was through with him for the moment anyway, and something much more interesting caught my eye.

The oven was deteriorating. True, the cooling system would create this effect over time, as rapid cooling of refractory materials causes cracking and crumbling in the materials. However, this was something different. It was more as if the oven was acquiring *wrinkles*.

It's believed that Adam—

Sleep, my Adam, in the arms of your love.

—would not have aged had he not fallen into sin. In some sense, the oven was alive and its sin was aging it. It was ravenous and willful for evil, but lines had formed under its skin. They were barely perceptible yet, but I saw them nonetheless. The oven was rotting from within. It appeared hardy enough to withstand the wages of sin for a season, but its end was certain. I was sure of it.

Later that evening we performed the next execution. Twenty more souls: 40 in all since the gypsy girl and her companion. The oven aged a little each time, and I felt hope ignited inside me.

24

In the wee hours of the morning, I slipped out into the mine shaft and worked my way through the darkness toward the intersection that led to Hayner's office. With my pack shouldered, I paused at the precise spot where Epicurus' words had first haunted me upon my advent to the Nachthaus:

If God is willing to prevent evil, but is not able to, then He is not omnipotent.

If He is able, but not willing, then He is malevolent.

If He is both able and willing, then whence cometh evil?

If He is neither able nor willing, then why call Him God?

My experiences since my arrival had cemented within me the answer to this ancient riddle. I smiled to myself in the darkness, said a quick prayer of thanks to God, and pressed forward. There was yet more work to be done.

At the intersection, I paused. There was no activity from the passage leading to the soldiers' quarters and torture rooms, and none up ahead with the prisoners and the shaft leading to the front of the mine. I stepped through the lit intersection and into the darkness of the shaft leading to Hayner's office. In moments I stood in front of his oaken door, unshouldering my pack.

I thanked the Lord for His grace in preventing my daydreaming enough to have left the first two messages in the Nachthaus. They had been cryptic enough, to be sure, but then, when is the Word of God not cryptic to unbelievers like Hayner? It had afforded me a chance to explain the meaning of the messages without being killed for it, and because of that I felt a little better about not having been as direct with Hayner as I should have been. At this thought, my internal wrestling match renewed itself with vigor, chained beings of light and darkness grappling inside me. I vowed that this time the message would be explicit.

I extracted from my pack a brush and the same specially mixed vial of solution I had used previously. Hayner had received his solvent in good order; he simply didn't realize it. I dipped the brush and began to paint the words. This time there would be no doubt.

I slipped into the storage room to check on Mirka, finding her asleep between the space in the drums of inferno fuel. It was only a matter of time before the Nazis found her, but I reckoned that now was not that time. Gott and Rolf had fashioned a space for her to hide inside the drums, with extra drums stacked on top, hiding the space.

She stirred behind the drums. I moved one out of the way to reach her. It scraped across the floor with a screech. I crawled into the space, which extended five feet into the stack, then took a 90-degree turn to the left where she hid. In a way it was like an artificial shaft inside the Nachthaus.

She sat up at my intrusion, pulling to her chest the sheet Gott had given her and adjusting her hair. I sat on the end of her pallet, my back against one of the drums. It was dark, but enough light entered between the cracks of the drums to allow me to see her movements and make out her features. She looked well-rested, but distressed.

"How long, Sascha?" she asked. "How long do I have to wait here?"

"There's no way for me to know that." I traced the branded circle in my palm, nauseated by the odor of my hands collecting in the confined space of the drums. "I've thought about posting Gott out in the mine shaft, about halfway up to the alcoves. He could get back here unde-tected if he saw someone coming. That would at least give you the freedom to get out of this hole for awhile. Maybe even an hour or two at a time."

Her features relaxed. "I'd like that." She pushed forward, the sheet dropping to her lap, exposing the tank top Gott had given her. Her shoulders looked like chiseled marble in the soft light. I tried to turn away, but she reached across the pallet and grabbed my hands. A draft of sulfur wafted into my nostrils.

"They're going to kill them all, aren't they?" Her hands squeezed, and then they shook. "Aren't they?" It was not fear or panic, but a regal resignation, as if this were not her first trial or tribulation. She spoke as a woman who had eaten from the Tree of the Knowledge of Good and Evil.

I dropped my gaze from her eyes, my chin sinking to my chest. "I don't know."

I knew she knew it was a lie. Her hands grasped harder. She knew it was a lie, and all I could hear was the blaring rat-a-tat of snare drums, the whoosh of the jets, and the roar of the inferno.

But they were so far away. They receded to the back of my mind like birds across a lake just after sunset, their calls fading into the blue of dusk.

Her hands held mine. I felt our pulses throb in unison. The warmth of her palms against mine, even through the branded circle, enveloped me. It encased me in a lush garden, a hidden oasis in the Nachthaus. My Katia faded away forever.

Outside, I could hear the scratching at the great door to the Nachthaus and the moaning of the forest, but they were as distant as the inferno. I was in the hands of an ivory goddess, and they held my entire world.

Sleep, my Adam, in the arms of your love.
In the arms of your love there is solace and bliss.
I slept.

25

I was dreaming of the Tree of the Knowledge of Good and Evil when I was expelled from the Garden. My nose snapped in two with the crack of a castanet, and when the stars cleared from my eyes, I was on the floor of the storage room, a few feet from the wall that had broken my nose.

Hayner stood over me, wiping my blood from his hand. My shirt soaked red until I could feel the warm ooze on my chest. In front of me, blood trickled down the wall at the spot where Hayner had slammed me. Behind me I heard Mirka screaming as they extracted her feet-first from the space in the fuel drums.

Hayner lifted me by my hair. It was quite a feat, given how short my hair was. Through the pain, I still wondered how he could be that strong. His wrists were coiled iron springs.

Hayner screeched like an entire flock of macaws. "Were Gott and Rolf party to this treason?"

I shook my head.

That seemed to enrage Hayner. He whipped out the crop with his free hand and used it to depress my broken nose. My legs went numb beneath me with the pain, but Hayner held me suspended in the air by my hair. "I said, did Gott and Rolf have a part in this treason?" He relieved the pressure on my nose.

The crop felt like a soldering iron jammed up my nostril. Through the pain I spit at Hayner, sounding more as a Nazi than I ever had. "Zay ver not infolfed."

Hayner pressed harder with the crop.

I screamed. "Zay ver not infolfed!" Speckles of blood spewed from my mouth and landed on Hayner's face.

Hayner grinned. His pythons emerged and tasted the blood with their forked red tongues. "We shall see, König."

Hayner motioned for the soldiers. Seconds later, Mirka dropped beside my feet, hunched over on her knees as if nauseated. Her hair swirled in front of her face, hanging to the floor. I heard a sob from beneath her hair, and the forest outside echoed with a lingering moan.

"Bring them in!" Hayner screeched.

The storage room door swung open. Gott and Rolf entered first, followed by Falke, stooping under the doorway. The flamethrower was strapped to his back. At the sight of the flamethrower, I felt for the sphere in my pocket, wishing it would light one more time. It didn't. I wondered if my grace was spent.

Falke pointed toward Hayner, his arm lifting like a drawbridge, and Gott and Rolf trudged over.

Hayner summoned Rolf. "Were you involved in this treason, Waechter?"

Rolf, staring at the blood on the wall, did not reply.

"Waechter!" Hayner screeched.

Rolf adjusted his goggles just faster than the speed of a clock's second hand. "I'm a civilian, Standartenführer. I don't have to ans—"

Hayner's crop struck Rolf on the side of the head with such force that I feared for his life. The enormity of Rolf's goggles seemed to absorb most of the shock. They flew from his head and skipped across the floor. Rolf sank to his knees, stunned from the blow, but appearing more concerned with finding his glasses. He groped about, hands feeling the floor in front of him.

"Obergrenadier Moench!"

Gott sidled to attention in front of Hayner in a silky manner that was memorable, even under the circumstances. He saluted Hayner. I couldn't tell if it was genuine.

"Dumme! Fool! Don't salute me!"

Gott lowered his hand gracefully.

Hayner eyed Gott's hand until it completed its downward arc. "One chance, Obergrenadier Moench. Were you involved in this treason?"

Gott's reply came without a hint of hesitation or consideration. "Nein, Herr Hayner."

Hayner's eyes bored into him. The daydream must have fought against his years of military experience and intuition— that, or he didn't care, knowing we were all trapped in the Nachthaus and he'd have time to get around to Gott and Rolf. "Take Waechter and get the oven stoked," he said. "We've work to do." Hayner turned to the soldiers. "Throw the girl in the oven. She can wait there while I deal with König. Falke, go with them and see that there's no trouble."

The soldiers lifted Mirka off the floor by her arms. I heard another sob as she was dragged through the doorway. The forest outside once more seemed to moan in response. Falke followed through the door without a word, the flamethrower in tow.

"Now we go to business, König, you and me." Hayner dragged me by the hair across the floor of the mine, pausing to tell Gott they had one hour to ready the oven.

When Hayner turned back toward the door, Gott gestured to me: *Should I do what he says?* I nodded and reached for the sphere in my pocket. I figured the torture room and oven waited for me, so I did not intend for the sphere to be lost. As Hayner dragged me through the doorway, I tossed the sphere, hoping Gott would catch it. He did, gracefully as ever.

Hayner hauled me through the hall and around the corner leading to the oven. Resisting him was useless; I was along for the ride. My nose bled on his shoes. I scanned the corridor for Mirka, but saw nothing. My heart collapsed under its own weight.

Hayner accelerated as we reached the inferno door. To my left, the philosopher- face would be appearing on the wall. With my hopes gutted, I wanted to reach him one last time. It was a difficult trick, with Hayner dragging me and my reduced height. I managed a glancing touch to the face's jowl as we passed, not much more than a fingernail. It was so quick Hayner didn't seem to notice and I heard the face say, *The time of testing is at hand. To him that overcomes . . .*

There was no time to respond. Hayner had me out the door to the mine shaft already. I was moving so fast my boots bounced up and down on the uneven floor. Hayner cackled.

"Ah, schoolboy. He who thinks he's the smart one. You could have done well here, schoolboy. But now you shall fail."

The forest outside groaned. So did my scalp, which was burning from Hayner's grip. We were halfway to the intersection and picking up speed, even on the incline.

"Do you hear that groaning, Hayner?" I knew where Hayner was taking me. After Mirka's discovery, I knew I had nothing to lose. Even armed with this knowledge, the threat came out academically. "You'll never make it out of here."

"Ah, schoolboy." Hayner stopped and lifted me to his face. In the dim light I could see his features: hardened like the walls of the Nachthaus. The dim light swirled around his hairless head. "Did you not realize, König, that in here I am God?"

His features moved slowly. They reminded me of the granite features of the philosopher-face. He was resolute in his reprobation. I knew then—not that he was God, but that he was man without normal restraint. He was the sin nature run amok, free to rule as it saw fit. He was isolated with the whim of his will and the power to enforce it. He was the burned corpse man without a luminous new man to battle.

Suspended in front of him, I seized his neck in my hands, squeezing with all the strength at my command. My broken nose stabbed stilettos of pain into my forehead as I twisted my face to squeeze harder. My hands reeked and I wished the stench would suffocate Hayner.

Hayner laughed. The harder I squeezed, the more self-satisfied his laugh became. He laughed so violently I could not maintain my grip. I dropped my hands.

"Sascha," he said, "what failed you?" He drew a deep breath through his nostrils, as if savoring the aroma of a home-cooked meal. It must have been my hands he smelled. He spoke out in his best German, but to me it sounded hackneyed. "Dummkopf! I vould haff given you ze girl. I vould haff given you vatefer you vanted. You could haff been second only to me."

He set me down and rubbed a hand through my scalp, proceeding almost in a fatherly tone. "Did you think I wanted out of the Nachthaus, Sascha? No, no, lad." He cupped his hands on the side of my head, patting a couple of times. "Nein, mein junge. I only want an avenue to travel freely outside. This is my realm, but the lone freedom I lack is to roam outside unmolested, unwatched, unsanctioned. I would never *leave* this place. If anything, I would expand its influence outside."

I vomited on his shoes. It was a combination of the pain from my nose, my stinking hands, and Hayner's revelation.

Hayner wiped his shoes on my leg, first the left, then the right. "Poor Sascha. All your schemes, all your defiance, all your prayers. And all along it was a child's dream. Wake up, poor Sascha. I want you to see how this ends for the fool."

26

Hayner lifted me by the scalp and carried me onward. We entered the intersection and headed right for his quarters. My nose throbbed with each bump and in cadence with a pounding that appeared to come from the front of the Nachthaus.

In seconds we were in front of his door. My inscription hovered on the door like a specter: *Every man's work shall be made manifest: for the day shall declare it, because it shall be revealed by fire; and the fire shall try every man's work of what sort it is . . . For our God is a consuming fire.*

Hayner released his hold of my scalp, and I fell to the floor on my back. "Ah, my little schoolboy," he said, "these are but words. Words of dreams. Dreams of the weak. They mean nothing. Life is for the strong, for those who *do*, not talk. Life is for those who assert their will. These are the only works that will be made manifest, for they are the only works that are real."

I felt better on my back. The pressure lifted somewhat from my nose and my head began to clear from the jostling ride I'd endured to get to Hayner's door. The drawback was having Hayner standing over me like a titan. Staring up at him from the floor seemed to augment his frame. The compact, sinewy build, the chiseled arrogance of the Nazi, the pompous trust in power. He was a colossus. Man at the height of his natural sinfulness, and I could not hope to stand against him.

Alone, anyway. There was still an opposing presence in the Nachthaus: the gypsy girl, the philosopher's face, the spark kindled between three Christian brothers. And it was more than that.

Something else was there—it was different than the power of man—but it was there. It was meek, like power without boundary yet under control. It was patient. It had borne my frailty in love and seemed to wait as the story played out in the Nachthaus. It was sovereign—I could feel its great power was somehow held in check, as if it derived from beyond the Nachthaus, dwarfing this world in its infiniteness. It was holy. It was other than the Nachthaus: pure, but more than purity; it was being itself. And soon, I sensed, the meek would come in power, its patience would call an end, the sovereign would exert itself, and the holy would always and forever still be holy, for it could do no other.

"You don't know the reality, Hayner," I said. "For if you did, you'd know there are greater forces at work here. You've been given a little time, a measure of power, that's all, and it's soon expended." I paused for a breath, gathering from what stores of courage I had left. This was not going to be pleasant, I feared, but this time I would not fail to deliver the message to Hayner. "The day is coming when all will be set right. But Hayner, it's not too late for you, even now."

He did not hesitate. There was no uncertainty in his features, no pause evident in his mind, no hint from the pythons that he'd even considered it. Hayner snatched me from the floor and raised me to his face, the two blue veins on his scalp writhing in concert with the pythons. "You're about to see a consuming fire, Sascha. Your own furnace, my dear Nebuchadnezzar. And once again, you'll not be able to stop it, or deliver the ones you love from it."

"God have mercy on your soul, Hayner." It was difficult to force myself to say it, and it was more difficult to force myself to mean it. I felt that battle raging inside me again, and I determined that I would follow the good, the luminous man, where it led me.

"Mercy?" Hayner said. Something pounded on the Nachthaus gate again. It was a hollow sound, like that of a battering ram against the great iron door. "Would you like to step outside, Sascha? Preach mercy to the savage? How long do you think it would be before they ripped you to shreds and sucked the lifeblood out of you? No, Sascha, mercy is an invention of the weak to confound the strong."

"Very well," I said. "Let us have our works tried by fire. Lead the way. We will see who stands."

Hayner grinned.

"But one last thing," I said, "the time for daydreaming is nearly done. The day of the Nachthaus draws to a close, and when daytime is over, the nightmares come."

Hayner didn't twitch. "Today is not that day, schoolboy."

27

The first of three executions began with German efficiency at 4:00 a.m., almost an hour to the moment after I had been rousted out of the storage room. Hayner and I walked to the inferno door, he with his arm around me like a loving father. It was repulsive. Gott and Rolf were already positioned in the control room. They signaled their readiness over the intercom.

The door from the mine opened, and the procession of soldiers and captives, trailed by Falke, proceeded as it had for the previous execution. This time there was no fighting, no protesting, no one needing to be shot trying to break out of the inferno, only the rattle of snares and the roar of the inferno. The execution too was a model of German efficiency.

Four hours later we achieved a second execution. Our works were tested by fire again as 20 more victims of the inferno perished. In four more hours we would execute the last of the prisoners.

Noon arrived with Hayner and I posted in front of the inferno door. He stood to my left. One more execution to endure and we were through. Until the next arrival of prisoners. The door was open and the soot from the victims of the previous two executions remained on the oven floor. The smell lingered in the air, though I had trouble smelling it through my broken nose. The stench of my hands was different. It was if I could smell that with my spirit.

At 12:01, Hayner's eye began to twitch, evidently at the tardiness of the soldiers in delivering the next round of captives.

Through the oven door, I noticed the continuing deterioration of the oven itself. The constant heating and cooling was taking its toll. The plate-sized chip I had seen over Mirka's head had now splintered and sent spider legs out in all direction. The oven's rear wall had cracked from the ceiling to the floor, and runners from the main crack were spreading in all directions like capillaries.

The oven was now not merely wrinkled, but it was also furrowed. It had its death inside it. Its guts were rotten. Its sin had found it out. Its works had been tried with fire and found wanting.

Hayner quit twitching when the door opened to let in the final contingent of captives. The snares blared and the procession continued as usual. The first squad of soldiers led, passing the oven door to stand at attention to Hayner's left. The captives followed, making the right hand turn into the inferno. These were followed by the last squad of soldiers and Falke bringing up the rear.

As the captives passed in front of me, I saw the gypsy girl— except it was not the gypsy girl. It was Mirka.

She marched to the cadence of the snares, head forward, eyes focused straight. She seemed to have regained her countenance and, other than a small bruise on one forearm, she did not appear beaten or molested.

Hayner beamed at her appearance, as if this were the main event. In a way, I supposed it was. She stopped in front of me at the entrance to the door and turned to face me. I expected Hayner to object, but he did not.

She reached her hands out and cupped my cheeks. Her hands, which had been those of an ivory goddess hours before, now were pale in the dim light of the Nachthaus. "Is there anything you can do?" Her eyes were stoic.

"Does it look like there is anything I can do?" As soon as the words came out, I looked away.

Mirka dropped her hands and turned toward the door.

I could feel Hayner's satisfaction oozing from his every pore. "Proving ourselves nicely, I see," he said.

I swung my right fist at Hayner's jaw with all my strength. He caught it like a leaf floating on the wind and began to squeeze. The pressure on my fist mounted. At first I felt the pads of his fingers compress behind my knuckles, then the bones in my hand began to creak. He stopped short of cracking them each in two. Oddly, the pain was the fiercest in my nose.

Mirka turned around and placed her hand upon Hayner's. "Please," she said.

Hayner considered it for a moment and relaxed his grip.

I repeatedly splayed my fingers to work out the pain. Mirka took hold of my hand.

"I know mercy," Hayner said. He looked as someone who had killed in the name of God.

"You're about to burn her alive, you—"

Mirka grabbed my head and forced it toward her. It was a violent twist. She leaned past my face and touched her lips to my ear, away from Hayner. "I wish we would have known each other in a different place," she said. "A different time."

With that, she kissed my cheek, turned, and strode into the inferno like a deposed queen.

The snares blared and the door began to descend.

Mirka stood in the doorway, eyes fixed upon me. The door eclipsed her head, her shoulders, her chest, her waist, her knees, her feet. It slammed shut and the snares fell silent.

"Give the order," Hayner said to me.

I saw Mirka's silhouette in one of the inferno's eyes. Her hands were upon the glass.

"I can't do it, Standartenführer."

"You must, Leutnant."

Mirka's hand fell from the glass and her murky silhouette disappeared like a ghost ship into fog. I remembered how devastating it had been seeing the gypsy girl's light snuffed out in the inferno. I reached for the sphere in my pocket, but it was not there. I felt naked. I reached behind me for the philosopher-face. I pawed at the granite—I knew I had my hand on him—but nothing happened.

The time of testing is at hand. To him that overcomes . . .

"I can't do it."

"You must." I saw in Hayner's eyes that I must. He would not relent this time.

Dear Lord, do not let me fail, I thought as I walked to the intercom. "Ready, Gott?"

"Yes, sir, Oberleutnant."

Hayner was staring straight forward in his stance in front of the door. I knew he was aware of my every move out of his periphery. The silhouette had reappeared in the glass slit window as well.

The snares blared as I gave Gott the start-up order. I had a dreamy sensation of a whirring noise as the fuel pumps kicked on. The shutters fell open with a thud, exposing the jets. There was a whoosh as the pilot light lit. Gott was ready for the final order.

28

Oh shame, where is thy blush? Rebellious hell, if thou canst mutine in a matron's bones, to flaming youth let virtue be as wax and melt in her own fire.

"Fire the oven, Gott."

There was a moment's hesitation before the inferno fired to life. It fired like an ancient star that felt its life ebbing away in a dark and unknown corner of space. But fire it did, and once again I was Nebuchadnezzar. The oven was seven times hotter than it had been when I arrived, and it conducted its work with raging vengeance.

As soon as the oven ceased, the snares quieted and a silence fell over the Nachthaus. In the distance, I could hear the pounding at the front door. The soldiers restrained my arms behind me.

Hayner strode to face me. "There may be hope for you," he said. "A day or two in the back rooms may reclaim you."

I didn't resist. There was nowhere to run, and even if I could fend off the soldiers somehow, I was no match for Hayner. I thought of breaking for my room—my firearm was there—but the soldiers would shoot me down before I reached the door. It might be better to die from gunshot, here and now, but I wanted to know how my choice to be faithful would play out without my forcing the hand. It could still end in death. I had accepted that, but I wanted it to happen as it should.

The soldiers must have sensed my acquiescence because they allowed me to walk toward the door. I hazarded one glance back at the oven. Over one hundred captives gone, including Mirka.

The air in the torture room hung stagnant with the smell of electricity. The light had been repaired and its dim shine illuminated what Hayner considered a reclamation center. I had a gnawing suspicion that Hayner had planted a seed of hope within me in order that I might suffer through the torture an extra day or two, just as he had planted the seed that I might escape the torture room by ordering the oven to fire for the last execution. I was only a vermin in a cage.

The plant-man at the rear of the room began howling and jostling his cage when we entered. He struck the bars with his stalks, and the vine protruding from his grass-ringed maw shot in and out with a whipping noise. His thorax fly-trap slapped open and closed.

The gargantuan roaches were caged on top of the island bar that stood in the center of the room. Their mandibles clicked as the soldiers escorted me past. One of the guards slapped the cages as we went by, agitating the roaches further, their razor-taloned legs spiking the metal floors of the cages.

At the end of the bar was the mess we had left earlier. The floor was stained with a mixture of blood and bug juice, and I estimated that none had left the room alive after me, neither man nor insect. The roaches in the cages might even be new acquisitions. I couldn't be certain.

My nose throbbed and I was beginning to feel the fatigue of not eating well. I was still soaked in the dried blood from my nose, and it occurred to me that the smell might be enticing the insects. I couldn't smell it; my hands were too pungent. I reached for the sphere, and remembered again that I had tossed it to Gott. There would be no repeat of the torture-room light show, no succor in the dark from the gypsy girl.

To him that overcomes . . .

Yes, but alone?

The soldiers prodded me to the metal frame torture rack. When I reached it, I grasped the metal framework to prevent them from strapping me spread-eagle to the frame. One of the soldiers rapped the knuckles of my left hand with a club, and I turned and swung my right fist at his face. He ducked it and thrust the club into my gut, knocking my wind out.

I doubled over. Two of the soldiers straightened me and pinned my arms to the frame while another two strapped my wrists in before I could recover. They stepped back a pace or two, apparently admiring their handiwork. I tested the restraints. They were horridly secure.

Alone? What if indeed no glory appeared over the Nachthaus? In my dream, I had scaled the Nachthaus's peak, only to find Hayner. On my climb, the bearded man in the cave had told me that *dreaming was seeing the world as it is not.* What if the Nachthaus were the stark reality and Hayner was its master, kept partially in check by the forest outside? What if the gypsy girl and the granite face were anomalies or, worse yet, *dreams?* Perhaps they were my wish fulfillment or my failure to face repressed fears of the human hydra of mortality, loneliness, grief, pain, meaninglessness, purposelessness, and nothingness?

The thought was debilitating, yet it dug into me like a parasite. Inside my heart, it began to suck the faith from my soul.

When the first jolt of electricity surged through me, my heart skipped. The second jolt stopped it momentarily, and when my heart lurched back on like a car taking off in second gear, I searched it for faith. The pain was immense, but the thought of losing faith was the pain of desperation.

A hot poker seared my right forearm, and for a moment the burning flesh overpowered the smell of my hands. A detached cry escaped my lips as if someone were screaming in the next room.

The physical pain was enormous. It was indescribable. Ineffable. But I knew even then that the dark night of the soul would be worse somehow. The fear that one is alone in an evil world. The hopelessness that great pain bows to no greater good. The despair that goodness is but a dream. The thought that all one's intuitions of right and wrong are but fancies. That grief is final. That horrible things are not put right in the end. That the horrid is not horrid after all.

To be forsaken. Forgotten. Utterly. But not truly forsaken, not truly forgotten, for there was no one to do the forsaking or forgetting in the first place. Beneath the mountain I wailed. I wailed in great pain, but mainly for myself, as there was no one to weep for me, nor did it matter.

The soldiers laughed.

I lifted my head from my chest and saw the insects. The guards had removed two from their cages and were carrying them toward me. The mandibles clicked and the roaches were salivating. Vanity of vanities, I thought. All is vanity. Meaningless! I hung my head.

29

Lord, how resolutely You direct each man to his end. It is the end of his days, the end of a professed faith in You, or the end of his lack of trust in Your goodness and graciousness, even in this dark world. I see the choice in front of me: I may either live or die whichever way I choose, but I must either now kill my faith or allow it to be faith. There is no other way. As for me, though You slay me, yet will I trust in Thee.

I remembered the prayer from the last time I had been in the torture room. This time, however, there *was* no choice. Not of mine, anyway. I would either live or die dependent on factors outside my control. It wasn't even "obey or not obey" anymore. My remaining choice was simple: faith or not faith.

I refused to look up. The insects were quite close now. Their feelers caressed my cheeks. The prickly and bulbous knobs at the end of the antennae searched my face, gliding across my temples, my upper lip, my chin, my broken nose.

The words of the prayer were distant in comparison with the horror in front of me. They were hollow, vacant, as if they were written and not believed.

One of the mandibles latched onto my chest, slicing a gash through the blood stain on my shirt. I saw through the tear in my shirt. The mandible had slashed a six-inch cut in my chest. It was a shallow laceration, but torture took its time.

I looked up at the soldiers. They were laughing again. It sickened me. I locked on to their eyes as they threatened me with the insects, thrusting the bugs at me and pulling them out of reach just as their jaws closed.

Their eyes were vacuous. They lacked fire. They were absent. They were the eyes of daydreaming men. The eyes of Pflanzen-Kriegerin.

Then a thought came to me. Hayner's eyes *were* full of fire. Hayner had embraced the evil, reveled in it. These men had merely accepted it. Taken it for the way things were, as if there were no reality but the Nachthaus and the forest. They were daydreaming. They might later claim a Nuremburg defense, but I knew they knew what they were doing. Either way, they were guilty.

I refused to daydream another moment, so again I awoke. *As for me, though You slay me, yet will I trust in Thee.*

The roach came forward now at face level. Its jaws clacked together, its saliva oozing from its mouth, its antennae sampling my bloody nose. Inch by inch it approached on the outstretched arms of the soldier. Its black eyes stared at me. Its mouth a gaping maw like the entrance to the Nachthaus.

. . . *allow it to* be *faith. There is no other way.*

Faith. In that terrifying moment I suddenly saw it: to die in faith was better than to live believing the Nachthaus was the sum total of our existence. I overcame. *Lord, into Your hands I commit my spirit.*

A great boom came to us through the walls. I thought perhaps the iron gate of the Nachthaus had been breached. The alarm engaged and began its rhythmic blare. The soldiers paused.

One went to the door of the torture room and looked out down the hallway. The light of the alarm flashed from the hallway, bathing him in red light as he motioned for his fellow soldiers. They moved for the door, stopping long enough to toss the roaches inside as they closed the door behind them.

It was a certainty of instinct that the roaches would come to claim their prize. I struggled against the restraints that held my hands. The burn on my forearm from the hot iron throbbed as I writhed my wrists, but the restraints held. The insects were approaching in formation along the floor, to the side of the island bar.

I thanked God my boots were on and that my feet were not strapped along with my hands. I kicked at the first roach and missed. My boot sailed above its head, and when it came back down, the roach clamped upon it. I wriggled my foot back and forth, trying to dislodge the roach's mandibles from my boot. This helped the jaws cut into the boot leather. I kicked with my free foot at the side of the roach, which let go.

The instant I felt the tension of its jaws release, I kicked. From that angle, I could not deliver a crushing blow, but the force was enough to back the roach up next to its companion two feet back.

We were at a stalemate. I continued kicking out at the roaches as they neared, and they continued to back up out of reach. They seemed to be testing the reach of my kicks, and timing them for a coordinated assault. I knew if they gained the metal framework and scaled it before I could stop them with my feet, I was lost. The placement of the framework prevented them from flanking me and attacking from the rear.

The alarm blared outside but was muted now with the door closed. I was forgotten here as I continued my battle with the roaches. They continued to test the perimeter of my kicks, always out of range, though I did manage to connect with one of the roaches' antennae. At this rate, they would wear me down, so I attempted a gambit. Lifting my knees to my chest, which put considerable strain on my wrists in the restraints, I waited.

My stomach muscles revolted at keeping my legs held up. A couple of times I nearly dropped them, but I each time I lifted my legs back up. The roaches seemed unsure and twittered around out of range, seeking me with their antennae. Then the first roach attacked.

Its quickness was remarkable. From a dead standstill it reached the metal framework almost before I could react. It had gained the framework with its front legs and was a foot up before the heels of my boots crashed down upon its back.

There was a sickening crack as my boots crashed through the roach's armored carapace. My full weight came down on the roach with velocity, and my heels pounded the floor right through the enormous insect. Its exoskeleton fractured and a gruesome blob of bug juice splattered across the floor in all directions. My boots were instantly soaked through with bug guts.

The roach emitted a hiss, but did not die. Instead, it renewed its attack with fury. My boots had it pinned it to the floor about six inches behind its head. Its jaws were arcing up behind my legs, snapping at the backs of my calves. Its legs ran wildly back and forth along the stone floor, trying to push its ruined body forward.

The jaws caught my pant leg below the back of my knee and shredded it. I couldn't allow it to catch my calf. I raised my legs again in order to launch a kill shot at the roach's head. However, my boots were caught in the thing's armor and I ended up lifting the entire roach.

Suspended in air from my boots, it was snapping at my behind, inches away. I tried to thrust my legs out sideways to split the roach in half, but its armor was too strong. The jaws underneath me chopped away. How long could the thing live like this?

I smashed my feet back down on the ground, which jostled the impaled roach further up around my ankles. The jaws were now a bit closer and they continued to search for my flesh.

The second roach must have sensed its chance, and it shot ahead for the framework. I lifted my legs again, the other roach still in tow, but the second roach got to the metal framework before I could bring my feet down again. With my feet stuck within the first roach, I could not knock it off as it climbed. I swung the first roach at it, but it resulted in only a glancing blow to its midsection.

Its taloned legs found footholds one by one as it climbed toward my head. The talons clinked on the metal as it struggled upward. It slipped once in its assent, sliding back a few inches before it caught hold.

I swung sideways at it again, but it was now above my feet. I pistoned my boots up and down, and shook off the first roach, but it was too late. The second roach had cleared my only line of defense.

I shouted at the vermin. I cursed it. I spit at it. I shook on the framework, trying to dislodge it.

It kept coming, inch by inch. Its jaws were now a foot from my head, and the antennae were searching for my neck and face. The roach hesitated as it found the soft flesh, savoring it. It cocked its head toward me and climbed.

30

The jaws snapped inches from my cheek. It seemed to be trying to negotiate a lateral move toward my head. That might have been better as it could have chewed my arm unrestrained.

It managed to come across an inch or two, and when it did I lurched at the roach, head-butting it. I caught the side of its jaws with pretty good force, but the bug didn't budge an inch. I kept my face planted against the outside of the mandible closest to me. That was my last stratagem. If it got loose now, it would have my neck.

The roach pressed back, trying to turn its head to work its jaw across my face. The jaw slid across my cheek until its tip was caught on my chin. It hung there precariously. I lurched my head away from the bug, and the jaws snapped three times in rapid succession. The first snap missed, and the second opened a two-inch laceration over my cheekbone as if I had cut myself shaving with a straight razor. The third snap removed a tiny portion of my earlobe.

I lurched back at the roach and again caught its mandible with the side of my head. The roach pressed back and began working its jaw across my cheek. Soon now it would have me. I wrestled against the restraints with no success. All my hands could do was stink.

The blood dripped from my ear and nose and chest and lacerated cheek. The roach paused to sample the blood with its antennae. It took its time, dousing its antennae and then transferring the blood to its mouth. The lifeblood must have sent it into a rage of thirst, for it reared its head back for the kill. This freed the roach from my last defense, and it had a clear shot at my neck. It would strike directly this time, and I was powerless to stop it.

It hissed, great white ooze erupting from its mouth. It arced one taloned foot into my chest to gain a foothold to power its strike. The talon lodged between two of my ribs. It reared back a final time.

The alarm blared, and red light flooded into the room as Gott opened the door, just as the roach began to strike. I felt the talon dig in, and the roach lunged, mandibles aiming for my neck.

Gott's athleticism had him across the room in a split second, but not before the roach closed its jaws around my neck.

Gott pulled the roach from me as the jaws began to clamp, and the jaws carved trenches in my skin as they were jerked away.

The front of the jaws clicked closed in front of my Adam's apple.

Gott threw the roach backward, and it hit a cabinet on the side of the room before landing in front of Rolf as he entered.

The roach teetered for a moment, then came to rest on its back, legs flailing in the air.

"Great Gregor Samsa," I said.

The caged plant-man howled behind me.

Gott had the restraints off, and I collapsed onto his shoulders. My arms felt like 50-pound weights were strapped to my hands.

There was a loud splat from the front of the room. I saw that Rolf had smashed a stool into the roach's head. I felt safe enough to sink to the floor next to the first dead roach, which was still twitching feebly.

Gott searched me for wounds, seeming to be most concerned with the fresh blood from my chest oozing through my shirt. He lifted the shirt and then dropped it. "Looks like you're scratched up quite a bit, but not in danger. Did you feel any internal pain?" he asked. "I saw several bad bruises under your shirt." Gott examined the laceration on my cheek.

"I'm t-tired and hungry." I also felt as though I had gone fifteen rounds with Max Schmeling. My voice shook from the shock and fear of what I'd just endured. "D-do you have any b-bacon?"

Gott started to lift me. "Let's go then, Oberleutnant."

I resisted. "I'd like to sleep, Gott."

Another splat came from Rolf's direction.

"Sir," Gott said, "do you hear the alarm?" He motioned toward the door. His face was uncertain. "It's not pleasant out there, sir. We need to get moving. There's a lot more where that came from." He pointed at the dead roach.

"And m-miles to go before we sleep, Gott. Miles to go before we sleep."

"Let's go, Oberleutnant." Gott lifted me again, and this time I assisted.

I staggered to the door along the opposite side of the bar from where Rolf's smashed roaches lay. I was beginning to tighten all over like my muscles were on strike. My nose was throbbing again, my ear stung with its missing lobe, the puncture in my chest smarted. I wanted to sleep: to be far away from this place, to forget.

With the plant-man hysterical in the cage behind us, we struck out into the corridor under the flashing red light and the measured cadence of the alarm.

The halls were barren. We saw not one creature, man nor beast, from the torture room past the officers' quarters, all the way to the intersection. There, we paused to catch our breath. From the front of the mine we heard commotion and sporadic gunfire mixed with the alarm.

"I'll need to get to the lab," I said, feeling stronger on my feet.

Another large boom came from the front of the Nachthaus, followed by what sounded like Hayner screeching.

Twenty minutes later we were back at the intersection. All armed with pistols, and me with my pack loaded. The extra weight of the pack increased my fatigue, but the pack was comforting at the same time. We crossed the intersection onto the wooden pier floor that ran in front of the alcove holding cells.

The cells were bare. Two of the doors hung open. There had been over a hundred souls caged there since I'd arrived, and who knew how many before. Now they were empty and the open doors seemed to testify what they had witnessed of human cruelty. I stared at the one locked cell, half expecting to see the gypsy girl.

More gunfire erupted ahead, followed by the forest groaning. It was the giant ship's foghorn, deep, foreboding, and sustained. It reverberated through the Nachthaus. I felt it as a harbinger.

I called to Gott and Rolf, extending my hands to them as they turned to face me. "The judge is at the door," I said. The biblical reference was out of context, but it seemed true nonetheless. I hoped the gypsy girl was right—that God and nature did not work together in vain. I was sure we'd find out as soon as we turned the corner to the front door of the Nachthaus. "I'm afraid these are our last moments here together," I said. "I thank God for you two, and I thank you for your courage in rescuing me and in seeing us through this."

Gott eyed the floor and traced his instep gracefully along a crack formed in the wood of the pier. Rolf, behind his goggles, appeared less heron-like now and more like an eagle. I offered my branded palm to Gott, who took it. Rolf gathered my other palm, and we prayed.

Even in the Nachthaus, where two or three are joined together . . .

31

Nature was not working in vain when we turned the corner to the great iron door of the Nachthaus. A pounding at the door occurred at ten-second intervals, as if the plant-men were ramming the door with a felled tree. The door had bent inward at its midsection, and had partially dislodged from its groove in the floor. Welts were forming on the inside of the door from the pounding, and with each strike the iron creaked against the rock of the mine as the door twisted in its casing.

The ram pounded the door again, and the metal twisted another three inches, scraping over the lip of the groove as it dislodged. I covered my ears from the high-pitched scraping noise of iron against rock. The door was stressed, and half its bottom had been twisted out of the groove. A small gap ran along the bottom of the door facing outward. Inhuman probes were searching the gap: antennae, a plant-man's vine, what looked to be the leg of a giant spider.

Hayner had assembled a skirmish line as before about fifty feet from the door. He appeared to have conceded the breach of the gate and was preparing for defense of the mine from full assault. A shot rang out, directed at the spider leg feeling its way under the door.

Hayner screeched at the soldiers. "Hold fire! We need every bullet." Behind the skirmish line, the Nazis had stockpiled every axe, knife, bayonet, shovel, and potential weapon they could muster, along with barrels of pre-made torches soaking in fuel oil. They had stashed two four-foot square box fans along with their supplies. Falke stood at the back of the line, flamethrower harnessed.

The Nazis had constructed a chest-high makeshift wall of timber, railroad ties, and loose rock across the mine, anchored into the wall supports on the side of the mine. It appeared Hayner's strategy was to inflict as much damage as possible on the enemy before falling back to deeper parts of the mine.

"Today," Hayner said, "you will fight as Germans." The door pounded as an exclamation point to the beginning of Hayner's speech. "You will hold this wall until all your ammunition is gone, and then you will hold it with axe, pick, and shovel." The red light of the alarm flashed on and off Hayner's face. He was ecstatic with the prospect of battle, and his face gleamed even more so than in the orange light of the raging inferno.

"This is the day of men, and you will drench yourself in the pulp and sap-blood of plants until none remain and we rise out of the Nachthaus to burn this forest to the ground. You will drive the heel of your boot into every vile creature that walks with its belly to the ground until their guts run like a river into the heart of this mountain. We will drive them into the outer wastes, left in the aftermath of our destruction of the forest, that they may burrow under ground and hide in clefts of rock like the vermin they are."

Another boom sounded at the great iron door, which slipped a full foot out of its bottom groove with a hideous screech. The lunatic howl of plant-men arose from outside, like wind rushing through the eaves of a house.

"The great vine shall come, mannschaften." Hayner removed a sinister blade from his belt. It flashed red in the alarm light. He cut a two-inch gash in his forehead horizontally between the two blue veins running up his scalp. Blood spilled from the wound as he matched the first cut with a vertical line bisecting it.

"Yes, the great vine shall come, and we shall cut him." Hayner slashed down with the blade, imitating a hacking attack against the great vine. "We shall cut him. We shall slash him. We shall hack him." With each sentence, Hayner carved his own forehead. His face ran with blood. Hayner made a final cut on his forehead. "We shall sever him from the forest, and leave him decomposing in his own sap on the ground."

The door to the Nachthaus boomed again, and Hayner raised his arms over his head, screeching. "Yes, today we shall fight like men!" On his forehead was a bloody swastika gleaming in the light of the alarm. The soldiers gazed at the door dreamily, frenzied.

We three huddled around the corner of the main hall and the alcove hall. "This is not our fight, Oberleutnant," Gott said. "Let's go back. Let them die. The plants won't search for us deep in the mine."

Rolf appeared to agree.

"Remember our pledge to the gypsy girl?" I said. "We have to see this through. All the way. Live or die."

Gott leaned against the corner, apparently unconvinced. He was both right and wrong. We had done what we had pledged in saving Mirka from the torture room. What more could the gypsy girl want? We were practically powerless against the Nazis, Hayner in particular, and we were utterly powerless against the force of nature, as men always are, ultimately.

Nature would win in the end, as it always did. Men pressed nature on all sides, but she outlasted them. I thought of other Nachthauses, now long languishing in the forests of Central America and Mexico, all but forgotten. How the tide of man had swelled against the forest. His temples of human sacrifice rose to the sky, but the tide always ebbed, and the forest reclaimed.

Nature is God's reclamation center, until all things are put right by Him. Until that time, she will groan in anticipation of forever abandoning her present duty. *Deus et natua non faciunt frusta.*

The forest groaned outside, and the pounding continued at the door. I could hear Hayner still exhorting his troops. And I also knew why Gott was wrong.

"You might want to check your pocket," I said.

Gott looked down at his pants. Rolf pointed. The sphere was heating up. The light was shining through his pocket.

"I suppose I agree or it starts to burn," Gott said. He moved a hand to the lip of his pocket and withdrew the marble. "I agree. We see it through."

I put my branded hand on Gott's shoulder. He didn't seem to notice an odor. "Very good," I said. "But it's not because you were scared of being burned, is it?"

Gott motioned for Rolf, who stepped forward a pace or two. "No, it's not," Gott said, placing a hand on Rolf's shoulder. "It seems right to me. I don't know why. It didn't burn. I felt courage in knowing what I should do."

Rolf placed a hand on my shoulder. "This is ridiculous," he said. "But I agree too."

I put my other hand on Rolf, who in turn grabbed Gott, who grabbed me. "The world is ridiculous," I said. "To have such beauty and behold it not—to want more—is ridiculous. To exchange it for this." I swung my chin at our surroundings.

"But what's more is that the glory of heaven would contend for such as we. *That's* ridiculous. And yet He does."

Gott removed his hand from my shoulder and placed it on his pocket.

"Put your hand back," I said. "That's His messenger, not Him Himself. As beautiful as her eyes are, they're not a pinprick of His glory."

Gott returned his hand, and we managed a prayer of thanks. It was a good prayer, full of thanks that the glory had overcome the darkness. And it mattered not now what might happen when the great iron door buckled and came crashing inward, unleashing the judgment of God.

32

We stepped around the corner as the pounding at the door ceased. Hayner quit pontificating and wheeled toward the door. The soldiers tensed at the silence.

It occurred to me that I might want to keep my presence hidden for the time being. Gott, Rolf, and I sank into the shadows at the side of the mine and waited.

Overhead the alarm blared. Only Falke seemed unaffected as he lumbered around ten yards behind the back of the skirmish line.

Again, the giant ship's foghorn sounded. This time the blast was sustained for ten seconds and it shook the walls of the Nachthaus around us. Bits of the ceiling crashed around us. The great iron door, twisted as it was, shook in its groove. The rampart erected by Hayner's men creaked, as did the columns supporting the mine. One of the alarm lights close to the front of the mine shattered, sending electric sparks cascading to the floor. Even Falke stopped his lumbering, and his oversized head gazed around the Nachthaus.

The great bellowing welled up inside us. It began in the midsection and radiated outward until the whole body was shaking from the sound. The vials in my pack clinked together as if even they were frightened.

Then it quit. The mine fell silent except for the rhythmic cadence of the alarm, which seemed a baby bird's chirping in comparison to the foghorn. After a few seconds of silence, I heard the monstrous footsteps that always seemed to accompany the horn. They trampled outside in the forest, shaking the floor beneath our feet with each step.

The footsteps ceased and another period of silence ensued.

Hayner leapt to the top of the rampart and turned to face his men. He lifted the blade over his head and unleashed his own sustained roar in response to the horn. The bloody swastika on his forehead pulsated in the light of the alarm.

In its own way, it was an impressive response to the foghorn, and I felt tempted to embrace the pride of man.

Hayner again urged his men. "This day the horn will be silenced." Hayner's voice ramped up. "This day—"

The foghorn blasted again, annihilating Hayner's words. Hayner's mouth quit moving. He turned his head toward the door, then turned back and leapt down from the wall.

The bellow of the horn continued unabated for what seemed like a minute. Then it fell silent.

We stared at the door. There was no movement there, no probing spider legs, no fingers reaching through, searching for a grip. The scratching had stopped. The pounding had ceased, and no sound came from beyond it.

With a sudden crash, the great door buckled upon itself as if a giant finger were pressing at its center. The door sprung from its grooves and pressed inward through the mine, propelled by a bulge at its center. It scraped along the floor and the walls as it shimmied back and forth. It pressed in far enough to demolish the door control shack we had defended during the last attack. The shack dislodged from the wall, rolled over, and was pushed forward along with the door. I saw the great vine behind the bulge in the door. The shack lodged against the mine floor, and the door veered left around it, smashing into the wall. The vine retreated out of the mine, undulating like a snake.

And just like that, the great iron door of the Nachthaus was breached.

We were now exposed to the wrath of nature. The judge was at the door, and I knew He had been all the time.

The great vine whipped back into the mine at an astounding speed. It covered the distance from the opening to the rampart in a flash, before anyone had time to react.

It struck below the line of railroad ties that composed the top of the wall. The wood shattered at the point of impact, hurtling splintered shrapnel in all directions. The ties flew backward into the first line of soldiers, breaking one soldier's leg.

The vine retreated for another strike. Hayner screeched for bayonets, axes, and blades to be ready.

The vine entered the opening again like the tongue of an anteater. We were its prey, and I thought the battle was already over. The vine breached the top of the wall again and impaled a soldier, propelling him past the corner where Gott, Rolf, and I hid.

The vine slammed the soldier back and forth against the wall behind us. We ducked as the great vine worked back and forth horizontally to both sides of the mine, trying to crush anything in its path.

As before, this was not the brown, wooden type of vine I had seen pictures of. It was a verdant green, with undulating sinews beneath its moist skin, patched like the skin of snakes and covered in places with live vegetation. It struck the wall over my head, leaving a greasy residue of oily sap.

I had underestimated Hayner. He rallied the soldiers, and they hacked the vine with every bladed instrument available to them. They attacked it as a pack of wolves. As it charged one side of the mine, the soldiers dodged and ducked, while the other side hacked. The vine had been successful in killing one soldier, breaking another's leg, and reducing the height of the rampart, but in the process it was absorbing significant damage.

It dripped oily sap from several lacerations, and the mine was beginning to smell like a greenhouse again. Hayner coordinated his hacks in one region, and I saw an exposed cord running through the center of the vine. It made two more passes back and forth and then receded, this time much more slowly. I figured this was from its wounds, and not the impaled and smashed corpse of the soldier dangling from the end of the vine.

Hayner roared as the vine retreated. With the door down, I was sure his voice would carry outside to the forest. When the forest did not respond, I began to think that perhaps the pride of men would carry the day after all.

I was wrong. At the door of the mine, they assembled. There were plant-men with their bulbous heads, exposed thorns, and flytrap thoraxes, covered with rotting undergrowth from the forest, vines dangling from their open maws. There were spiders standing four feet high with clacking jaws, hairy black legs tapering down to razored feet suspended from their midsection, and a foot-and-a-half-long barbed stinger hanging below them. Roaches like those in the torture room were the frontal assault. They crawled over each other as the column began to advance.

The column moved forward through the breach at a disciplined pace, and behind them was a rearguard of the giant ape-like creatures I had seen trying to pull the door open with their hands. Their hands were disproportionately big for their bodies. The giant apes stood nine or ten feet tall, and their hands dragged the ground as if it were more comfortable to drag them than hold them up. Each finger must have been a foot long. The apes roared as they entered, exposing a set of dagger-like teeth.

There were bears, crocodiles, lions, packs of wolves, and birds of prey. It was as if Noah had saved them all for a time such as this.

Hayner steadied his troops. "Ready firearms! Shoot on my command." The rampart had been reduced by the vine to the height of Hayner's waist. The front line of soldiers was bent over it, guns aimed at the advancing column. The second line stood behind the first, with a third line of rifles behind them, with the rest of us bringing up the rear.

Hayner removed himself to the third line. "On my command, we'll shoot them down like the beasts they are," Hayner said. "This is the day of men. Hold fast, meine Brüder!"

The column advanced with discipline. The front was now even with the great iron door as it lay against the side of the mine. I wondered how long Hayner would wait before giving the order to fire.

The column was yards in front of the bulwark when it halted. I could see through the breached door that the column of Nature's army stretched out the front of the Nachthaus with no end in sight. Gott was correct. We had no chance against these numbers. Hayner, however, still seemed confident.

In the flashing of the alarm lights, we could see those who stood arrayed against us. The roaches' antennae swayed back and forth, the plant-men were whipping and howling. They all stood awaiting something, I supposed. But what?

Perhaps it was one final opportunity extended to the world of men in order that they might awaken. Perhaps the sight of tooth, claw, fang, and mandible were meant to shake man from his sinful stupor. We stared at each other: man and beast, man and nature, neither side blinking.

Hayner arose from behind the third line with a bottle in his hand, a rag protruding from the spout. He lit the rag and a flame engulfed it. He threw the bottle over the column. At the same time, two other things happened: two soldiers next to Hayner depressed plungers, and the great foghorn sounded.

33

The kingdom of men had refused the final offer of harmony from nature. When the foghorn sounded, the roaches rushed the waist-high earthen and wood wall erected by the soldiers. Half of them took flight toward us, the buzzing of their wings drowning the sound of the alarm.

Hayner's firebomb struck the ground in the middle of the advancing column. The Germans had laced the mine with fuel oil, and the whole of the Nachthaus became an inferno. Fire raced across the floor in all directions and scaled the walls. The flames rushed all the way to the rampart, where it halted in front of the Nazis.

The Germans had also placed incendiary bombs at the entrance to the mine and back along the walls to a depth of 25 feet. The soldiers operating the plungers had timed the strike perfectly, and the resulting firestorm engulfed the mine. The explosion incinerated everything in its path, blasting out the mouth of the Nachthaus like a dragon spewing forth its fiery breath. We ducked as the concussion of heated air blasted over us.

The plant-men took the worst of the blast, their vegetative bodies vaporizing in the conflagration. Their wild cries erupted one moment and silenced the next. Their vines caught fire and appeared as sparklers as they whipped in and out of their mouths while the bodies burned away.

One of the spiders, its legs and torso ablaze, scaled the wall and reached the ceiling. It hung like a chandelier lighting the carnage beneath it, spewing filaments of fiery webbing onto the burning column.

The ambush created a bonfire at the entrance to the Nachthaus. I couldn't see how far outside the fire had reached, but inside it was devastating. The entire enemy column had been destroyed or was perishing in fire. The odor of burning flesh and plant matter was nauseous, and several of the soldiers vomited. I chose to watch the spectacle from around the corner to the alcoves, where the air was fresh in comparison.

The roaches had escaped the blast and firebomb in their initial charge. The flying roaches sailed over the wall as we had ducked the heat of the blast, and they were into the second line of soldiers before a shot could be fired. They inflicted two or three casualties due to the swiftness and surprise of their attack—the Nazis had not counted on them flying—but were cut off from the decimated column and were quickly dispatched.

Hayner shouted a victory cry and leapt onto the wall to meet the charge of the ground roaches. The first one to the wall soared at Hayner. Hayner caught it in midair, rammed his fist through its torso, and ripped it in half. He screeched, threw its severed halves against the side walls, and challenged the remaining roaches.

The pythons shot out of him, hissing. The roaches hit the wall in unison, scaling it with their taloned feet. Hayner smashed one, stomping it behind the head. It splattered against the front of the rampart. He grabbed another by the mandibles, ripping them apart and off the roach's head with a vicious sideways pull.

The rest were over the wall in an instant. But, cut off from support of the vanished column, they were destroyed by the waiting soldiers, who clubbed them to a pulp with the butts of their guns.

The front of the mine was a firestorm, and nature was ablaze. It writhed in agony and, outside, the wolves howled and the forest moaned. A cloud of smoke permeated the mine. We had lost three men. Nature had lost its entire column.

Hayner ordered the box fans engaged. The fans had been wired into the electric cable on the ceiling powering the lights, and the fans were placed in front of the wall. The smoke from the fire and incendiaries was increasing, now that the victims were beginning to smolder. The fan blades rotated slowly at first and then picked up speed. The smoke wafted toward and then through the entrance to the Nachthaus.

Hayner addressed his men against the backdrop of smoke and fire. His swastika had clotted over, and it now appeared to protrude from his head with an eerie three-dimensional effect. One of the pythons was licking it. "Yes, my brethren, as I have prophesied, the world belongs to men. We are its masters, you and I. We take when we see fit. We give out of a position of strength, never as the compelled."

I surveyed the scene ahead. The smoldering remains of nature lay before me as far as I could see, even out the entrance to the Nachthaus. How could I have been so wrong? Was man's *will to power* the final arbiter of the Nachthaus? It hadn't seemed possible moments before, yet what my eyes now saw said differently. Where was the judge at the door?

My fears and insecurities of this world beset me like a swarm of lost souls. I was in a dream and unable to run from them. They would encircle me and drag me down into their unholy slumber.

What if there was no judge? What if the Nachthaus were not evil, but existence? What if it was all there was? This world, nothing more, its good and evil nevermore, or simply never.

What if Hayner's ethic were not an ethic but a description of reality? A state of affairs. What if it were like gravity, energy, matter, time, space? Brute facts that simply *are,* with no arbiter, moderator, or ultimate judge.

The Nachthaus pressed against me, the mountain weighing down upon me. I felt the urge to sleep, to remove myself from Hamlet's crushing thought: *for there is nothing either good or bad, but thinking makes it so.* Indeed, the Nachthaus would be a prison, or more so, an outpost—an outpost of wickedness.

I saw the alcove cages. There had been flesh and blood people in those cages who had been sent to the torture rooms and the inferno. There had been the most beautiful creature I would ever lay eyes upon, with eyes of galaxies. All snuffed out under the ethic of men. How could it be that this was not evil? That it was the outworking of natural causes alone assaulted my most base intuitions. Deceit, lust, greed, murder, hate, rape, torture, pride—could they be the amoral byproduct of the Nachthaus with no ultimate distinction from love, joy, peace, patience, kindness, goodness, faithfulness, gentleness, and self-control?

But how not? The kingdom of man had prevailed, and there was no fit arbiter among us.

Sleep, my Adam, in the arms of your love.

I stumbled back around the corner, sideswiping Gott and Rolf, who didn't seem to notice. They were staring at the carnage, entranced by Hayner's ongoing speech.

"Who is judge but us, my brethren?" Hayner screeched. "Man is the measure of all things!"

The foghorn blasted again. Forms began to appear in the smoke at the entrance to the Nachthaus. This time they were not marching with discipline, it was an all-out frontal assault.

"*Deus et natua non faciunt frusta. Ex malo bonum,*" I said. The words barely came out, but they came. I whispered, though I was trying to scream. "God and nature do not work together in vain. Out of evil, good comes."

This time I added to the phrase. I was getting closer to a solution to Epicurus' riddle: "Evil exists; therefore, God exists. Evil exists; therefore, hope exists." Evil did exist, after all, and it would be a silly shell game to think it didn't. The judge was at the door.

We saw them coming through the smoke. They came, all creatures great and small. They came as a mighty army with banners unfurled pouring through the opening of the Nachthaus. They roared through the smoke as if reality had shown itself to the dream. They came, one and all: wolf, bear, ram, roach, wild boar, raven.

The Nazis froze. I suspect they realized at the last that the kingdom of men was founded on shifting sands, that those who wished to rule would find themselves in a universe that did not care.

Hayner snapped out of it first and ordered the first volley. The front line of rifles fired from behind the wall, and the charging animals were cut down next to the great iron door, which still rested against the wall of the mine. They slammed hard into the floor of the mine.

The charging beasts behind them leapt over their dying comrades and continued at full speed. The second line of Nazis fired, and the front line of invaders was again destroyed.

The enemy line had moved forward ten yards by the time the third line of Nazis fired. Hayner blasted a raven from the air with his pistol and ordered his entire contingent of soldiers to fire at will.

Gunfire rang in the Nachthaus. The Nazis displayed deadly aim in the tight quarters, and they inflicted heavy casualties on the invaders. The bodies began to pile up, and soon it was difficult to secure a good aim as the animals were crawling in, around, and over the bodies of the slain. The mine was now flowing with blood, and the attackers splashed through it as they approached.

It appeared the Nazis might win another battle until a colony of bats swooped in. The bats honed in on the Germans, flying in by the hundreds. The Germans were powerless to shoot them all, firing sporadically into the air. Bullets ricocheted off the ceiling, and the bats dove into the crowd of Nazis, landing on their heads, biting their ears and noses.

With the gunfire disrupted, nature renewed its charge. Plant-men poured over the wall, howling wildly: *Wooooooooooooooooooo! Wooooooooooooooooooo! Wooooooooooooooooo!* Their thorny appendages lashed out in all directions. Their vines shot out their mouths, circling around soldiers' necks, tightening like constricting snakes. Their Venus flytrap midsections opened, revealing a pink lining dripping with sap. The vines constricted and pulled the soldiers close and, when the soldiers blacked out, the flytrap jaws closed over them.

Hayner ordered a general retreat, and the men fell back to the cache of hand weapons and torches. Hayner organized the remaining two lines of firearms, instructing them to fix bayonets, while the torches were lit and the weapons were distributed to the rest of the soldiers.

At last, Hayner spied me lingering around the corner of the alcove cave. The pythons surged to the corner and hovered in front of my face, tongues darting, eyes compressed, and nostrils flaring. "You're next, Sascha, after I dispose of these vermin." Hayner returned to the battle and the pythons shot back to the front, though I noticed from that moment forward they kept an eye on me.

Falke lumbered past me and trundled down the wooden pier in front of the alcoves, flamethrower in tow. "Best to come with me," he said.

Another swarm of roaches poured over the wall and advanced on the soldiers. The soldiers fired away, splattering the bugs, but it took several bullets per bug. Hayner was occupied readying his reserve unit, and without his guidance the soldiers had drained their supply of firearm ammo.

The plant-men mounted another charge and were atop the first line of gunners. I sensed the battle turning and noted another column of attackers massing at the front door. The second line of gunners retreated to the back line, bayonets at the ready. Hayner ordered the lit torches tossed onto the plant-men, and they went up in flames howling.

Hayner tossed a lit torch to Gott, who caught it effortlessly. He flung a shovel to Rolf, and to me, a trowel. I inspected the tiny instrument, chuckling to myself.

As Hayner ordered a full-scale retreat to the intersection, the great vine emerged in front of the massing column at the front door. It whipped back and forth across the mine as if counting its dead.

The soldiers filed past us at double speed and caught Falke at the intersection, where they assembled inside the passage leading to the lab. There were around fifty left.

Hayner met Gott, Rolf, and me at the corner. "This will be the last charge," he said, looking back at the door. "Everything's as it should be."

He placed a firm grip on my shoulder and squeezed. It should have hurt, but I couldn't concentrate on anything but the swastika on his forehead. It was healed, and had somehow become part of him. The two veins in his scalp had joined with it and his blood coursed through it naturally. It pulsated in concert with his expressions.

I thought of the plant warrior corpse I'd seen with the swastika carved in its head. If Hayner were to fall, would we later meet a muscular Pflanzen-Krieger wearing his uniform?

"I'd die for my country and mankind here today, if I were you," Hayner said to me. He released my shoulders and set off down the pier toward the intersection. He had made it to the end when the great vine shot forward, heading right at us.

34

We stomped down the pier as fast as we could go, Gott outdistancing Rolf and me easily. By the time we reached the middle alcove, the vine had reached the corner and made the turn. I urged Rolf ahead.

When the vine turned into the alcove passageway, it entered beneath the pier and shred the wood to bits as it pursued us. The planks splintered into the air one after another in all directions as it came toward us. It was closing fast, and by the time we reached the third alcove it was only ten feet behind us.

The splintering wood hit me in the back as I reached the last plank of the pier. The vine would be inches behind me. I dove from the last plank, expecting the vine to impale me in midair.

The last plank shattered, raining splinters down upon me as I hit the ground. Vials in my pack clinked together, out of reach of the vine. I rolled left as I hit the floor, and the vine shot past me into the line of soldiers in the passageway leading to the lab.

Falke blasted it head-on with the flamethrower, and the vine recoiled back down the alcove passage, still burning at its tip. It whipped around the corner leading out of the Nachthaus. There were a few moments of respite before the next line of attackers, fronted by rams and wild boars, charged into the alcove hallway.

I rose and darted for the protection of the passageway. I pushed through the line of Nazis and made my way down into the darkness behind the lines. There were two more plungers. The Nazis had rigged the alcove to blow.

"Best to come with me," Falke said again, lumbering by.

Hayner gave the order, and the plungers plunged. This time, though, the timing was off and the front guard made it through the ambush. All the rams and boars made it through unscathed, along with a pack of wolves, three plant-men, and a bear.

The firebombs ripped through the alcove corridor. It was a more compressed space than the open mine, and the resulting heat incinerated every creature left inside. Several fuel drums planted by the Nazis in the alcoves exploded. The hall would be impassible for a while.

The rams crashed into the line like a tsunami of horns. I ran farther into the passageway, my wounds aggravated by the dive to avoid the vine. Gott and Rolf followed.

The rams decimated the first line of Nazis, breaking legs, kneecaps, and shins. I estimated twenty men were crushed in their initial charge and lay maimed on the mine's floor. The wild boars had pounced with surprising speed, gashing and slashing with their tusks. The wolves feasted on the wounded, ripping at them with bared teeth.

The rams, boars, and wolves might have killed them all, but they clogged up in the passageway. One boar gored its fellow, two of the rams interlocked horns, and the element of surprise was lost. The men regrouped and hacked the pack with bayonets and assorted hand weapons until the animals collapsed.

Amid all the confusion, I saw Hayner locked in a struggle with the three Pflanzen-Kriegerin and the bear. The plant-men had him cornered against the wall, in front of the dying boar. Their flytraps opened and they approached, vines flagellating, thorns exposed.

Hayner caught the first vine an inch from his neck and twisted his hand around it, making a fist. He jerked the plant-man forward like it was a 98-pound weakling and smashed its bulbous head with his other fist. The thing's head exploded, spurting juice all the way across the passage.

He dropped the vine and sent a right cross into the second plant-man's mouth. His fist rammed through its mouth and out the back of its head. The plant-man collapsed. One of Hayner's soldiers cleaved half of the third plant-man's head from behind.

Then Hayner's pythons erupted from his chest. He rushed the bear. With a screech, he grabbed the bear's right wrist with both hands and twisted it until the bear's arm snapped. The bear roared with pain and slashed Hayner across the chest with its other paw. Four gashes opened on Hayner's chest from his right armpit to his left hip.

The bear bared its teeth and lunged, jaws snapping around Hayner's head. He ducked and jabbed the bear's broken arm. The bear recoiled, allowing Hayner to close behind it. He jumped on its back, slid an arm around its neck, and pulled backward. The pythons coiled around the bear and began constricting.

The bear staggered into the intersection under the light. It rammed backward, smashing Hayner against the wall. Hayner sank the hook in tighter under the bear's neck. For a moment, I thought I saw the swastika light up. Hayner gave a final lurch and the bear's neck snapped. It swayed, wobbled a moment, and collapsed.

It was enough for me. My body ached. We were down to twenty or thirty men, and the fire up ahead in the alcoves was dissipating. The alarm had even burned out. Unless the Nazis had another trick, they were doomed in the next rush. I called for Gott and Rolf, and we started to make our way to the lab.

Two-thirds of the way down to the lab we caught up with Falke. Behind us, the last charge had commenced and we heard the clash of claw and fang against bayonet, hoe, shovel, and axe. It would be a rout.

"The Standartenführer will be along soon," Falke said. "You could try to lock him out of the lab, but I doubt it would work for you."

We slowed to Falke's pace, which was a relief for my bruised gut and punctured chest. He trudged along at the same pace as always: comforting in some ways, unsettling in others.

"How would you know this?" I asked.

"I've seen it repeated enough."

I strained to see Falke's face so I could measure his words. I could make out the outline of his butterknife nose, but that was all.

"You're confounded, I see," Falke said, his arm free of the flamethrower rocking back and forth with his gait like a pendulum. "The Standartenführer will be along right on time. Best to come with me. The Standartenführer doesn't like to be kept waiting."

"How long have you been here, Falke?" I asked.

"Long enough, sir."

With that, we were at the outer door of the lab and oven complex.

Hayner rushed up alongside us. "Mach schnell! They're coming, and we've got to bar the door!"

We barred the door and slid as much furniture and fixtures in front of it as we could.

It seemed a silly gesture—the scratching began almost instantly once the door was barred. Whatever was out there would enter when it desired to. I reckoned it would enter right on time.

Gott, Rolf, and I sat with our backs to the inferno, under one of its glass slit eyes. The philosopher face stared back at us, its lines a bit more faint than the last time I had seen it. Hayner paced in front of us, rehashing the battle and priming for his next move. Falke stood at the far end of the oven by the corner that led to the lab.

"What now, Hayner?" I asked.

Rolf shuffled next to me, his eyes shifting beneath his goggles. Gott cautioned me with an open hand. I waved him off.

Hayner stopped pacing. "We wait, Leutnant. We wait until the vermin tire and leave. Then we walk up front, kill whatever stragglers there are along the way, mend the door, and call for reinforcements."

"Rolf, could you get us some food and something to drink?" I asked.

Rolf seemed happy to get away from Hayner. He sprang up and strode off in the direction of the lab.

"I think I'd like to help him," Gott said. He waited for approval, which I granted, and then followed Rolf.

Hayner stooped down in front of me. "Now that your lackeys are gone, schoolboy, what did you have in mind?"

"I'd like us to take a walk," I said. I nodded at the philosopher-face. "You and me."

Hayner eyed the wall, then turned back to me, swastika gleaming. "Do you think I'm naïve, schoolboy?"

"It's a test of courage, Standartenführer. Not worldliness."

Hayner scoffed. "It's foolishness, Sascha. This is your weakness." He held his palms out in front of him, gesturing. "Stories, myths, gods, religions, moral sensitivities . . . all weakness. The Nachthaus is rock, Sascha. Firm." Hayner slapped his palms on the floor for emphasis. "Do you see it? We have a structure here. A hierarchy." Hayner stretched out his palms again. "A man's worth is defined by his relation to others. I tell men to go, and they go. I tell men to do, and they do. That's reality. That's all the right and wrong that exists."

I spit on the side of the inferno. "That's a devil's hierarchy and a devil's ethic."

"You say that because of your status in the hierarchy," Hayner said. "You say that because you resent being told what to do."

"Then you're saying you resent God because He tells you what to do." I couldn't resist a wry grin. I took note of my resistance and figured I'd better think later on what that meant in relation to Hayner's hierarchical theory. I had resented the Nazis. That much was true.

"God," Hayner said. He floated his hands in the air around his head. "Dreamy. Ephemeral. The hope of those at the bottom of the hierarchy." He pounded the floor. "Real. Now. Tangible. That's what counts."

I pointed at the philosopher's face. "He's made of rock," I said. "The rock you say is real and solid. So why do you fear?"

Hayner threw his chest out, and I knew I had him. He offered me a hand and lifted me up. "I still intend to strangle you once we get out of here," he said. "No magician's trick will change that."

I ushered Hayner over to the face and invited him to touch it. He did not hesitate, placing his hand on the face's mouth.

Nothing happened. Hayner stared at me, grinning. "Poor schoolboy."

I wasn't sure why. Maybe the face didn't like Hayner. Maybe it had nothing to say to him. Maybe he was too far gone.

I grabbed Hayner's wrist.

Gott chimed in from the corner by the lab. "You sure you want to do that, Leutnant?"

"*Ober*leutnant." I looked dead at Hayner. "I'm sure."

I placed my hand on the face.

35

Hayner and I found ourselves back in the valley surrounded by hills we could not climb. The crag stood before us, and we knew there was no sense in attempting to scale it. Our own weight doomed us to the valley. We would wander it forever, were there not someone back at the Nachthaus to knock us off the wall.

Hayner had changed. He was a weakling here now. He still had the swastika, but his powerful frame had shrunk. He was emaciated and under five feet tall. The pythons were tiny black filaments waving around his eyes.

My nose quit throbbing. I reached to touch it, tentatively, discovering it was no longer broken. I slid my hands down to my cheek—no laceration. My earlobe was back. The puncture wound in my chest had disappeared. My gut was not bruised.

Not only was my gut not bruised, it was sculpted muscle. I held my arms out straight, admiring the chiseled curvature they now possessed. Energy flooded my body as if I had jumpstarted an internal dynamo.

The surge of power intoxicated me, and I beheld Hayner with disgust. His shriveled form inched away from me, backing step by step until he reached the crag at the center of the valley. His shrunken head darted back and forth, apparently seeking a route of escape.

I was on him in an instant. "How does it feel, little man?"

Hayner cowered, holding his arms in front of his face.

I slapped him. A welt developed on his cheek. "How does it feel, little man?"

Hayner darted to the left, but made it only a step away before I grabbed him. My new body was undeniable. I sensed it wasn't the body, however. It was my being. Somehow it had amplified in this space. The body was the outward representation of my will.

I lifted the puny worm by the back of the neck, squeezing hard enough to make him squeal, but not hard enough to break him. His bones squeaked and ground under the power of my grip. The power was glorious, my will unrestrained.

I drank the power deep. It was ambrosia and I would never have my fill. I was man, and man was the measure of all things.

I slammed Hayner's face into the crag, breaking his nose, which bled profusely. His blood splattered on the crag, and it appeared to me as a rosebush, a cultivated thing of wild beauty.

I was the measure of all things in this valley. Here I could create a paradise. I would create a paradise out of this horrid valley, a paradise where goodness reigned and evil was banished, and nothing could prevent me from willing it.

But evil would need to be banished, so I entered the door as judge. I lifted Hayner to my face, for I wished him to know the reason he was about to die.

"Evil must be destroyed," I said, and I increased the pressure on his neck. Hayner's withered body writhed and flopped in the air below my grip.

I was about to close my fist around his neck when someone shouted for me to stop. I turned to see Gott approaching. He seemed to glide across the wasteland of the valley.

He was in front of me in moments, and I relaxed my grip on Hayner. Hayner gasped for air.

"You must not do this," Gott said.

I presumed Gott didn't recognize me in my new form. "It's me, Gott. Things will be different now. We can make our own world here. I can see to it. We'll construct a new and beautiful Nachthaus, one of our own choosing. One of great splendor."

"I know, Oberleutnant," Gott said, "that's what frightens me. Men are not capable of such things."

"You don't understand," I said. "I can do as I will here."

Gott backed up. It was so slight that if I had not had my new form, I wouldn't have noticed it. "That's the problem, sir."

I lunged at him. Even with his grace, Gott was powerless to evade my grasp. I lifted him to my face. "Evidently you're a problem, Obergrenadier," I said. "And all problems must be dealt with. Hayner's a lost cause, but perhaps we can reclaim the likes of you, Gott."

I closed my eyes and began to envision. At first it was a pinprick of light in the recess of my mind, but it grew, slowly at first, into an ever-increasing glow. Before long, it was roaring in my imagination. I opened my eyes, and a flaming pit of fire was cut into the valley floor at my feet.

I held Gott out over the pit. His legs spasmed from the heat of the inferno. He pleaded with me. "You must not do this."

"You may join me, Gott." I pleaded with him. "You know how much I loved you, Gott. Why would you force me to do this?"

"Don't you remember the gypsy girl's pledge, Oberleutnant? We were pledged to help the helpless." The flames licked at Gott's feet. He was showing visible signs of succumbing to the heat.

"But that's what I'm doing," I said. "Helping the help-less. Building a new world without the likes of him." I cocked my head at Hayner.

"It won't work!" Gott screamed the words at me through his pain.

I screeched at him. "How can you say that? I'm good, Gott!" My mind flared like the pit of flames below me. "You're jealous that I have power. You speak as a man that resents his master! You'd not do the good I intend!"

Gott seemed to be on his last breath. He choked his words out. "Take a look at yourself, Oberleutnant. It won't work."

Gott held up the gypsy girl's sphere, and I saw my reflection in it.

My sinful nature stared back at me in the reflection from the sphere. It was grotesque. The features of my face were recognizable, but they were misshapen and malformed. My eyes were greedy orbs of pride. My tongue slithered out of my mouth, setting all it touched on fire. My hands grabbed and seized and clutched, ever desiring, never satisfied.

My heart was an onyx stone, cold and hard, deceitful above all things. Who could trust it? My appetites swirled within me, lusting. My spirit despised and hated. And my sinful nature had disguised itself in a cloak of goodness.

36

I awoke on the floor of the Nachthaus, sprawled out in front of the inferno. Gott was lying to my left, Hayner to my right. Rolf stood over me. When I composed myself, I realized he was asking me if I was hurt.

I turned toward Hayner and he cringed, sliding back on his rear end with his hands in front of his face as fast as he could. Gott must have touched the face, and Rolf had then pushed us all off the wall.

I turned the other direction and reached for Gott, asking him if he was injured. He was inspecting his feet and legs. "Would you mind not doing that again, Oberleutnant?" Gott said. His eyes let me know he understood. I apologized to him anyway and he waved me off.

"Magician's tricks." He was Hayner again, and he was standing over me. The aftershock of the vision was gone. "A test of courage indeed. But I have a *real* pit of fire awaiting you, schoolboy."

My nose began to throb, and my body reverted to the cache of numb pain it had been before I'd touched the face. I wanted to sleep. I muttered to myself, "It won't work. It couldn't work. How could I have not seen it all this time? I deserve whatever happens to me, and anything that doesn't happen to me is a matter of grace and mercy." I looked back at Hayner. "Do what you will. I'm not afraid anymore. I wasn't afraid before, because I was dreaming. I'm not afraid now, because I'm awake. God forgive me."

Rolf bent down over Gott and me and grabbed our shoulders, smiling the smile of one content in the fulfillment of his duty. We grabbed his and each other's shoulders. We held our grip there for a moment. I'm sure each of us expected it to be the last time, and we had accepted it. Our destiny with the inferno awaited. Three young men cast into the furnace.

Hayner broke the embrace by jerking me to my feet, lifting me by my neck. His grip was stout, and I could feel my vertebrae shifting beneath his grasp. I didn't resist. It felt good to let go, to hang there, knowing I was held by a larger set of hands— hands infinitely more powerful than Hayner's, and hands that cared for me despite what I had seen in the Nachthaus. Despite what I had done.

"What are you blabbing about now, school—" Hayner's rhetorical query was interrupted by a slam at the door.

The judge was at the door, and our barricade could not hope to deter him.

Falke trudged over from his post by the lab and took up a position at the door to the inferno. "They'll be along now soon," he said. "Best get prepared. The judge will not be kept waiting. He's always right on time."

"Why, you insolent whelp!" Hayner launched an uppercut at Falke.

Falke caught Hayner's fist in front of his collarbone. Falke paused, holding the fist, perhaps squeezing a bit, judging by the look on Hayner's face. "You know better than that, Standartenführer," he said, and then released the fist.

Hayner sulked away and rummaged through the barricade for a weapon.

Gott and Rolf and I smiled, and turned toward the door to see what might come next.

37

The barricade against the door rattled as the pounding outside began. Final things were here, and I welcomed them. My body ached and I could not heal it. I was exhausted but could not sleep.

Hayner discovered a steel pipe in the barricade pile and retrieved it, taking a few practice swings. He positioned himself ten feet in front of the door, pythons out. He seemed enthusiastic for another fight.

We stood by the oven door, the three of us in a line, me still with my full pack across my shoulder. Falke stood behind us.

The inferno waited to our left, its door yawning open. Its deterioration had increased in both scope and effect. There was not a square foot of the wall that was without structural failure. The floor was littered with refractory material. The inferno was not just wrinkled now, not just old; it was decrepit. I didn't think it could stand another blast, but I knew it would collapse yet desiring to burn.

The pounding at the door continued, and then the latch failed. The door pushed open a few inches with the barricade restraining it. The door pounded back and forth against the junk stacked in front of it. Two more pounds at the door rotated the barricade sideways, where it tipped over and spilled to the floor.

A horde of plant-men entered two by two through the door. They swarmed into the lab complex like an invasive plant species into a pristine lake.

Hayner burst the first plant-man's bulbous head with the pipe. He pivoted and disabled a second and a third before retreating a step. Hayner might hold them off indefinitely if there weren't so many.

Hayner swatted away a couple of thorn-studded stem thrusts, and then blasted a bulbous head and struck another in its flytrap thorax. The pipe lodged a second before Hayner pulled it free, but that was enough time for three vines to wrap around it.

The vines contracted, ripping the pipe from Hayner. Hayner dove backward to avoid another set of thorns.

"Is our pledge fulfilled, Oberleutnant?" Gott asked.

"I'd say so, Obergrenadier."

Gott, Rolf, and I stepped into the oven. Hayner retreated to the oven door and braced for a final stand next to Falke. He was having success in fending the plant-men off by grabbing their vines and ripping them out of their heads or eluding their thorny swings and ripping their arms off.

The plant-men spilled into the oven after us with their wild *Woooooooooooooooooooooooooo* howling. The sound was deafening in the oven, and the speed of the plant-men caught us off guard. Before we could retreat they were behind us. It was a horrible error in judgment brought on by cockiness, and we were no longer smiling.

The plant-men closed in upon us, flytraps opening. We stood back-to-back-to-back in the center of the inferno. I had figured to die here, but in fire, not in the clutches of a plant-man. Sap oozed from their traps.

Gott erupted in pain. "Ahhhhhh!"

I looked down to see him grasping his leg. But he wasn't grasping his leg in pain—he had reached into his pocket and brought out the gypsy girl's sphere. He tossed it to me and I held it aloft.

The plant-men froze as the sphere burst into a galaxy of light rotating around the inferno. The light accentuated the oven's deterioration, and I saw its dark soul rotting away from the ravages of its sin. The furnace was rotting from within.

A vine coiled around my wrist and ripped the sphere from my grasp. The sphere went out and flew into the corner of the inferno, where it came to rest on the floor. Rolf dove for it and was struck down by three vines. The plant-men pounced on him.

A vine coiled around my neck and constricted. Two more grabbed me, one on each arm, and pulled me forward. I saw a flytrap open in front of me and I was carried toward it. My air was gone, my lungs burned, and my head began to reel. I fought for air, even breathing through my broken nose.

I felt my legs elevate. The horde of plant-men were feeding me to their partner. My head entered the trap, and it closed around my shoulders.

The pulp was tepid and juicy on my cheeks as I slid in. The sap burned my skin and the inside of my mouth. I saw the digestive juices bubble up from the gullet at the center of the trap.

As I began to pass out, I tried to reconcile myself to my fate. The judge would soon be at the door of my life, and then there would be no excuses of evil, but only what I had done in the face of it. Had I done enough with the time allotted to me? Had I honored my faith by resisting the evil around me? Had I honored the One who had died that I might wake from my sinful slumber?

In those last seconds I saw that the greatest evil that had ever occurred was also the greatest good: *God made Him who had no sin to be sin for us, so that in Him we might become the righteousness of God.* That we might see where we once were blind. That we might wake where we once were asleep in the arms of the prince of the power of the air, and in the Nachthaus. *Ex malo Bonum.*

I felt the vine torn from my neck. It left a rope burn from its recoil. I was yanked backward and found myself on the floor of the oven. I sucked in a putrid gasp of air, which reeked of compost. I retched a ball of sap from my throat and breathed again.

Falke had three plant-men in his left hand and me in his right. His left foot pinned two more and he had shielded an opening to the control room door with his massive frame. Gott and Rolf called to me from behind the door.

"Your time is not now, Sascha, and no one may go before his time," Falke said. Vines were coiling around every available inch of his six-foot-eleven height, around his arms, neck, legs, knees, ankles, even around the flamethrower. He was covered in thorns as if he had fallen into a briar patch.

"Come with us, Falke," I said, slapping a vine away from me.

"You know better than that, sir."

"Falke—"

"For everything there is a time, Sacha." Falke nodded toward the control room. "Don't keep them waiting."

I took Falke's hand—his wrist was swamped by vines. "Thank you, Adalbert." I thought he smiled, but I wasn't sure.

Falke's bulk held off the plant-men long enough for me to get through the control room door ahead of swatting thorns and whipping vines. The last thing I saw before closing the door was Hayner's hand smashing a plant-man's head outside the oven door. Then they fell upon him.

I shut the door, hit the latch, and slid the bar in place.

38

"How long will the door hold?" Rolf asked. He was tinkering with the controls to the oven. There was a scratching at the door from a thousand thorns.

"I'm more worried about how long *I* can hold up." I had added plant-men vine and sap burns to my collection of ailments. "Leave those controls alone. We're not firing the oven."

They looked at me with disbelief, but I knew they knew we wouldn't fire the inferno. It wasn't right. We had killed enough plant-men and animals, creatures only following their instinctual instructions. The creation always does what it is told. It has no obey or disobey paradox. It is only man who disobeys.

"We'll leave them be," I said.

Rolf disengaged the oven.

"What about Hayner?" Gott asked.

I shook my head, telling them what I had seen while closing the door. As if to confirm the story, we could hear scratching through the door.

"Can we go, then?" Gott asked. "We've fulfilled our pledge, right?"

We had fulfilled our pledge. I was proud of Gott and Rolf for not shirking in the midst of such evils. Somehow, that made everything mean more. They had been tested with fire and had persevered. They had overcome.

The time of testing is at hand. To him that overcomes . . .

"Can we?" Rolf asked.

"Yes," I said. "Let's go. Our work here is through."

We gathered 'round with our arms on our shoulders again, rejoicing in the iron bond that had formed between us in such a brief time, and the bond we had formed with our Creator. We held it for a moment, relishing it, and then walked around the corner of the control area and down past the generator sitting on its I-beams.

Gott reached the wall first, where the generator exhaust pipes entered. He removed a façade from the wall below the pipes and set it to the side, exposing a tunnel big enough to allow even a large man easy passage.

Mirka stepped out through the hole in the wall.

I pushed by Rolf and caught her in my arms, lifting her in the air. "You waited?" I kissed her before she could answer.

"No, I came back," she said. "I got everyone out as you asked, but I couldn't leave you here."

I kissed her again. "You came back!"

I had discovered the tunnel by what some would call accident, by what others would call coincidence, and by what I know was Providence. While we'd been purging the fuel lines before welding, Rolf had dropped his hammer on my toe, and in my anger I had cast the hammer against the wall, under the piping. A large rock had dislodged from its mooring, and we had discovered the tunnel.

In the end, I saw that I had not thrown the hammer with extra power from the Nachthaus in my rage. I had thrown the hammer meaning it for evil, but God had meant it for good. *Ex malo bonum.*

The engineers who had created the crazy and dysfunctional operational system for the oven had evidently commissioned the tunnel for the generator exhaust and oven cooling system piping. It followed a direct and easily traversed route where it joined with a natural cave and led to the surface.

Gott, Rolf, and I had removed the rest of the false front, explored the tunnel, and later fashioned a façade to hide it from the Nazis.

In our discovery, our three-way pact had manifested itself. We had stood by and watched the gypsy girl and her companion perish in the inferno. But that had been the last.

We had saved them, one and all, ushering the condemned out of the inferno, through the control room, and out the tunnel before the furnace had fired. They had wept with joy as it occurred to them they were rescued. They had hugged Rolf and Gott, blessing them even as they disappeared down the tunnel.

We camouflaged our deception by frontloading the control room with plant-men from the lab cold locker, enough to make the ashen remains plausible to the Nazis upon inspection. Once or twice, a plant-man, no longer frozen, had reanimated in the oven, strengthening the illusion. One of them I had seen pounding the glass slit eyes of the inferno before incinerating.

The captive who was shot trying to fight his way out of the oven was unfortunate, but it had provided the final validation of the illusion to Hayner. When I'd kicked around in the ash and found the bullet still there on the floor of the oven, whatever latent or buried suspicion he may have had was erased.

We had saved them all. We had honored our pledge. And, as we walked out of the oven control room and into the tunnel, I wished we had been given more time to save more. But I knew better than that. We seized the time that had been given us, and we had confronted the evil in front of us.

We paused inside the tunnel: Mirka, Gott, Rolf, and me. We took one last look at the other message I had left on the walls of the Nachthaus:

And that, knowing the time, that now it is high time to awake out of sleep: for now is our salvation nearer than when we believed. The night is far spent, the day is at hand: let us therefore cast off the works of darkness, and let us put on the armor of light.

39

The mouth of the cave was not much bigger than a man's body, and I had to push my pack through it before exiting. I scratched my shoulders against its sides crawling through. It was obscured by the forest undergrowth, and though our freed captives trampled the ground coming through, I had trouble locating the cave entrance once outside, though I knew right where it was.

The trampled undergrowth was the last I ever saw of the captives, with a few exceptions. I trust the forest ensured their safe passage out, perhaps to Ploiesti, maybe down to the Mediterranean or the Black Sea, where they booked travel on a freighter to a long and productive life. I don't know, but that's my hope and the way I like to think of it.

I wanted nothing more than to find a cool patch of grass under a welcoming tree—preferably one without vines. My body and my mind yearned for release, but a greater desire to distance us from the Nachthaus competed with the urge for sleep. And the forest was still foreboding and I wasn't certain I could find a welcoming tree without vines, without plant-men, without marauding insects.

The gloom permeating the forest hung thick. The forest still moaned. The eternal twilight still reigned. It felt odd to be outside again, without walls. Something was watching us, or *somethings* were watching us. We were helpless out here, defenseless, at something's mercy.

The four of us walked on a path between the mountain and the perimeter of the forest, the barren rock on one side and the teeming wildness on another. We trusted neither and we were caught in between. The way was easy, without roadblocks, without adversity, and we were a mile or two along the base of the mountain before we stopped to rest.

We sat on the path, as there was no need for shade. We chose a spot where the path rose at a sharp incline and rested with our backs to the rise. We were defenseless, but hadn't we always been? I had been in Hayner's grasp, had been unable to prevent the inferno from firing, had been at the mercy of the invading forest. It was always and only grace and mercy that kept us from the evil.

I fell asleep with these thoughts, my Mirka nestled into my shoulder.

Gott rousted me from sleep. He told me I had been out for hours. I was lying next to the path with my back to the incline. Gott helped me up. My sore body had seized up with the sleep.

Rolf and Mirka were looking worriedly back the way we had come.

"What is it?" I asked.

I had only to glance down the path to see what the problem was: Hayner was coming.

He was a hundred yards or more behind us along the path, but he had seen us. His eyes were focused on us as he trudged between the forest and mountain, dragging one leg behind him. He wore nothing but boots and the remains of tattered pants. His body was an open sore, cut from innumerable welts and lacerations from the Pflanzen-Kriegerin's thorns and vines. One arm flopped loosely beside him, as if it were broken or out of joint.

He didn't seem able to outrun us, but I figured he would never stop. Gott and Rolf looked at me for direction.

"Mirka," I said, "hand me my pack." She searched around in the grass and carried it to me. "Go ahead and get to the top of this hill, all of you."

Mirka protested, refusing to leave.

I decided to leave it alone and focus on Hayner. I set the pack down and opened it, wishing I had concocted an exploding vial or two and not just these acid vials. I hadn't felt right using my vials during the final onslaught, but it felt right now. This was self-defense, not judgment.

Hayner had limped to within seventy-five yards.

"If this doesn't stop him," I said, "get ready to run."

"Do you think the three of us could handle him?" Gott asked.

"No, I don't think we could." I sighed with pain in my chest. I pressed against my puncture wound. It was warm and tender. Infected. I felt faint. "Get Mirka ready. See to it she gets out of here if there's any way." I reached in the pack for a couple vials.

"I'm right here, Sascha," she said, "and I'll not be ordered around like your Obergrenadiers."

I caught a glimpse of her. Regal. Beautiful. I smiled. "I know, *liebling*. If things go bad, though, please let them get you out." Then I added something: "This is not your time."

Hayner was moving faster now. He was around fifty yards out when I lofted the first vials at him. My body revolted at the throwing motion, and the vials went high in the air, landing 20 yards ahead of him. Two of them splattered on the path, the other landed in the underbrush on the forest side of the path, failing to burst. The broken vials spewed a noxious cloud that obscured both Hayner and the path from view.

I retrieved more vials as we waited to see what would happen. I instructed Gott and Rolf to pick out a couple vials each, which they did. Moments later Hayner emerged from the cloud, wheezing, but moving toward us.

"You and me, schoolboy!" Hayner screeched, his thins lips parting with satisfaction. "Falke said it wasn't my time yet! I killed everything and now I'm here to kill you, schoolboy!" Hayner's pace seemed to increase, as did his resolve. "I pried that door of yours out of the wall like I'll pry the brain out of your head! Free my captives, will you? You'll be the first victim in the new Nachthaus!"

I nodded at Gott and Rolf, and we launched our vials. Hayner was inside 20 yards now, and his muscular bulk offered a good target.

My first vial struck him in the midsection and failed to burst. It fell in front of him, and his foot crushed it as he passed.

Gott's first vial crashed on the kneecap of Hayner's good leg as it stepped forward in mid-stride. The vial shattered, splashing Hayner's leg with acid. Hayner roared and kept coming, his leg melting.

Rolf's vial struck the shoulder above Hayner's bad arm, bursting. A plume of acidic smoke rose above his head, trailing him as he pursued us.

We launched a second volley. My vial smashed dead center into his chest from about ten yards. Gott's erupted on Hayner's right collarbone. Rolf hit the instep of Hayner's good foot, shattering it on his boot.

Hayner was engulfed in a chemical cloud that arose from his burning skin and trailed him as he limped along. His ribcage was exposed from the chemical burns, and I could see his lungs expanding and contracting. His pants had dissolved. His good leg, if it could still be called that, was exposed down to the femur. I could see the tendons working under and around his bare kneecap.

And still he came.

I reached into the pack, rummaged around, and came out with one last vial. "Get Mirka and go! Now!"

Gott and Rolf started to hesitate, but must have seen my eyes. They grabbed Mirka, who was still protesting, and headed up the incline.

Hayner had closed to five yards and was grinning at me. The pythons were out and hissing. The giant veins on his scalp were pulsating through the swastika. He started to say something that I did not wish to hear. I slung the last vial at his head.

It impacted his forehead and exploded. The acid ate into the swastika and dripped down his face. A chemical cloud enveloped him.

He never broke his limping stride. Hayner came at me, the skin melting off his face. One eye was gone, and his facial bones were exposed in several places. His thin lips burned off, revealing clattering white teeth. He reached for me with a hand that was mostly exposed bone.

I ran.

Gott and Rolf were out of view over the incline. They had succeeded in taking Mirka with them. Good men, those two. As good as men can be, that is.

I slipped on the pack and slammed down on the path, a few feet up the incline. The breath went out of me, and I felt something spurt out of my puncture wound. The top of the incline was ten feet above me, and Hayner was closing. The top of the incline seemed like something out of a dream. I could crawl and crawl and never reach it.

My vision was blurring and the top of the hill wavered. I reached out for the earth and pulled myself forward, sucking in dust from the path.

Hayner screeched behind me, his words slurring. "You'll sleep soon, schoolboy!"

I looked over my shoulder. He had limped to the edge of the incline, measuring it with his one good eye. His head cocked to the side to get a better look. He was almost as malformed and hideous as my sinful nature had been when I'd seen it in the valley.

His good eye gawked at me through his ruined flesh and exposed skull, full of hate. His hand scratched the back of my calf, searching for a hold. If he got me now, I would never make it up the hill.

I clawed at the dirt, pulling myself up the path foot by foot. My broken nose scraped in the dirt. I twisted sideways, pushing myself with my legs. Slowly, I climbed.

As did Hayner. He limped up a step, then planted his bad leg behind himself on the incline for leverage. He reached out as he could, searching for my leg, pausing a few times to wipe pus from his good eye. I kicked at his skeletal hand as it groped for me.

I reached the top of the incline ahead of Hayner. Another small victory for the liberal arts. I swung my legs over the top of the hill and let myself roll.

40

The path ended abruptly at the bottom of the hill. I came to rest against the side of the mountain, with the forest in all other directions. No sign of Gott, Rolf, or Mirka.

That presence was back—the one I had sensed the first time I had touched the philosopher face. I was beset by it and adrenaline surged through me. I discovered my last store of strength and took off into the woods.

Branches scraped my face, clawed at my body. I pressed on into the darkening woods, wishing to escape the presence that pursued me. Darkness surrounded me, and soon I would be lost in the depths of the forest. And then I understood my foolishness, and stopped.

I once had a teenage friend who got hit in the jaw by a bigger kid over a girl. I remember telling my friend to stay down while the bigger kid was cajoling him to get back up. When it was all over, my friend told me he was glad it happened because he never had to be afraid of being hit again. When you take the hardest punch, the rest are easy.

I had taken the hardest punches, so why was I running? Evil had pursued me, had wooed me, had threatened me, and by the grace of God alone I had overcome. Now it could have me if He so wished. I turned to look the presence in the face, as I had done while touching the philosopher face. It vanished in front of me, dispersing into the forest like leaves on the wind.

I saw Hayner trudging along, following my trail. He spied me and doubled his limp. I determined to run from him no longer. Two minutes brought him to me.

He stood in front of me, hunched over, panting. "Ah, yes, schoolboy," he said, "the final lesson has arrived." His triangle ears had been burned off his head. His eye, which had been black in the Nachthaus, was now a shattered patchwork of blood vessels. Hayner raised his hand to strike.

"Before you do that," I said, "let me ask you something."

Hayner paused, his exposed teeth grinning at me in the darkness. He leaned in, arching his head sideways on his neck to see me better. "What, Sascha?"

"Do you know it's not too late for you?" I had once been afraid to speak of him about such things, but I had been hit hard and I was no longer afraid.

"You would still try to pull the wool over my eyes, even now?" Hayner said.

His *eye*, perhaps. Given the look of him, it wasn't a bad idea. "No, Standartenführer. I mean, even now, if you would, you could still find forgiveness."

Hayner spit at me. With his lips gone, the spittle dribbled out of his mouth onto his burnt chin. Hayner struck with his fist.

But his hand never reached me. Out of the forest, the great vine had come. It wrapped one vine around me and one around Hayner. The vines constricted around us, trapping our arms to our sides. My puncture wound spurted, and the pressure of the constriction exited through my broken nose.

We were lifted through the forest, branches slapping us, twigs scratching our faces. Upward we went until we crossed through the forest canopy. Behind us, the mountain rose into the clouds, and under us was a carpet of green formed by the treetops. The great vine pulled each of us to its face.

I didn't see it at first, but as the vines pulled us closer, it appeared to me. The face was in the canopy itself, and appeared as a collage of plant life, treetops, branches, and bird nests. It was like one of those pictures with random dots, where if you stared at it long enough, something appeared to you inside it.

It drew Hayner in until he was nearly touching the treetops. The wind blew, the treetops swayed, and I could hear in the breeze the moan of the forest. It was a softly textured voice. It spoke one word: *Why?*

Hayner screeched and bit the vine with his exposed teeth. He managed to lacerate the vine, and a drop of sap oozed out.

The vine began to constrict. I saw the coils moving around Hayner, squeezing tighter. With his last breath, Hayner screeched a curse, which was cut off in mid-phrase as his air was forced out of his lungs. Hayner's bones began to crack like dead tree limbs. His body went limp, and his head sagged against the vine. His one blank eye stared out lifelessly.

The vine reared Hayner's body back 50 yards in the air and hurled it forward at the mountain. Hayner's body struck the mountain and plummeted down out of sight. *Deus et natua non faciunt frusta.*

I was then pulled closer to the face, which was animated by a light breeze. As the breeze blew and the treetops swayed, I heard the moan of the forest and its one-word lament: *Why?*

The vine that held me constricted as if the forest had asked this question countless times and was accustomed to bad answers. Yet it waited for me, and I answered the best I could. "Mankind exchanged the truth of God for a lie, and you suffered in the process," I said. "I beg your forgiveness."

I'll never be sure what it meant, but a drop of water fell from the sky, landed on one of the face's eyes, and then rolled from its eye to the forest floor below.

The vine loosed its coils around me. The vine that had held Hayner rose in front of me and brought a tapered point at its end toward me like a spear. The coils parted around my chest, and the tapered point stabbed me in my puncture wound.

I convulsed in the vine, and my eyes saw stars. The pain was brilliant for a moment, and then it was gone. The second vine retracted from my chest and disappeared into the canopy. The vine constricting me loosened so I could move freely. Feeling my puncture wound, I found it was gone.

The second vine returned from the canopy and daubed my nose and my cuts with a salve it had brought up from below.

"Thank you," I said. "I don't deserve this."

The face in the canopy smiled, and then was gone.

The great foghorn blew. I heard the giant footsteps below me, and then I was moving. Soon thereafter, the vine deposited me in a paradise garden. Gott, Rolf, and Mirka slept there, and I joined them, drinking deep the sweet elixir of sleep.

41

That was the story I told my accusers and to my judges after they asked me if I had anything to say in my defense. The beady-eyed man ran his frail hand across his widow's peak and leaned back. De vemen looked to him for instructions. The other assembled officials—my jurors, I suppose—mumbled to one another.

"Mr. König," the man said, "you sit here accused of complicity in the heinous and brutal murders of a multitude of innocents, and *that* incredulous tale is your best defense? It would have been decent of you to have simply denied the charges and not wasted our time."

Having been hit hard, what was this man to me? I sat there, old and alone in the world. To die is gain, indeed. This world is evil in its indifference.

"Furthermore," the man said, "we would still like to know of your accomplices."

I rattled my handcuffs. "Would you let me out of these things?" I asked. "You're not scared of an old man, are you?"

The beady-eyed man looked back to one of the accusers lining the wall of the room, and then nodded at one of de vemen, who came around the table and unlocked my chains. She pulled them off hard, the chains unraveling around my arm like a plant-man vine.

"My friends . . . " I said, thinking back to Gott, Rolf, and me standing in a circle, our arms on each other shoulders. "Precious friends. I never found two more like them."

I leaned forward, elbows on the table, hands over my eyes. How those two had stood tall in the Nachthaus, never flinching in fulfilling the gypsy's pledge. To find friends such as those in this life is a rare beauty.

The four of us had awoken in the garden. The vine presented us with the lush bounty of the forest. We supped, and then the vine escorted us out. The forest gave us safe passage to its border, and from there we followed byways and back roads to the coast of the Black Sea.

From there, Mirka was able to link up with the Ukranian underground and we surrendered ourselves to the Allies. Between Gott, Rolf, and me, we were able to supply the allied forces with enough German intelligence to earn ourselves citizenship anywhere in the west. We strategically omitted tales of the Nachthaus, but the bombing raids of Ploiesti in '43 were one of the results of our handiwork, one I've never been proud of.

We omitted tales of the Nachthaus because we knew no one would believe them, and it would jeopardize our futures. It was self-serving, but what was our alternative, the asylum? As I sit here and recount this narrative, no one's going to believe me now, and they wouldn't have then. That's the power of the Nachthaus—it's always singing a lullaby, cradling men to sleep.

I entered the U.S. as Sanford King, found my way to Texas, and lived there until they finally found me. In 1949, I married Mirka, and she immigrated to the States, where we lived until her death in '72 from pancreatic cancer. After Mirka's death, I served as a custodian at the University of Texas Medical Branch in Galveston.

It was always rumored by the locals there that there was a face on the wall outside one of the buildings on the UTMB campus, right off of Port Industrial Avenue, before it was erased by Hurricane Ike. I can tell you that was no rumor. The face followed me halfway across the world to Texas. We had some good talks, he and I.

Gott, Rolf, and I split up when we reached the States, knowing that the Nachthaus would be discovered and that its atrocities would create a manhunt for all involved. I never saw my friends again. Gott went to Broadway under an assumed name, and with his physical prowess, became a regionally known personality. He passed away in the mid-nineties. By all accounts, Gott led a full life, and I thanked God for that.

I lost all contact with Rolf. I like to think of him in his lab coat, goggles on, teeth sticking out from his lip, now very old, researching cures for cancer. He disappeared out of my life like my Katia, whom I always remember now as an image in a discarded black-and-white photograph, lying dusty and forgotten on the floor of the Nachthaus. While I'm here I should look for it.

"And so," I said, "I'm the lone witness you have of what happened at the Nachthaus. Funny thing is, I'm telling you the God's honest truth, just as it was."

"Nazi swine cannot tell the truth," the beady-eyed man said. "It's not in them. Leaving aside your unbelievable tale of walking plants and giant spiders, would you have us to believe that you saved a hundred captives from the Nachthaus and yet not one has come forward to confirm this incredible tale? Yet we have records of thousands of deaths by torture and by the oven."

I stood from my chair, but without a threatening gesture. De vemen coiled to strike, but the beady-eyed man held up his palm. "What is it, König?"

I ripped open the front of my jumpsuit, exposing the scar from my puncture wound.

The beady-eyed man waved me off. "König. Do you expect us to be—"

I held my palm out to him. In it was the perfect circle where the gypsy girl's sphere had branded me. "Have you ever seen a circle this perfect?" I asked. "Measure it, if you like. I'm telling you the truth. Look at it! There's no scar tissue!"

The beady-eyed man's pupils expanded for a moment, and then collapsed. "I suppose next you'll claim to have stigmata. I've heard enough." The beady-eyed man looked around the room at his companions, and everyone seemed to nod at him. "Sascha König, we find you guilty of crimes against humanity. Ours is a private council, and we execute our own sentencing. Do you have anything final—anything *new*— to say before we sentence you?"

"Whatever you have in mind to do, do it quickly," I said.

But I knew what they had in mind to do. I had always thought I would die in the Nachthaus inferno. They had called me Nebuchadnezzar, and the name suited me fine, for I had made the oven seven times hotter.

42

I didn't need them to tell me. De vemen stood me up and held me until everyone in the room, including the beady-eyed man, had cleared out.

De vemen marched me out the door with a nightstick uncomfortably pressed in my right kidney. I exited the door to encounter a gauntlet of witnesses leading to the inferno. These would be the families of the victims. These would be holocaust foundation dignitaries. They beheld me with disgust.

De vemen forced me to walk slowly through the gauntlet. I was spit upon, called names, cursed, and struck. They thrust pictures of loved ones in my face. One doused me with a vial of urine and feces.

I walked on through the gauntlet thinking what a destroyer evil is, how it corrupts everything it comes into contact with. How, by its nature, it is restless and never satisfied.

Evil is a virus, and we are all infected by it. These folks would return to their lives after this day's events concluded. They were farmers, accountants, and garbage men, leading normal lives, most of them blissfully unaware of the communicable disease they carried within them, spreading it with whomever they came in contact.

They were not as bad as the Nazis, but I knew it was a matter of degree only, and that their lesser degree was on account of grace: the common grace of the Holy Spirit that restrained all men from being as bad as they could be, and the special grace that leads some men to a knowledge of their sinful nature. I thanked God for letting me see my own in the valley—and through the Nachthaus, as hideous as it was. And is. I prayed: *Father forgive them, for they know not what they do.*

As the strikes and curses and epithets mounted, I cried. The gauntlet roared with more vigor as they saw my tears. They thought I was crying for myself, but I was crying for them. I knew I deserved whatever evil befell me; my experience in the Nachthaus had taught me that. They did not know, which meant that, here and now, the Nachthaus had prevailed. It was vibrating again. Its walls shook. The Nachthaus was the world, and it would carry on infected until the Judge came the final time. Even now, I heard scratching at the door and the forest moaning above the din of the gauntlet.

I turned the corner to the inferno and saw my old enemy in front of me. Its glass slit eyes were jaundiced. Its face was riddled with scars, and its skin was mummified. Evil was a destroyer, and the inferno was suffering the wages of sin. I stood in front of it as they raised the door, close enough to the wall to brave one last touch to the philosopher- face, who had followed me back for my finale in the Nachthaus.

I touched the wall, wondering if my old counselor had one last parting word to share. He did: *Wake up, O sleeper, rise from the dead, and Christ will shine on you. The final time of testing is at hand. To him that overcomes . . .*

I thanked him.

The door opened, exposing the guts of the inferno. Its interior refractory had collapsed. It was a hollow shell, deteriorated by its evil to near nothingness. I stepped into the furnace. As I did, I thought I saw a hulking silhouette behind the screaming crowd, lumbering around the door leading to the mine. If he was there, and somehow I think he was, I know what he would have said to me: *Now it is time, Sascha . . . and He is always on time."*

The door closed behind me.

43

I stood in the inferno waiting for the flames to engulf me. I had spent my life receiving forgiveness for burning the gypsy girl in the oven, and now I would experience her fate firsthand. I remembered that night long ago when her light had been squelched in the flames. One moment the oven was filled with brilliant light; the next moment it was gone.

I had seen true evil in the Nachthaus, and I had seen it in the recesses of my own heart. But my hope was this: if evil was real, then good must also be real. And where there is goodness, there is hope; and where there is goodness, there is God.

God has His reasons for allowing evil. In my case, it was to bring me to Him.

The whirring noise began. It was the fuel pumps engaging. I had heard it several times outside the inferno, but inside it was infinitely more terrifying. The oven whirred like airplane propellers. I resisted the urge to run to the door, beat on it, and plead for my life.

In the back corner of the oven, under some of the fallen wall material, a dim light began to rise. My first thought was that it was the pilot light somehow shining through the wall. It was a ridiculous thought.

My mind slowly pieced together the events of the past like a puzzle. The light grew in intensity from under the rubble, and now it illuminated the entire back wall. I remembered being trapped in the inferno by plant-men, and then it occurred to me what it might be. I hastened to the corner of the oven.

I kneeled down, tossing the fallen pieces of the oven wall aside. It was the gypsy girl's sphere. It had remained here hidden all these decades, and now it was glowing again for me.

I picked it up and rushed to the window. Its light now flooded the entire oven. Certainly they could see it! I beat on the window, screaming above the whirring of the fuel pumps. "Look! Look! I was telling the truth! Here's your proof! Please! Look at this!"

I pounded on the glass. I pressed my face against it, imploring the crowd outside. They seemed to cheer more wildly in my distress.

The gypsy girl's sphere dissolved in my hand. Its light vanished. Gone.

In a flash, a column of light appeared next to me. Out of it walked an angel with the face of the gypsy girl and the eyes of galaxies.

"Sascha," the angel said, "will you even now daydream during these last things?"

I was ashamed. The angel was right: A hundred-year-old man beating on the window to save his life, after all he had seen. The horror of man's sinful nature.

"Fret not, Sascha," the angel said. "This too is forgiven."

The tears streamed down my face as I finally, after all, understood the depth of grace required to quench the fire of man's sinful nature. Tears of joy and of horror—tears of grace.

The pilot light kicked on, and its *Whoooooooooooosh* sound filled the oven. I knew I was now only moments away from the flames.

The angel took my hand. "Ex malo bonum."

"God forgive me," I said.

The shutters flew open inside the inferno. The roar of a hurricane ensued as the flames filled the oven.

It stung for a split-second. It was like a dry twig snapped, and then I was outside my body. The last part of Epicurus' riddle fell into place: this life is such a fleeting thing in the face of eternity. With the snap of a twig, I was facing eternity, and the pain and evil already seemed distant, like a dream I could barely remember upon waking.

I looked back at my body, which had burned away, falling as soot to the floor of the inferno. My sinful nature remained, and it was as hideous as it had been in the valley. It screamed and writhed as the flames consumed it. To the end, it fought and clawed and cursed. Then it was gone; my old man was no more. I stood amazed in the flames—I was at last cleansed of my stinking hands.

And suddenly there was someone else in the fire, one that looked like a son of man.

I cannot and will not describe His glory, except to say that the gypsy girl's eyes were as dung in His presence. I fell at His feet.

He lifted me from the floor of the oven, the flames swirling around us. He wiped the tears from my eyes as if He were wiping the stain of the Nachthaus off me forever. At last, I had been completely refined in the refiner's fire.

He pointed at the oven's control room door. It swung open, revealing a glorious, indescribable realm. I walked through the door in the arms of my savior.

Yes, they called me Nebuchadnezzar, and it was a good name, for I had been in the fire seven times hotter, and seen one like a son of man carry me through the flames.

Soli Deo Gloria
Marc Schooley
May 2010

AWARD-WINNING FICTION FROM MARCHER LORD PRESS

BY DARKNESS HID
BY JILL WILLIAMSON

WINNER OF THE 2010
CHRISTY AWARD
(VISIONARY CATEGORY)

ETERNITY FALLS
BY KIRK OUTERBREIDGE

WINNER OF THE 2010
ACFW CAROL AWARD
(SPECULATIVE CATEGORY)